RAGE

A Frank Kelly Novel

Vaughn F. Keller

This is a work of fiction. Names, characters, events, and locations are figments of the author's imagination or are used in a fictitious manner. Any data used, has been taken from public records.

Printed in the United States of America

Paperback ISBN: 978-1-951854-49-2

Cover design by Karen Phillips
Edited and Formatted by Riverhaven Books

Titles by Vaughn F. Keller

Frank Kelly Mysteries

Behind the Neon
The Unwilling Pawn
Dirt
Rage

Collections (Short Stories, Poetry, Essays)

Glimpses
The Corner of my Eye

Novels

Tír na nÓg (A Family Saga)
Portofino Summer

"I want my president to be the biggest American chest thumper out there. If you cross him, he will slit your throat, and I get that out of President..."

Brian Mast, Congressman
for the 21st District Florida
Campaigning in Iowa,
August, 2023

To Herbert S. Keller

A believer in the idea of America

Chapter One: Camp Liberty

The new owner told them to come get their files or he would burn them. As they drove away after retrieving the three boxes, Charles told his wife, "I can't believe they changed the name. *Camp Liberty*, what a joke. Bunch of right-wing nut cases parading around like they're in the army or something."

Bonnie didn't respond. She was crying.

Charles and Bonnie Spitzer had no choice but to sell. Their dream had turned into a nightmare. They were young though, and they were confident they would rebound from the financial disaster they and the universe had created.

Theirs had been a good dream. Everyone they told about it loved it – a summer music camp for troubled teens deep in the Maine woods. They would keep the previous name of the camp, Camp Nebizun. They liked the Abenaki meaning, *Water is Life*. The camp was located where three different streams flowed into the eight-mile-long lake on the outskirts of tiny Sparta, Maine. The camp came with one mile of lakefront property.

Music would be its unique offering. The young couple went about recruiting music teachers they knew, and they had it all covered: brass, woodwinds, percussion, strings, and voice. To work at the camp, there were three requirements: love teaching, love teenagers, and love music.

One of the reasons the Spitzers fell in love with the camp was the amphitheater, built into a hill overlooking the lake. It was perfect for performances. They imagined parent weekends with the families sitting on blankets and chairs watching their children perform. The camp would be expensive, though: campers would pay $7,000 for the seven-week program.

The location was remote. Sparta had fewer than a thousand people, and the camp was four miles from the center of town. Bonnie's father called it a "sneeze" town: "One good sneeze while you're driving through, and you'll miss it." What there was of a center consisted of a general store selling liquor, gas, and basic groceries, a post office, a volunteer fire department, and a library open Wednesday afternoons and Saturday mornings.

The Spitzers were fine with Sparta's size. They reasoned that the camp's one hundred and sixty acres of beautiful woodlands on rolling hills would provide more than enough opportunity for adventures. They planned to develop a ropes course in and among the trees. It would be a medium-sized camp with only ninety-six campers, but troubled teenagers, boys and girls, would need close supervision.

There were sixteen rustic cabins arranged in four groups of four. Named for a composer from Bach to Wagner, each cabin had eight bunks: six for campers, one for a counselor, and one for a counselor-in-training. You entered each cabin through a screened porch that functioned as a multi-purpose room for rainy days. It stretched their budget, but the Spitzers installed electricity in each cabin. Most of the campers would be new to camping, and removing them from their phones and tablets would be an unnecessary challenge. Campers would be able to access Wi-Fi in the dining hall. They purchased a large generator to supply power to the entire camp in case power was disrupted.

The dining hall, along with multiple buildings for crafts and sports activities, maintenance, an office, and a small infirmary clustered together around an open area near the waterfront. The former owners had called it "The Parade Ground." Charles and Bonnie decided to call it "The Gathering."

The waterfront area had a sand beach overseen by a high wooden tower. On shore were racks for canoes, kayaks, and six sunfish sailboats. Nearby, there was a long dock with four row boats and an ancient skiff with an outboard motor that was used to retrieve campers who strayed too far away from the camp when sailing or paddling. A short distance

2

away was a softball field, ranges for rifle targets and archery, a basketball court, and a field for soccer. While focused on music, the camp would offer a full camp experience, with the exception of archery and rifle.

Charles and Bonnie borrowed money from their parents and took out a second mortgage on their home. The previous owners, the Colby family, agreed to give them a mortgage on the camp at an excellent interest rate. Neither of the two Colby children was interested in owning a camp in a remote part of Maine, and the market for summer camps in 2019 was not great, so the senior Colbys were delighted with the arrangement. The Colbys liked this young couple and their dream. They did not want their legacy turned into a logging operation.

Recruiting campers and staff was more difficult than Charles and Bonnie had expected. Because they were both music teachers in Framingham, Massachusetts and knew music teachers throughout New England, they thought attracting students and staff would not be a problem. They were wrong. Nebizun's fees were a disincentive for most families, and the kind of counselors who were capable of providing both music instruction and work with difficult teens were rare and expensive. Former campers had no interest in the new structure, which focused on music and behavior. During the first year the Spitzers owned the camp, it was only two-thirds full – less than break even. Then a virus devastated the world with a pandemic that disrupted every economy on the planet. Camp Nebizun did not open during the summers of 2020 or 2021. The Spitzers put it up for sale in December of 2021.

***

Camp Nebizun was exactly what Lieutenant Colonel Gordon McKnight (ret) was looking for. He, too, had a dream.

To most people, Gordon McKnight appeared to have taken his forced retirement well. Neither his mother nor his two sisters knew he was smarting from the United States Army's decision in 2015 to retire him after thirty-three years of service. Only his older brother, Doug, and his father knew how devastated he was. "Bitter" was the word they used with one another. "He's also embarrassed as hell," his father told Doug.

Not empathic towards his younger brother, Doug replied, "He should be. There are too many morons trying to play Lone Ranger."

"What do you know about it? You never served," the father replied to the older son.

The timing was against Gordon McKnight. In 2015, the Army had an abundance of lieutenant colonels and did not consider Gordon for promotion to full colonel. He had failed the "up or out" requirement for military officers. Twice the sobriquet "loose cannon" had found its way into his fitness reports, and some thought he was lucky to have made it to thirty-three years.

When he retired at age fifty-five, Gordon first tried his hand at teaching high school social studies in St. Augustine, Florida. He found his high school students lackadaisical and only marginally interested in social studies. Gordon didn't like them, and they didn't like him. His problem wasn't just with his students. Parents complained about "the Colonel" – he insisted his students use his military rank. They complained about his political pontificating in the classroom and his zealous grading practices. In three years, no student received an "A." The school district did not grant him tenure, and in 2018, Gordon McKnight found himself looking for work. Once more, a policy had brought rejection, but this time, it was "tenure or out." Childless, wifeless after two divorces, and rootless, an increasingly embittered Gordon McKnight headed North.

Downeast Range and Retail in Portland, Maine, was more than happy to hire a retired U.S. Army lieutenant colonel and former high school teacher as a small arms instructor and salesperson. Gordon told his brother and father, "These are my people. Not like those idiots in St. Augustine." On a Zoom call, he told them, "We still have a big 'Buzhardt for President' sign hanging in the store's front window. People who come in here know what a disaster Goodman will be if he's re-elected. He's an idiot. That'll never happen. People aren't that stupid."

His father said, "Yeah, we'll see. Who knows who'll run against him since Buzhardt can't? You sound good, Gordie – better than you have in a long time."

"Yeah. I'm good. Starting to make some connections here. Good stuff. Got some ideas, too."

While in Portland, Gordon became familiar with and made connections with the Maine Militia and other militant groups active in the area. Members of these groups often came to the range to fire their weapons or to purchase them from the retail store. Gordon talked to them about their programs and activities. He started jotting down notes at night. One night, he wrote, "They have no plans. Nothing!!!" He became convinced that none of these groups would make any difference in the country's direction, a direction Gordon considered disastrous. He told his brother, Doug, "They talk a lot, but that's it. They play dress up like a bunch of little girls."

He began a serious reading regimen. Among other books, Gordon McKnight read *Bedford: A World Vision, The Turner Diaries*, *The Camp of the Saints*, and *American Crusade: Our Fight to Stay Free*. The reading transformed him. He now understood how America had changed from what it was supposed to be. Replacement Theory was no longer a theory to Gordon. It was happening. Whites were becoming a minority in their own country. Black and Brown people had to be stopped. Of all the books, *American Crusade* by Pete Hegseth impressed him the most. When he read, "Leftists have surrounded traditional American patriots on all sides, ready to close in for the kill: killing our founders, killing our flag, and killing capitalism," he began forming the precepts for a different kind of militia, one based on discipline and action. This group would make a difference and bring about change. He realized that violence was acceptable. As Hegseth had written, "Our American Crusade is not about literal swords, and our fight is not with guns. Yet." Gordon concluded that 'yet' had arrived. It was 'now.' He started writing his ideas down. It took him several months, but eventually, he finished writing a manifesto to guide the creation of the Defenders of Liberty. He called it, *We Must Defend Ourselves*. He sent it off to several publishers and was disappointed when he started receiving form rejection slips. Undeterred, he printed it himself and gave it away at the store. He sent copies to his parents, sisters, and brother for them to read and distribute. He replaced the bitterness that had enveloped him with resolve. He knew what was needed. He knew what he had to do.

He'd need money. He had read about the work of a billionaire, Joshua Whitman, who was using his wealth to turn the Ship of State in a new direction. The 'new' direction, Whitman claimed, was really old. It would return America to the founders' intentions with limited government, no involvement in foreign lands, and an end to interminable immigration. Whitman not only supported conservative political candidates who fought for these causes, but he also funneled money to private militias. Gordon McKnight decided to seek him out. First, though, he went to his brother, because Doug would know Whitman; Doug knew everybody.

A Washington, D.C. insider, well known as a lobbyist for conservative causes, Doug was connected. Although separated by five years and with different mothers, the two brothers were close. Gordon knew his brother funneled large sums of money to the Hamilton Society and other right-wing causes. During the family's pandemic-constrained Christmas of 2021, Gordon shared his plan for the Defenders of Liberty. His brother was encouraging. "It sounds like you've given this a lot of thought. Do you think you can pull it off?"

"Yeah. There are a lot of angry people out there. Afghanistan withdrawal. Ridiculous Covid shit. People are pissed off."

"Talk is cheap. How many are…"

"Real Patriots?" Gordon suggested. "Enough. It doesn't take a lot."

"Now you sound like the Three Percenters."

"More discipline; more secrecy. Smarter. Much smarter. No tattoos announcing who the hell you are."

After Christmas dinner, the two brothers went for a walk with their father. Talk quickly turned to politics. The brothers' father, Glen McKnight, said, "We never should have lost the 2020 election.

Goodman's a disgrace. We can't lose again. We've got to stop this leftist, woke bullshit. It's destroying us. Pretty soon, you won't be able to take a shit without government permission. Fucking libtards."

Gordon responded, "I know. It's even worse than we thought it would be. Afghanistan will go down as one of the worst defeats in American history. Total disaster, pulling out the way Goodman did. Should have been impeached."

Doug added, "Worst president, maybe ever. You're right, Dad. Goodman cannot be re-elected, and he won't be."

"Bullshit. There's a good chance he'll win a second term. People are that stupid."

"Not going to happen. I promise you."

"Sure. Sure. You going to stop it? You and what army?"

"You wait. You'll see. We've got a lot of time."

After a mile, the senior McKnight left his sons and returned to his house and the other family members. The brothers kept walking.

Doug said, "Tell me more about this group you want to start."

A half-hour later, Doug told his brother, "I know Josh Whitman. I'll talk to him. What will you need to get this Defender thing up and running? Money? How much? If we're going to get this country back on track, we'll need a group like that. Tell me again. What are you calling them?"

"Defenders of Liberty."

"Right. Good name. Do you think you can pull it off?"

"I know I can."

"What's your first step?"

"I want to buy this camp in Maine. I want to develop it into a training ground for new American revolutionaries who want to take America back."

"A militia group."

"No. I keep telling you – more. We'd work with militias and be part of the militia network, but this would be a new force with a philosophy behind it, a set of principles. Duty, honor, country. Quick strike capacity.

7

Not parading about in masks like these Patriot Front assholes. A group that will actually make a difference. Not a bunch of losers. A highly disciplined team. Full-time commitments. No weekend bullshit. A group that can strike hard and fast to support true leaders, not political hacks."

"Okay. I got it. We need to talk more, a lot more. Gordie, I need to fill you in on some things that are going on."

"Like what?"

"There are some people I know who are working on some stuff, just the way you are. Big plans."

That weekend, the two brothers laid the groundwork for the creation of the Defenders of Liberty. It would begin with the purchase of the camp. Doug focused on the legal structure and the financing. "We'll set it up as a non-profit, call it a survival training camp. We'll give scholarships and stipends to the people you recruit, call it training. You're thinking ex-military, right?"

"Absolutely. But I want guys who see past the bullshit, who know what the military should be."

"How many are you talking about?"

"Fifteen. Maybe twenty to start. We'll make the pay comparable to what they were making in the military but as stipends, not wages. We're going to be training them."

"You'll have to feed and house them. In addition to buying property, how much are you going to need to get started?"

"I don't know. Three or four million."

"Not a problem. You're talking about a serious effort here. We're going to want others to have skin in the game. We'll start with Whitman. I'm sure he'll go for it. He's fed up with what Goodman's doing to this country. Fucking traitor."

"You think Whitman'll be interested?"

"I know he will. He's already got some things going."

"Like what?"

"If I told you, I'd have to kill you."

Gordon laughed. "Come on. Cut the bullshit."

"How serious are you about this?"

"Very. I already told you."

"As I said, some things are going on. If I tell you, you cannot mention a word to anyone. Anyone. You understand."

"Yes."

"There's a group, a small group, that plans on taking back the presidency. Changing things. Whitman's a key member of the group."

"You? You a part of it?"

"Yes."

"Taking over the presidency. You serious?"

"Very. We have a candidate."

"Who?"

"You know John Pope?"

"Pope. No shit. Of course I do. I served under him. He's all over the news. Christ, he's been on every goddamn talk show there is."

"We don't think any of the current crop of potential candidates can get elected. We think people will get behind Pope."

"How? Every time someone asks him, he says he's not interested."

"That's on purpose. There's a plan."

"You going to tell me?"

"In time. I will tell you this. By the end of the primaries, people will be pleading with Pope to run."

"You're thinking primaries already. Christ, they're not for another three years."

"Iowa caucus. January 15, 2024. It takes planning. So go slow. No missteps. No broadcasting. Just buy the camp and get it up and running."

John Pope. Gordon McKnight knew him. He'd served under him in Iraq and revered the man. Pope, a West Point graduate, had also attended the Command and General Staff College and collected many medals during his years in the Army. Gordon had heard Pope refer back to Douglas MacArthur's *Duty, Honor, Country* speech many times, and every time he did, Gordon felt encouraged by his decision to make a career in the military. Gordon knew Pope had lost favor in the military establishment because of his outspoken views on Democratic administrations and the "Gutless compliance of the military to wokeness." Pope was adamant that, "Queers and trannies have no place in the military, absolutely none." He was also convinced that women did not have the strength or the intestinal fortitude for battlefield commands. Since leaving the Army, Pope created a boutique consulting firm and became a favorite of conservative news organizations and several "patriotic" organizations.

Gordon asked, "You sure about Pope? Every time anyone suggests it, he says he's not interested."

"I'm sure. Don't worry. Pope's open to giving it a shot. Support structure's almost in place. Money's coming in, and two different groups have been formed. One will become public right after the first primary debate, the DPP, the Committee to Draft Pope for President. When people see what losers the crop of possibles is, they'll want a fresh face."

"That's not until…"

"Sometime the summer of '23."

"You said *two* groups."

"Yeah," Doug said with a smirk.

"That's all you have to say? Yeah."

"It will never be public."

"What's it called?"

"The committee. That's it – The Committee. It runs the show."

"Who's on it?"

"People who care about this country."

"You?"

"Yes."

"Whitman?"

"Yes."

"Who else?"

"Some names you would recognize."

"You're not going to tell me."

"No, I'm not. I've already told you more than you need to know."

"Okay. So Pope. I like it. It makes sense. Does he have a chance?"

"Yes. First, he has to be nominated."

"Why not start now?"

"Don't worry about it. As I said, there's a plan."

"What about the other candidates?"

"What about them?"

"They're not just going to…"

"Self-destruct? Some of them will. You may be able to help us with the ones who don't."

"How?"

"Not now. I'll let you know. I can't tell you more right now."

Doug McKnight did not tell his brother the plans to ensure Pope would be the candidate in 2024. The Committee was still formulating them, and Doug didn't want his brother to get locked into one scenario. What Doug knew was that everything depended upon controlling the primaries. Ultimately, only one candidate would be left: General John Paul Pope.

***

Gordon McKnight closed on the camp purchase in late August of 2022 and immediately went about winterizing ten of the sixteen cabins, the dining hall, and three of the buildings that had been used for different camp programs. He even insulated the large barn that was the maintenance hub of the camp. Throughout the camp, thermopane replaced ancient wood windows and doors. He installed heat pumps to make the cabins and buildings comfortable whatever the weather. One building became an armory. He hired locally, and the people in Sparta were happy to get the work. During permitting and construction, Gordon told town officials he was converting the camp into a training center for adults to learn survival camping and leadership skills.

Tyler Chase, the Sparta Select Board chair, visited the camp frequently. Gordon offered Tyler the use of camp facilities for a family reunion, and Tyler used one of the camp's cabins during deer season.

Tyler was thrilled that the camp would be back up and running and bringing money into Sparta. Gordon assured him that he would hire local people whenever he could.

Gordon was busy. He hired contractors to reset all the water pipes below the frost line. Latrines gave way to composting toilets. Local relationships were established to enable the camp, actually a small city with all of the services of a small town, to function smoothly. Every one of the camp systems was in some way related to a service provider in the town. Gordon paid attention to detail. Even the 'pig man' was contacted to ensure the slops from the dining hall would find their way to the 'pig man's' farm.

Gordon's most significant problem was providing sufficient Wi-Fi bandwidth throughout the camp. It was limited in the dining hall making it inadequate for a patriotic movement that would eventually reach throughout the country. He hired a consultant to set up a camp-wide system. The Wi-Fi system was the biggest single investment he made. When installed, the enormous motorized discs and repeaters could bring service to every building in the camp. Once installed, Gordon invited Tyler Chase and some other Sparta men to come to the camp to watch sporting events. McKnight told them, "You bring the food; I've got the TV and the beer." Once in a while, Gordon sponsored an 'adult night' when he would stream adult films for Tyler and a few of his friends.

Doug was delighted with the progress his brother had made when he came to visit Camp Liberty late in October of 2022. He brought his family with him, in addition to Whitman and some close friends who shared his political views and were interested in hunting, even though it would be a week before the season opened. Only Whitman got a deer during the visit. Doug's two sons caught a meal's worth of trout.

For Gordon McKnight, the final evening was the critical event of the visit. At dinner, his brother gave him the go-ahead to use the camp to train Defenders for the time they would be needed to protect the country from the overreach of the government and to ensure that John Pope received the nomination for President of the United States. Doug approved funds to develop an extensive arsenal and begin recruitment during the summer of 2023. Until then, he could train any interested weekend survivalists or rent out cabins. When Gordon said he wanted to start using the name Defenders of Liberty publicly, Doug and his friends agreed. They also agreed that elements of the *Militia Manual* would guide the recruitment process, especially the need for secrecy.

When they were leaving, Doug pulled his brother aside. He said, "One thing. You want to call it Fort Liberty. We don't think that's a good idea. Take that sign down. Okay? You need to keep a low profile. Remember, you're training people in survival skills. 'Camp' sounds less militaristic. Do you have a problem with that?"

"No. Security, though. Security's going to be like a fort."

"Of course. How are you going to recruit?"

"I thought I'd start with gun shows. I'm going to go slow at first. But we'll be ready. Summer of '23. Don't worry. I'll have teams ready when you need them."

Chapter Two: The Blizzard

He's walking towards me, firing his gun, one shot after another. I know one will hit me. He's too close for all of them to miss. One hits me in the neck, the carotid. I put my hand up and feel the blood spurting from the wound. There is no pain. Another bullet grazes the top of my head, and blood flows down, covers my eyes, and I can't see. A third hits me in the chest. I fall down backward onto the pavement. I am weak and growing weaker. I'm dying. I know I am dying, and I don't want to. I fight it, but I am going deeper and deeper into death. I gasp once, twice, and with the third gasp, I wake up. The nightmare is always the same.

If Frederick Douglas's shot had been a foot higher, I wouldn't wake up this morning or any morning. But, instead, the only shot he got off hit me in the chest, and the Kevlar vest I was wearing kept me from being killed. I had to go to the hospital for evaluation but left the next day with nothing more than a big bruise and a couple of very sore ribs from where the vest had dispersed the impact.

Since I started seeing a therapist, I don't tell Eve about my nightmares. After I was shot, she wanted me to quit my job and stop being a private investigator. "Go back to teaching. You liked teaching. Get an adjunct job at the University of New Haven. You said they had a good program. Sell your shares of Nutmeg." For a couple of days, she even considered calling off the wedding if I wouldn't quit. We talked, and then we talked some more. I promised her I would be careful. She did marry me. Then we bought a condominium on the water in Milford, Connecticut, and I wake up with her every morning.

I did think about it – quitting. She was right. I'm not a kid. I have two adult children and might become a grandfather in a year or two, maybe less. I have nothing left to prove. When I first went to work at Nutmeg Security and Investigations, I did feel like I had something to prove. I wanted to prove I could do what I taught when I was a criminology professor specializing in investigative techniques. I've done that. I've solved real cases. I've found people who went missing. I've protected people who were in danger. I've cracked a murder case that the police had given up on. Between my academic credentials and experience as a practitioner of the investigative arts, I was pretty sure the University of New Haven would give me an adjunct position if they had an opening and a budget. I might even do it for free, although given what adjuncts typically make, it might as well be for free.

I don't need the money. When my late wife, Patricia, was killed in a car crash, she left me wealthy because of an insurance policy I didn't even know existed. I also inherited the three homes she owned outright and was renting. Money is not an issue. So, what's stopping me? Why not quit? The truth: I love what I do, and I'm pretty damned good at it. I love the puzzles and the problem solving. I love the adrenalin rush when I take on a complicated case.

When I told Eve this, she said, "But it almost got you killed."

"But it didn't. You said you understood."

"I do. It's just…"

"I know. And I told you. I'm going to be more careful. Remember the research I showed you?"

"I know what it said. Safer than being on a police force."

"Most dangerous thing is a paper cut."

"You got shot."

"Outlier. Like getting hit with lightening."

"They were bullets."

I couldn't very well deny that. Eve knew this conversation would not go anywhere. Being the wiser of the two of us, she said, "I will worry. Don't ask me not to."

How much do I love the work? As much as I tried to explain it to her, she never fully understood, so I stopped trying. There was no way I was going to tell her I looked at myself in the mirror one morning and said out loud, "Come, Watson, come! The game's afoot?" I knew she wouldn't understand my channeling Sherlock Holmes. Hell, I wasn't sure I understood it.

***

The blizzard began last Thursday. New England is a land of surprises when it comes to weather – a full-blown blizzard in December, just in time for Christmas shopping. Knowing I wasn't going anywhere, my dear wife let me sleep. She's the early riser of the two of us. The religious life – she was once Sister Patricia of the Sisters of Mercy – disciplined her to get up early for morning prayers. Dispensed from her vows, she is now Professor Eve Karam with academic appointments in theology and political science at the College of St. Joseph in Hartford, Connecticut. My wife has not one but two doctorates. Smart, this one.

When I finally woke up, I looked out the bedroom window but couldn't see anything. The wind had driven the snow so hard that the big bedroom window overlooking the harbor had become another wall. If it were paint, Sherman-Williams would call it "Glacier White." No light came through.

I got out of bed and looked around. I was prepared to let Blackie, my Schutzhund-trained German Shepherd, out for his morning constitutional, but he wasn't there. Eve must have taken care of him. I reached for my cell phone, a bad habit but one I could live with. When I am not in the office, I forward the calls from my direct line to my cellphone. There was a voicemail message:

> *Mr. Kelly. My name is Jim Perry, and I'm calling about my son, Mark. A week ago, he went to a gun show in Portland, Maine, and we haven't heard from him since. It's like he's disappeared. No one knows where he is. I've talked to his brother and his friends. No one has seen him or heard from*

him. He took the week off from work, so they don't know where he is. They want him back because of the snow. My wife called the Portland police. They checked their databases, and he wasn't arrested or anything. No accidents. Since he's thirty-two, there's nothing more they can do. Would you give me a call? I think he's probably okay, but I'd really like to know where he is. I think he would have told us if he'd gone hunting or something.

"Hunting or something." A thirty-two-year-old male was on vacation in Maine. There had been no accidents, and he had not been arrested. He had been gone a week. He was probably okay. I knew I would call Perry back eventually, but right now I had a more pressing problem.

When I bought Nutmeg Security and Investigations from my partners, Sam and Meg DeRosa, the plan was for someone other than me to run the security part of the business. The last thing I wanted to do was be in charge of protecting condominium swimming pools from teenagers. We did a lot more than that, but the swimming pool comment was my obnoxious way of expressing my preference for the investigative side of the business. Sam and Meg had met a young man, Marvin Cahill, at a security conference in Florida, a young man they liked very much. They thought he might be the right person. He seemed smart and ambitious, understood the security business, and was tired of being the number two person where he worked. He was a bachelor, so he didn't have to wait until the end of a school year to move a family with kids. He could come in two weeks if need be. After several Zoom conversations, we struck a deal with Cahill. He would take over the security division of our company.

So, on Thursday morning, he flew into Hartford, and we arranged for a limousine to pick him up and drive him to New Haven. The plan was to meet on Friday morning to solidify his employment and future partnership. He'd go back to Florida for Christmas and start right after the New Year. He would camp out at the Residence Inn in New Haven, at our expense, until he found a place to live. Things were all going according to plan until Cahill and the blizzard arrived together.

The blizzard was a big one. On the first night, twenty-eight inches of white stuff came down. And it came with high winds and gusts up to sixty miles an hour. Everything closed, and the governor told us to stay home. There was no way I could get to New Haven from Milford Friday morning for my planned breakfast meeting with Cahill. Fortunately, I still had cell service. I called him and told him. He told me there was no power at the B&B where we had housed him. The B&B had water but no heat and no lights. Eve and I were in the same predicament at our condominium in Milford, but at least we had each other.

That was Friday. Saturday was the same, and there was more snow. I talked to Cahill and he said they still had no power and they were running out of wood for the fireplace in the parlor. The snow stopped Saturday night. On Sunday Cahill managed to get to the airport in Hartford and flew back to Miami. He had made up his mind about employment with Nutmeg. He left his *mind* on my voicemail: "Sorry, but this isn't going to work for me." In a long, rambling message, Marvin Cahill explained that he loved Miami, hated the cold, and could not imagine being trapped like that ever again. I could have responded with, "What about hurricanes?" but I knew that wouldn't work. That was the last I heard from him.

When I called Sam and Meg to tell them what happened, my former partners said they were sorry they were leaving me in the lurch but couldn't cancel their trip. Clearly, they were more concerned about their flights to the Caribbean the day after Christmas than my predicament. They were scheduled to leave Tuesday morning. Their heads had retired, and they were getting their bodies to follow – a week at a Sandals Resort, all-inclusive, not a care in the world.

Nutmeg Security and Investigations was mine to worry about. My darling Eve was not overly sympathetic. "Get used to it, Kelly. You asked for it. You're the boss now." I was not looking forward to going to work Tuesday morning. I knew I'd be facing a host of security problems caused by the blizzard: alarms not working because of downed power lines, personnel not able to get to their posts, and gates unable to open because of snow drifts. I didn't have any active investigations at the time, so I had no excuse. I owned whatever security issues the blizzard had created. And then what? I would have to find someone to replace Cahill.

First, though, there was Christmas. Our original, pre-blizzard plan called for Eve and me, along with my daughter Molly, her fiancé Stan, and my son Ben to drive to Bay Ridge in Brooklyn to celebrate with Eve's family. It would be midnight Mass at Our Lady of Lebanon Maronite Cathedral, followed by a day of eating Lebanese delicacies with Eve's mother, brothers, sisters, and their families. Loud, raucous, over-the-top fun. Then the two-hour drive back to Milford. A very long day.

The remnants of the blizzard were making driving extremely difficult. The governor was still asking people to stay at home to make clean-up from the snow easier. Reluctantly, Eve called her mother to give her the news. We had Christmas presents, but we didn't have food. In my family, Thanksgiving and Christmas are both Turkey meals. Off we went, a great hunter and his mate, looking for a turkey with all of the assorted fixings plus pies and the required vegetables. Every turkey we found was frozen. A flurry of text messages with the younger generation debating fish, fowl, or beef, led to the purchase of the largest roasting chicken we could find. That would legitimize the cranberry sauce and stuffing. Potatoes for mashing, frozen bags of green beans and corn, two pounds of frozen shrimp, the last apple pie in the store, and it was beginning to look a lot like Christmas, and a very white one at that. Since we were the bringers of the wine to Bay Ridge, we were well-stocked in that department.

Midnight Mass was still a must; sorry, Governor. We all went, and the 'kids' spent the night. Christmas day was quiet by comparison to the Bay Ridge experience but lovely. After dinner, we went for a walk along the harbor where the snowplows had managed to carve out one lane for traffic. No one was out driving, though, so it was peaceful. Enough snow does that. Everything slows down; things get quiet. We did as well.

At breakfast, Eve asked how she could help. I didn't know. I told her about Jim Perry's call but confessed my mind was not on a thirty-two-year-old who was probably shacked up with a new honey someplace in Maine.

"He could be hurt," she said, ever the empath.

"His parents don't seem that concerned. Perry didn't say anything about them heading to Maine to look for him."

"True. But they did call you, and there is the slight issue of a blizzard that might deter them from traipsing off to Maine."

"I'll call him back."

"I know you will."

***

Despite their focus on getting to Jamaica, Sam and Meg apparently felt some responsibility for Cahill's desertion. When I arrived at the office, their backup plan for Cahill was sitting at Sam's desk. Their oldest, Vicki DeRosa Russo, was on the telephone. Her head was down, blond hair falling, covering her face. From her end of the conversation, I could tell she was talking with one of our security people who was reporting in. When I tapped on her open door, she raised her head, smiled, and waved.

On the floor, her sprawled-out teenage son was wearing earphones and playing a computer game on his iPad. He was all arms and legs. Of course Paulo was here. No school. Christmas vacation. I wondered where his younger brother was. Sam and Meg's daughter had come to the rescue, and it looked like Nutmeg would continue to be a family affair, at least for today. But for how long?

Blackie left my side, went over to the teenager, bent down, and gave Paulo a lick of welcome. Lost behind earphones and attention to his game, he was surprised by the dog licking him. Paulo rolled over and started wrestling with the hundred-pound black, hairy intruder. I left what was, at least temporarily, Vicki's office; Blackie stayed.

20

When I reached my desk, I wasn't ready to start. Coffee first. Our computer guru, Jackie Forrest, had managed to get in and was just leaving our break area when I arrived. She said, "Some storm, huh? Not even January. Can you believe it?"

"Yeah. Everything okay with the power outage?"

"No problems. I've checked. The generator kicked right in. All the backup systems worked perfectly. We're fine." Shifting topics, she said, "So, what happened to the new guy? Cahill. I only Zoomed with him, but he seemed like a good fit."

"The storm. Apparently, Marvin did not figure New England weather into his deliberations."

"Seriously? So, is Vicki taking over?"

"Taking over? What do you mean? I'm just glad she's here today."

"Oh. I thought she might be taking over."

"Taking over what?"

"You know…" Jackie paused. "You didn't know?"

"Know what?"

"Vicki. She wanted to do this right along."

"Do what?"

"Join the firm. Head up security."

"Join the firm? What are you talking about?"

Jackie ignored my question and quickly left, saying, "I've got some stuff to do. By the way, I never did like the name Marvin." Her rapid departure left me with several questions that needed answering.

I started back to my office but stopped to see if Vicki was still on the phone. She was. My questions would have to wait.

When I reached my office, I played Jim Perry's message twice. The father was worried but did not sound frantic. I wondered how his wife was handling her son's disappearance. Perry said she had been the one to call the Portland police. Perhaps she didn't share her husband's equanimity.

People go missing – a lot of them. Six hundred thousand people are reported missing every year in the United States. The vast majority of them show up within the first few days of being missed, and only a tiny fraction of them are ever harmed. A week was on the long side, but young men did things like that, taking off and not telling anyone where they were going. Thirty-two was a bit old to be pulling that kind of stunt. Eighteen-year-old, sure, but thirty-two?

I kept thinking about that. Mark Perry was thirty-two. His age bothered me. Abduction and murder were possibilities but highly unlikely. Had he bought a gun and decided to go into the wilderness after the gun show? Maybe try out a new weapon? Maine has a lot of wilderness, and wilderness claims over a thousand lives each year because of weather or accidents. Sometimes the people are never found. I had no idea if Maine had been hit by the blizzard the way Connecticut was. Maybe he was in a hotel someplace without power. Christmas, though. Had he made it home for Christmas?

I called the number Perry had left. A woman answered. I said, "This is Frank Kelly. Mr. Perry asked me to give him a call."

"I'll get him. Is this about my son?" I didn't know what Perry told his wife about getting in touch with me, so I put on my smile voice and added a boundary, "I haven't spoken with Mr. Perry yet."

"I'll get him." She shouted, "Jim, it's Frank Kelly."

A couple of seconds later, a man answered, "Kelly?"

"Yes. You left me a message."

"Yeah, I did. I thought I'd hear from you before now."

Okay, so is he being demanding or is he anxious? It was Christmas for Christ's sake. I tried to ignore it, but I found something about his voice irritating. It was as though I was a waiter and had gotten his order wrong. "How can I help?"

"I told you. My son's not been heard from for a couple of weeks, and no one knows where he is. Cops want nothing to do with it."

"I must be confused. I thought you said a week." Let's get our facts straight. "Have you filed an official missing person report?"

"Not yet. I didn't want to embarrass him if everything's okay." He didn't add "or if he's just being stupid" to the end of his sentence, but he might as well have. Why was he so irritated, and with whom?

"Has this ever happened before? You know, your son not being in touch with you for a while."

"No. Maybe a day or two, even a week. But when his mother calls him and leaves a message or texts him, he gets back in touch with her within a couple of hours." So, Mom communicates with Mark.

"I understand. You said he had gone missing for a week once before. Where was he that time?"

"With his brother, but his brother says he has no idea where he is."

"Where did the two of them go that time?"

"Vegas. See Connor MacGregor fight."

"Do you think he…"

"Went to someplace like Vegas? Nah. It's been a lean winter for him." Perry said that with a finality that implied he did not approve of his son's economic standing.

"You said he's had a lean winter. Could he be looking for a job? Maybe got a new one, just hasn't told you yet?"

"Possible, but he would have called by now. Someone. Would have called someone. It's Christmas. He didn't call. You get that?"

"Yes. I understand. Does he live with you?"

"Hell, no. He's got his own place. We've already been there. I've got a key. Nothing." I heard Perry's wife saying something in the background. Perry ignored her.

"You said friends hadn't heard from him either."

"No, and he's got to get to work, or he'll lose his job." Again, the concern about economics. Had the Perrys been providing Mark with funds?

"Does Mark have a girlfriend? Wife?"

"Divorced. I know he's seeing someone; we haven't met her." Again, I heard Perry's wife in the background. Her voice sounded demanding. "My wife wants me to tell you that all his guns are gone."

"All his guns?"

"Yeah. He's a collector." Again, his wife was saying something. He didn't tell me what it was this time.

"Tell me about the guns."

"What about them?"

"Did he have a lot of them; what kind?"

"Why do you want to know that?" Again, "stupid" was implied. Maybe Jim Perry was just generally irritated with the world.

"I'm just wondering what kind of weapons he might have taken with him if he was going to a gun show and why he would take all of them. Do you find that unusual?"

"I told you. He's a collector. Maybe he wanted to sell some or trade them. I don't know." Somehow, that was supposed to be a definitive answer. Or, the message was, "Stop asking questions about his guns." So, I stopped. The type of weapons would remain unknown for now.

I said, "You might want to call his friends and see if any of them know how to contact the woman he's been seeing. She might know where he is."

"And if she doesn't?"

"Let's go one step at a time. In the meantime, would you email me his contact information, full name, address, telephone, email address, where he worked, and any social media that he uses."

"What do you want that for?"

"Just in case he's posted something that might help us. Also, send me four or five current pictures."

"Four or five?"

"If you would. People look different in different pictures."

"I guess. What's your email?"

"Frankkelly@Nutmegsecurity.com. No 'e' before the 'y' in Kelly. Nutmeg security is one word. Also, would you send me your contact information, as well."

"You've got my phone number; what more do you want?"

"Just address and all your phone numbers – your wife's, too; you said you had another son. Any other children?"

"No, just Mark and Luke. Why do you want their numbers?"

"So, I can get in touch with them." I didn't say, so we can learn more about you, your wife, and your sons.

After I hung up the phone, I buzzed Jackie. "Hey, in a couple of minutes, I'm going to forward you an email with information about a Mark Perry. Would you do a deep dive on him?"

"Anything specific?"

"No. Whatever you find. No rush. The guy's missing. Parents are worried, but he's thirty-two. He was headed to Portland, Maine, to attend a gun show. That was a week ago."

"Quite a while. Disappearing for Christmas. That's strange. Anything suspicious?" Jackie loved a mystery.

"Other than the fact that his parents have no idea where he is? No."

"Okay. Got it. Will do."

Back in the dark ages, when I started studying and then teaching investigative techniques, doing a deep dive would take weeks and trips to multiple places to collect information: courthouses, newspapers, and any place the target might have spent money. Microfiche was the investigator's friend. Today, for a few hundred dollars a year, you can subscribe to a wide range of software companies that have developed applications to do the work for you – in a matter of minutes. Police have even more resources at their disposal, and Nutmeg's friendships with police departments, thanks to Sam DeRosa, are important. A few after-work drinks can go a long way to keep these relationships intact.

***

I had just finished lunch when Jackie knocked on my door. "I've got the stuff on Perry."

"Come on in. You get lunch yet?"

"Yeah. I'm good."

"So, tell me."

"Guy's a right-wing nut case."

"That's succinct."

"You take a look at the Facebook groups he's in and the sites he's following, and you'll see what I mean. Here goes: Guy's ex-Special Forces, 3rd Group at Ft. Bragg in North Carolina. Served eight years. Two deployments to Afghanistan. Honorable discharge. Divorced. No children. His ex-wife had him in court once on a domestic complaint. Younger brother, Luke."

"There's no Matthew or John?"

Jackie looked at me and shook her head, "Really?"

"Okay. I'll stop. "How did you find out about the domestic?"

"Court records. His wife divorced him rather than go through the reconciliation process."

"Any other assaults?"

"No. He's a gun nut. From the pictures he's posted, it looks like he's got at least fifteen weapons, and they are a variety package. None are meant for hunting. He belongs to a gun club and was second vice president last year."

"Work?"

"Three different jobs since he got out of the service. Primarily as a laborer, landscaping. Some restaurant stuff. I can't find anything that would indicate he has any special skills other than firing a gun and beating up on his wife."

"You called him a right-wing nut."

"Facebook likes and comments. Conspiracy sites. Forums he belongs to on Mastadon. Some stuff I didn't even know existed. So, I went a little deeper into the dark web. I've printed out some of the comments he's posted. The guy is certifiable. He makes your normal alt-right wing conservative look like a left-wing liberal."

"Violent?"

"Oh yeah. He was on a team that was training warlords."

"So?"

"Training warlords, Frank. Afghan warlords. Torture."

"Got it."

"Any changes over time?"

"Yes. He thinks President Goodman was a traitor because he didn't pursue the Taliban into Pakistan. That's when he started talking about the overthrow of the government."

"Overthrow?

"Overthrow. Insurrection Get rid of the traitors. All of it."

"Dangerous?"

"Given his background and interests? You think?"

Jackie handed me a thick file.

I asked, "Any guesses where he might be?"

"Yep. Maine or New Hampshire."

"Why?"

"Web message exchanges with folks in both places. Militia types. Nice people he's hanging out with. Try this: 'America needs to be retaken by whites.' 'Extremism in defense of liberty is no vice.' I'm telling you, Frank, this guy is over the edge."

"That extremism quote, that's Barry Goldwater."

"Who's that?"

"Former Republican candidate for president. Senator from Arizona."

"It's also this guy up in Maine Perry's been communicating with. That saying of Barry Whoever is close to the name of a group in Maine: The Defenders of Liberty. Defenders for short. They were at the gun show this guy went to. Had a table."

"How do you get all this stuff."

"Most of it's easy."

"The not so easy?"

"Oh, that. You don't want to know. Don't worry, though. I used my own computer for anything marginal."

"You're right. I don't want to know. Is this Defenders group just an internet kind of group? Do they have a place? Organization?"

"All of the above. It's in the file. Let me know if you want more."

"Thanks. Let me start with this. I'm not at all sure this guy is missing. He's just missing from his parents, my guess."

"Missing a few screws is my guess."

"Feeling a little judgmental, are we?"

"No little about it. Wait until you read this stuff. One thing bugs me. I get not telling his parents what he's into. What about his brother and friends?"

"Maybe he's too far out for them, too? Or..."

"They're not leveling with the parents."

"Where's this place in Maine?"

"You ready for this? They call it Camp Liberty, and it's in Sparta, Maine."

"You're joking. Sparta?"

"It's Maine. Maine is crazy with names. There's a China, a Poland, Mexico, Norway, and Peru. Try Hope, Liberty, and my new favorite. You want to guess?"

"Okay. What?"

"Purgatory. Can you imagine a kid going off to college... 'Where are you from?' 'Purgatory.' You want more?"

"Names? No. I think that does it. Got a little sidetracked?"

"Who me? Never. Oh, and the Defenders of Liberty is not the only group in Maine. They're all there: American Warriors, NSC131, Patriot Front, Three Percenters, Bluttstamm..."

"Bluttstamm?"

"German. Means blood tribe. Neo-Nazi group. The biggest group seems to be the Maine Militia with chapters all over the state."

"You're kidding. Chapters?"

"Yup, and the Defenders of Liberty think those people are a bunch of, to use their words, 'Weekend pussies who play dress up.' Some of them..."

"Are capable of violence. And you think..."

"The Defenders are worse. Absolutely."

"One step at a time."

Chapter Three: Another DeRosa

I was in the middle of reading the file Jackie had given me when Vicki knocked on my door, "Am I interrupting?"

"No. Come on in."

She walked over and sat down in one of the four chairs at the small conference table in the office. "I'll bet you were surprised to see me when you walked in this morning."

I got up and took one of the other chairs at the table. "I sure was. Tell me what happened."

"Mom called and told me what happened with Cahill. Asked if I could give you a hand. So here I am." Her voice changed, and she became formal. "Frank, I'd like to apply for the position of director of Nutmeg's security division."

"Vic, are you serious?"

"Very. I wanted to do it before, but my parents, especially Dad, were, to put it mildly, against it. They didn't think I could handle it with two teenagers at home. When I pointed out I was already working a thirty-six-hour week as a dispatcher in Stratford, Dad said that was different. You should have heard him."

She had mastered her imitation of Sam. I tried to keep a straight face when she said, "There, you can do your shift, go home, and forget about work. Security at Nutmeg is a twenty-four-hour-a-day job. You've got personnel depending on you and clients to think about. It's not the same."

"What did your mother say?"

"Mom wasn't as bad, but she wasn't for it either."

"What were her reasons?"

"Similar to Dad's. She thought I should wait a couple of years."

"What do you think?"

"I'm forty-one years old and can make my own decisions."

"Vic, I don't want to get…"

"In the middle of something. I know. Please note, though: who did they call to help out when Marvin Cahill chickened out and ran back to the warmth of Miami? Can you believe that? Where on earth did that guy think he was moving to? New England has winters. He didn't know that?"

"I guess not. So, your parents called you?"

"Mom. Yep. I used to work here on and off when they were in a jam. That was before your time. Anyway, here I am. So, what do you think?"

"I don't know. Your dad's right. It's a big job. It's selling as well as managing. How comfortable…"

"Am I about taking it on? Very. I've been around this business since they started it. I've filled in on security when they were in jams. I sure know Connecticut better than Cahill, and I know a lot of the staff already."

"Yeah, you do."

"So?"

"I think we should wait until your parents get back to make a firm decision. Your parents are under a consulting contract for the coming year, and I wouldn't…"

"Want to, I know, get in the middle of something."

"We're also going to have to fill your mother's position. Have you considered…"

"Being the finance person? Running the office? Not my thing. I want to be out in the field like my father was. My B.A. is in criminal justice. My plan after college was to apply to the police force in Fairfield."

"I didn't know that. What happened?"

"A really stupid first marriage, then kids, then a divorce and starting all over."

I could see she was serious about doing this and was excited. Maybe keeping it in the family was a good idea, and the thought of not having to worry about it would be a load off my mind. I realized I hadn't paid much attention to Vicki since I joined Nutmeg. I just thought of her as Sam and Meg's daughter and mother to their two grandchildren. High energy. Bright. Beyond that, I didn't know her.

"How about this for now? I'd love it if you could fill in. I'll pay you what we were going to pay Cahill. What about your dispatch job, though?"

"I gave them notice over a month ago. They know I've been looking, but we agreed I'd stay on until they replaced me or I found something. Our agreement was I could leave with two days' notice if I found something before they hired a replacement. They've been dragging their feet. I can be available full-time starting on Friday. In the meantime, I can help out."

"You already gave notice?"

"I did. I've been looking. I started when Dad said he didn't think I could do the job at Nutmeg and you were going to offer it to Cahill. That sounded like a done deal, so I started looking for something else."

"Vic, I'm sorry. I didn't know you were interested."

"Not your fault."

I was irritated that neither Sam nor Meg had told me Vicki was interested. We should have at least discussed it.

Vicki continued. "I'm bored dispatching. It was great when the kids were young. Now, it's tedious. Same old, same old, day in and day out."

Okay, Kelly. It's your company now. Make a decision. "Can you work today?"

"Yes, until three. I'm on the four-to-midnight shift. I'll let them know when I go to work tonight. I can work here from nine to three tomorrow and Thursday and start full-time on Friday."

"What about…"

"The kids? They're well-trained. And Fred's used to cooking dinner and supervising homework."

I had met Fred. I knew he was her husband, but until now, I didn't

31

know Fred was husband number two. There was a lot about this woman I didn't know.

She continued, "It's one of the bonuses of being married to a teacher who gets home by five most days. They'll manage just fine."

"I know all about that."

"That's right. You taught."

"Okay. Let's plan on meeting tomorrow morning. We'll go over the client list and the staff assignments. This afternoon, I've got to get going with this new client."

"Someone new?"

"Name's James Perry."

"What's it about?"

"I'm not sure there's much to it. His thirty-two-year-old son hasn't been in touch with his parents. Name's Mark. His brother and his friends claim they don't know where he is. The guy went to a gun show in Portland, Maine. Portland police have nothing. He hasn't shown up on any hospital intakes."

"He just vanished?"

"Seems like it. Only been a week, though. Doesn't sound like a warm and fuzzy character. He may have gotten hooked up with a radical right-wing group of vigilantes. Militia types."

"Let me know if I can help."

"What you're doing is more help than you can imagine."

***

Vicki left, and I went back to the file that Jackie had prepared for me. As usual, Jackie had gone beyond what I asked for. She anticipated what I didn't yet know I would ask for. One folder was labeled "legal." I started there. First up was the Heller decision: *District of Columbia v. Heller, 554 U.S. 570, 621 (2008) (citing Presser v. Illinois, 116 U.S. 252 (1886))*. It was the second time the Supreme Court ruled that the Second Amendment did not give a group the right to form a militia apart from the governance of the state.

Given where Mark Perry was headed and his Facebook likes, Jackie had focused on Maine law:

> Prohibition on private military units: Maine law makes it a crime for groups of people to organize as private militias without permission from the state. *Me. Stat. tit. 37-B, § 342(2)* provides that "[n]o group of persons, other than federal or state military forces, may join together as a military organization or parade in public with firearms." Prohibition on unauthorized wearing of uniforms: In Maine, it is a crime "for any person not an officer or enlisted man in the federal or state military forces to wear the duly prescribed uniform of any military forces," "any distinctive part" of a military uniform, "or a uniform any part of which is similar to a distinctive part of a prescribed uniform." *Me. Stat. tit. 37-B, § 266(3).*

Despite Maine's law, the Maine Militia claimed to have chapters in thirteen of Maine's sixteen counties and a membership of thousands. They were not secretive about their existence. Jackie included a clip from an old Bangor Daily News article. In it, the reporter interviewed Mack Page, the leader of the Maine Militia. Jackie had highlighted some paragraphs:

> "The Maine Militia also makes a public showing each year at the Searsmont Memorial Day parade. Marching in full dress uniform and carrying the American flag, the Maine flag and the Maine Militia flag emblazoned with a rearing black bear, the honor guard has added a touch of military dignity to the parade," Page said.
>
> "Initially, some residents took issue with the idea of having a militia participate in the parade," said Searsmont First Selectman Bruce Brierley, but no longer.

***

John [Page] spoke about the militia's training exercises and general preparedness. Members have stockpiles of tents, blankets, and other things that might be needed in an emergency. Each county [chapter] must have a supply of 50 gallons of gasoline, kerosene, and diesel fuel on hand, and each Maine Militia member must have a "three-day pack" with them, containing enough first aid, food, and water to survive in case of emergency. They practice winter camping and other survival techniques, along with learning how to march in sync.

***

In part, the gun requirement helps to weed out felons, whom they don't accept, he said. It's also to teach safe usage to its members – and because, again, they'd rather be prepared. Just in case. "I'd rather have a gun and not need it than need a gun and not have it," Page said.

***

In order to join, a would-be member needs a rifle with 100 rounds of ammunition, a knapsack, and eating and cooking utensils. But militia members said they also look toward the future and being prepared for what might arise.

***

This country's in trouble," Page said. "Things are getting very bad, and they're only going to get worse."

Jackie added a note: "This is the group the Defenders consider pussies." On another note, she wrote: "Remember the Rise of the Moors group that got arrested on July 3, 2021? They said they were going to Maine for 'training.' I wonder where that would take place? Possibly Sparta and the Defenders of Liberty? Or maybe Belfast and the Maine Militia?"

I remembered the Rise of the Moors group and what happened in 2021. Traffic was tied up on Route 95 in Connecticut for hours. The group's van broke down, and when the Connecticut State Police stopped to assist, the group scattered. They were armed to the teeth – heavy-duty stuff. It was the first time I had heard about or thought about a black militia group. The Rise of the Moors did not believe they were subject to American laws. They learned they were.

It was clear that Maine wasn't enforcing its laws if the Maine Militia was marching in uniform in Searsmont. Why was there no enforcement? Was it not caring or not wanting to get into a legal fight about the constitutionality of the Maine law? Or was the sheriff's department sympathetic to the beliefs of the Militia? I jotted down my questions on a legal pad. Did Maine state officials know about the Defenders of Liberty? If they had a table at a gun show, they must know. Was Mark Perry working the table? Was Mark Perry at Fort Liberty in Sparta, Maine? I kept writing down questions.

There was another note from Jackie: "From his pictures, it looks like Mark wears a Thor's Hammer medal around his neck. Maybe he's into Odinism. A lot of white supremacists are. Maybe he went to Sparta for a Blot."

What the hell is "Odinism?" A "Blot?" Did Perry worship Odin, the Norse God of war and death? Who is this Mark Perry? Jackie wrote: "Sparta sounds like Ulysses, PA. Neo-Nazis are welcome." I knew Maine had a KKK history. Maybe it wasn't just history. Ulysses? What happened in Ulysses, PA? More questions.

Still another file described the movement called 'Prepared Citizens.' These were civilians – nurses, pilots, construction workers – preparing themselves for a civil war or an invasion. The leader on one weekend retreat where his group of trainees had gathered to learn how to use firearms began with a prayer: "Lord, you would use them as assets, to be protectors in this world, in a world that's full of evil." These groups were all over the country, average citizens who feared some catastrophe and wanted to be prepared with pistols, rifles, and assault weapons. Their instructors were usually former military or police. I wondered if there was a group like this in Fairfield or New Haven.

Other than a vague "find Mark," I realized I hadn't clarified what Mark's mother and father wanted from me, so I called them. Again, I got Mrs. Perry on the phone. "Have you found him?" she asked.

"No. We need to straighten some legal things out before we start to do an intensive search."

"I'm worried about him."

"I understand. Anything in particular you are worried about?"

"Nothing I can put my finger on."

"But you are worried."

"He hasn't been himself lately."

"In what way?"

"He's been saying things."

"Saying things about…" I felt like I was pulling gum out of a child's hair without hurting them.

"Mark's always been very conservative, but lately, well, ever since President Goodman's policies in Afghanistan, he's been…"

"He's been…"

"Different."

"How?"

"Saying things." More goddamn gum. Okay. She's afraid to tell me. What has her son been saying? I decided to be direct with her.

"It sounds like you're very concerned about Mark and that something has changed. Knowing what those things are will help me find him. Can you be specific?"

"Things like… well, he said he wishes he had..." She stopped talking.

"He had?"

"He feels like he has missed out on some things."

"Some things?"

"You know. That thing at the Capital."

"You mean January 6th?"

"I'm sure he didn't mean it."

"Mean what?"

"He said that President Goodman is a traitor and needs to be shot. It's time to take our country back. Things like that."

"It sounds like you're worried he might do something that would get him into trouble."

"My husband doesn't think he would… but I…"

She stopped herself, censoring. I waited. Nothing. When it became apparent she was not going to continue, I asked, "Anything else?"

"He started talking a lot about this general."

"A general…"

I could hear a man shouting, "What are you telling him? Here, give me that!"

Jim Perry got on the line. "Ignore her. She's exaggerating. He hasn't changed. There's nothing wrong with him. We just want to know where he is."

I had a decision to make: get involved in their conflict or leave it alone. I decided to leave it alone for now. She could elaborate on the changes she saw in Mark, but I had enough information to let my imagination do the rest. I also didn't want to listen to Jim Perry defend his son, so I got down to the business I had called about.

"Mr. Perry, my apologies. There are a couple of things I should have discussed with you the last time we spoke, and I failed to do so. First, we need to talk about our fees, and I need to send you our contract for our services and our confidentiality agreement. Would you like me to email these to you? Electronic signatures are fine."

"Sure. Do that."

"Okay, I'm going to do that right now. When I have gotten these back from you, I'll call again. I'll have some questions for you."

"Sure."

"Okay, your email is…"

"I sent you everyone's contact information from my email."

"Thank you. I'm sending these right away. As soon as I get them back with your signatures, I'll call."

I waited. I expected to get the signed documents back within minutes. It didn't happen. I waited. After twenty minutes, I decided to stop waiting and went in to talk to Vicki to find out how things were going on the security front. She was on the phone, so I went back to my office.

Sticker shock exists in all businesses. I wondered if that was taking place. Nutmeg charges different rates for different staff members, anywhere from $40 an hour to $250 an hour, depending on who is doing what. We also set upper limits on the number of hours we would not exceed without agreement from the client. All of this information was included in the contract I had sent Perry. I had set an initial limit of $5,000 to find Mark Perry. I had set it that high in case I had to make a trip to Maine to find their son. It may have been too high for the Perrys.

An hour went by. Nothing from the Perry household. I stopped checking my email and concluded they were not interested, they had a lead on their own, or that Mark had gotten in touch with them. Such is the life of a private investigator. Then the telephone rang. It was Jim Perry. He got right to the point, "Five thousand dollars is a lot of money. We can't afford that. We don't know if there's anything wrong."

"I understand. Perhaps you would like to wait a few more days to see if you hear from Mark."

"No. We don't want to wait. Can't you do it for less?"

I knew the reaction to our fees was not dissimilar to what dental patients experience when they find out what a root canal and crown are going to cost. People have no idea how expensive investigations can be.

I answered, "If you would like to set a lower top limit, I can do that. I had anticipated the possibility of one trip to Maine. That doesn't mean it would be necessary. We might find Mark in a few hours of digging. It's impossible to know."

"Okay. Yeah. I guess. Alright. How about you let me know when you hit three thousand?"

"I can do that."

"Okay, good. I'll get this right back to you."

Five minutes later, I received the contract, and I called Perry.

"Thanks for getting these to me. I know you want me to find Mark, and I'm going to continue working on that – we already have done some digging. But what would you like me to do when I do find him?"

"What do you mean?"

"Well, do you want me to call you and let you know I have found him and that he appears to be alive and well and where he is, or do you want me to provide you with the specifics of what he is doing, or would you like me to approach him and ask him to get in touch with you and your wife – that you are concerned? Mark is an adult. By searching for him, I am intruding upon his right to privacy. Although this may seem like a remote possibility to you and your wife, Mark may not want you to know where he is. My question is, what is the degree of intrusion that you would like me to perform?"

"Wait a minute. Let me talk to my wife." It took several minutes. I waited. Finally, he got back on the line. "Tell him we're worried about him and ask him to get in touch with us."

"Okay. I'll be in touch."

***

That night, over dinner, I told Eve about my discussion with Vicki. She said, "I know you love Sam, but it doesn't mean he's perfect. He knows the job and what it's taken out of him. Maybe he was just being protective of Vicki."

"Or his grandkids."

"That, too."

"You know what I didn't think about until now, Vicki's younger than Sam was when he started the business. He started it from scratch. Vicki's taking over something that is well-established, thanks to Sam. He may be thinking about how many hours he had to work when he got started."

"True."

"There may be something else." I waited for her to say something, but she didn't.

"What?"

39

"Didn't Marvin Cahill have military and security experience? Maybe Sam thinks those are absolutely necessary."

"Possibly."

"And one other thing."

"Yes."

"Maybe Sam doesn't think a woman can do the job."

"With Meg as his wife? Really?"

"Daughters are different. My father was much more protective of me than my brother."

"I guess."

"And…"

"More?"

"Sam helped you on your more dangerous cases. Perhaps he simply doesn't want to put his daughter at risk."

"Sam didn't have to do that. He wanted to."

"And you don't think Vicki might? She is her father's daughter. And didn't she say she wanted to be in the field? Dispatching is boring and tedious. Weren't those her words?"

"Do you think…"

"She may actually want to do what you do."

"Really?"

"Possibly. Who knows?"

"I should talk to her about that."

"No, you shouldn't."

"Why not?"

"Trust me. Some things just need to develop over time."

Over dishes, I asked, "Do you think Henry knows anything about hate groups?" Henry was Henry Gore, a professor of political science at the University of Connecticut and Eve's former doctoral dissertation advisor. Henry had helped me understand the political scenarios in the case that almost got me killed and led to my nightmares.

"Possibly. And if he doesn't, he'll sound like he does. Henry likes to think he knows everything."

"But he doesn't."

"Close, but he knows everyone. He can certainly point you in the right direction."

"I'll call him."

"Do call him. He'll love it, especially if you take him to dinner. I have a question."

"What?"

"Is this case going to get dangerous?"

"No. Why do you ask?"

"Hate groups. Guns. Militia crazies. Really?"

"All I'm doing is looking for this guy. He might show up tomorrow. Nothing more."

"You promised."

"To be careful. I know. At most, I'm only allowed a paper cut now and then."

"Good. I'm not going into any more hospital rooms because of your job."

"I know."

Chapter Four: Help

It was Eve's idea; I was resistant. No one in my family ever had a "mental illness," and no one in my family ever needed psychotherapy. My parents both thought psychotherapy was nonsense. They were of the "pull yourself together" generation. My nightmares hadn't gotten that message, though, so three months ago I agreed to "try it out." Eve dug around and found someone who was "Smarter than you are and knows his stuff." I didn't ask her about the "smarter than you are" comment.

That's how I came to have a regular four o'clock Wednesday appointment with Stuart Nevens, M.D., Distinguished Fellow of the American Psychiatric Association, and Harvey S. and Helen T. Shapiro, Professor of Psychiatry, Yale University School of Medicine. He told me to call him Stu. His office was in an old home on "Psychiatrist Row" in New Haven. Parking was always a problem, but it was worse today because of the snow piles from the blizzard.

When you entered the front door of what was once an elegant home for a single family, you found yourself in a wide hallway. Stu's waiting room, once the parlor, was to the right – bay window facing the street, comfortable leather chairs, white noise machine whirring away. Local magazines with articles about the current hot New Haven restaurants were stacked on an old oak table. Oak. That was what struck me the first time I walked into the room – beautiful old oak panels, trim, and doors. It was comforting.

The stairs in the central hall led to the second floor, with three more offices belonging to a psychologist and two social workers. Across the hall from his waiting room was Stu's therapy office, probably the original dining room. His office had double doors to the hall. Privacy. Everyone wanted privacy. I certainly did. Eve was the only one who knew I was seeing Stu, except for Blackie. With Stu's blessing, Blackie came with me.

This room was different – sparse, muted colors. Somehow, his office communicated: "Here we do important work." Stu was like that, too. He was friendly, but he wasn't going to be my buddy. Shorter than me, a bit overweight, and with a seemingly never-ending supply of sweaters, Stu was as comfortable as his waiting room. We laughed at times but didn't tell jokes.

He always surprised me. He saw around the corners of my psyche where I didn't even see the corners. During this Friday afternoon visit, I told him my dreams had become intense the last few nights. He didn't say anything – space, silence, emptiness. Work Kelly. You do the damned work. Stu never said that. His silence did.

It was pretty damn obvious, always the obvious – Mark Perry, militia, danger, being shot, the hospital. Stress working its way out in nightmares. And then the questions: Why was I doing this? To find Mark Perry? Proving myself? To whom? So often, the first person who came to mind was Patricia. My late wife, killed in that car crash with her lover. Patricia, who had wanted a "real" man, not a college teacher. A "real man" made things, she would say. Her lover did. He built homes; she sold them. What did I do? I taught. How often had she said, "Those who can't, teach." So, after she died, I left teaching and showed her. I'd showed her again, and again, and again.

And then there was dear old Dad, my father, the lawyer. He was always saying, "Community College. Why are you teaching at a community college? You've got a doctorate."

"Because that's where there was a job, Dad. And I like it." It was simple. So simple. I should have asked my father for absolution because I committed the sin of not wanting to become a lawyer like him. Dad approved of my son, Benjamin, who was a lawyer.

43

Proving myself. The same old shit. And then somebody shot me and the nightmares came. Is that what proving myself got me? And now, I owned the firm and was married to the world's most intelligent, most wonderful woman. Take that, Patricia; take that, Dad.

Stu said it once in a way that I laughed at and then wanted to imprint on my psyche: "Shit is not destiny." This was the same old "prove yourself" shit, and I had choices. My choices. Choices. I could choose to tell Jim Perry, "No. Go find your own son." Why wasn't Perry doing that? I didn't know. I had to find out. I could tell Perry "No."

"So why don't you?" Stu asked.

"I don't want to. I'm becoming curious."

"About?"

"Who is this young man with his fifteen guns taking off for a gun show and then disappearing?" It was like that before my other cases. Curiosity is what drove me. I had wanted to know about the underbelly of the sex trade and terrorists and political campaigns. My work at Nutmeg had been a wild ride of encountering worlds I knew nothing about, and I loved it. Would curiosity kill the cat or me? Risk versus reward. I asked Stu, "Is there a Sherlock Holmes syndrome?"

"I don't think it's in the DSM-5. Maybe we'll get around to it in the sixth."

"You don't think I'm nuts doing this?'

"For what? The curiosity or the risks?"

"Both?"

"What do you think? You're the one who lives with them."

We talked about how I had learned to manage stress over the years. Running, meditating, working out. I had not gotten back into my routine since I was shot.

Stu asked, "Do you think your routine might help?" Always with the questions. Of course it would help. Again, the obvious. I once asked Stu what therapy was really about. His answer surprised me: "Most of the time, it's about coming to grips with the obvious."

When I left Stu's office, I called Eve. "I think I'm going to head to

Takuma's. Okay if we eat late, or do you want to go ahead and eat without me?

"Late is fine. Do you want to do takeout? Pick something up on the way home? That way, you can stay as late as you want."

"Yeah. Let's do that. Thai?"

"Sure. Say hi to Takuma for me."

"I will."

She knew. She always knew. I'm convinced I'm married to a Lebanese sorceress.

***

Takuma's Dojo is a martial arts center housed in an old three-story factory building in Bridgeport. There are multiple "studios," and students and practitioners of all ages find their way there. At Takuma's you can study every martial art. You can also study Yoga, which Eve does. There is even a basketball court that is open to the neighborhood kids. On the top floor is a meditation room and a Japanese Zen Garden.

I had taught a variety of martial arts there for years but stopped teaching after I was shot. It wasn't physical; I was only bruised. Somehow, though, I didn't want to discipline myself physically. I wanted a "time out" from teaching. I missed it, though.

This afternoon, I started in the meditation room. I sat zazen for forty-five minutes. Breathing, simply breathing, concentrating on every breath. Blackie lay at my feet, just touching me. When my concentration gave way to my "monkey mind" spinning away, I would remind myself to let go of the tension in my body and return to my breath. I was out of practice. It took me fifteen minutes before I felt myself let go, first in my body, then my ego – the ego, always the damned ego. Always the last to let go.

I didn't want to lose the sense of centeredness from the meditation, so when I went downstairs, I found an empty studio and started doing Tai Chi. Takuma considered me to be a Tai Chi Master. Given my awkwardness, I wasn't sure he would award me that honor today. I wondered if the other forms of martial arts I taught would also feel as rusty. It was time to get back to work. I knew it would be hard. Age was not going to be my friend.

Before I left, I went to find Takuma. He was finishing teaching a Taekwondo class to a group of middle-school-aged boys and girls. In his sixties, Takuma could pass for forty. Lithe. Eve said the word was created for him. When he moved, he flowed, all five feet nine inches of him.

Takuma's grandparents and parents had been interred during the Second World War, even though all of them had been born in Los Angeles. After the war and their release, his grandparents stayed in Los Angeles, but when Takuma's father was old enough, he headed east and away from the memories of imprisonment. Eventually, he settled in Boston, Massachusetts, where he became a nurse. That's where Takuma was born and raised. I always got a kick out of the Boston accent of this Japanese martial arts master.

Ater receiving a degree in exercise physiology, Takuma decided to, as he put it, "Become Japanese." He went to Japan for ten years and became a student of Zen Buddhism and a wide variety of martial arts. When he returned to the United States, a friend from his time at UMass, Boston, encouraged him to come to Bridgeport and join him in managing a rehabilitation program at Bridgeport Hospital. The following year, he found the abandoned factory building and a business incubator program that enabled him to launch Takuma's Dojo. Now, twenty-five years later, it was a magnet for martial arts training in Fairfield County.

Seeing me, Takuma motioned me toward his office, and I followed him. Blackie followed me. Once inside, Takuma invited me to sit. "Tea?" he asked.

"Please."

"It is good to see you, my friend."

"And you. Eve said to say hello."

"I see more of your wife and daughter these days than I do of you."

"I know."

"I'm glad you are here."

"So am I. I felt very old today."

He didn't say anything. Takuma and Stu. The silent ones.

I continued, "It's good to be back."

"It's good to have you. Are you ready to teach?"

"No, I don't think so."

"The Danbury police are interested in a Krav Maga class. I have told them you are the only one qualified to teach it."

Krav Maga is a salad of techniques – aikido, judo, karate, boxing, wrestling, and anything else the instructor thinks might work. It was created for the Israel Defense Forces. It is not concerned with health or well-being. The goal is to maim the opponent. It is for the street and is intended for defense and disabling. It is not "clean" fighting. Takuma hates it. He says there is no aesthetic to it. He's right, but he allows me to teach it to law enforcement agencies.

In response to his question, I said, "Not yet."

"Soon?"

"Soon."

"In the meantime, you will remove the accumulated rust."

"The rust, if not the years."

"They are together. Are they not?"

"They are together."

"May I have the privilege of helping?"

"Yes."

He looked down at Blackie, "And your companion?"

"I've kept up with his obedience training. We haven't done any tracking or protection work since the event."

Blackie is highly trained in Schutzhund. Technically a sport, there are three domains in the training: obedience, tracking, and protection. Blackie had protected me more than once.

"He is well?"

"He recovered quickly from his bruises and sprain."

"So, we need to schedule gym time for Blackie as well."

"Yes. We are both rusty."

We got out our calendars and started looking at dates. I didn't schedule anything for the following week, not knowing what would happen with our efforts to find Mark Perry.

***

When I got home, Eve asked, "How did it go?"

"With?"

"Either. Stu or Takuma. Only if you want to talk about it."

"I don't think I do. Do you mind?"

"Of course not. What did you bring your starving wife?"

"Mango chicken from Siam Cuisine."

"I knew there was a reason I married you. Oh, Henry called. Said he got your message."

"Why did he call you?"

"Wants me to do a chapter in a book he's working on."

"Congratulations."

"Thank you. He asked me if I knew what you were calling about. I hope you don't mind. I told him what I knew."

"And he said…"

"What I told you he'd say, let's get together for dinner and talk about it. Can you do tomorrow night? Hartford?"

"Sure."

"And he said he might bring someone with him."

"As in…"

"He didn't say. I told him he should talk to you about it."

"I'll call him after dinner."

Talking to Henry Gore was usually an exercise in deciphering his hyperbole to arrive at a modest understanding of what he was trying to tell you. Henry was faithful to form when I called him a little after eight.

"So, Kelly. How's my favorite sleuth?"

"Good, Henry. How about you?"

"I would be fine if it weren't for thoughtless university administrators and uninterested students. The world around them has changed, and

48

neither group seems interested in paying attention. Meanwhile, Babbler's supporters (Henry never referred to former President Buzhardt by his real name) continue to wreak havoc on education. May all the gods and goddesses help us if they ever regain power. I've considered changing professions, perhaps farming, but I'm too stubborn to leave the crumbling halls of academia."

"That bad?"

"Worse. Much worse. I won't bore you with the details. Your wonderful wife tells me you are in need of my assistance."

"I am."

"I stand ready to assist in any way I can. Eve said you are about to involve yourself with very nasty human beings, anarchists, who wouldn't know the meaning of the word."

"Yes. I'm curious about what makes them tick."

"You and your curiosity. I love it. So, you want to know about the inner workings of these monstrosities parading around as human beings."

"Yes."

"Don't we all."

"Do you think…"

"I can help? Probably not. However, many academicians are on the job trying to understand this…this collection of antediluvian miscreants who parade around like children playing dress up."

"I…"

"You want me to get back on track? I will. I have a young colleague, a Cambodian lass named Heng Pho, who's doing a postdoc here. She did her dissertation on this ticking time bomb that's getting ready to explode."

"I'd like to meet her."

"You will. Tomorrow night. You are buying these two poverty-stricken academics dinner, are you not?"

"Of course."

"And Eve will be with you?

"Of course."

"And we will dine at Salute?"

"If you like."

"Absolutely. The best Giobatto outside of Rome. Oh, and a word about Heng – this is very personal for her. Her parents were able to escape the killing fields of Cambodia when they were children. She has been back there several times trying to understand how Pol Pot and his thugs got control and decimated an entire country."

Chapter Five: The Crew

Gordon McKnight knew how to be persuasive. He could string together a series of talking points in an uninterrupted stream that could not help but impress someone with his enthusiasm and command of information or disinformation. Mark Perry had been impressed with him during their telephone call, but when Mark met him in person at the gun show in Portland, it didn't take much to convince Mark that he wanted to become a "Defender." Mark knew he needed a change. Even the weather had been against him.

The winter had been very warm, and Mark was broke and disgusted. His employer, Hennessy Landscaping, had more than enough contracts for snow removal, but they, and consequently their workers, only got paid when it snowed. December, so far, had passed with not one call for snow removal. November had been a total bust. The usual fall clean-up jobs had fallen way off.

Mark had picked up some day laborer work here and there, but nothing he could count on. He used his truck for a few junk removal jobs but, again, there was nothing he could count on. Even tips from his second job as a valet at Savin's Restaurant had slowed down. When Mark saw the internet notice that Camp Liberty was recruiting ex-military to train civilians in survival skills, he knew he had to learn more about it. His telephone conversation with McKnight had begun with an exchange of background information. Twenty minutes later it was obvious Camp Liberty was more than a survival training organization. Mark had to make the trip to Portland.

When he arrived at the gun show, Mark sought out the table for the Defenders of Liberty. McKnight was the only one there. McKnight got up to greet him when he saw Mark approach. Tall and slim, McKnight's hair was as close-cropped as a brand-new army recruit. He wore a T-shirt with an image resembling the American flag on it. Where the field with fifty stars was usually found, there was a different image. It read *2nd Amendment* and was surrounded by thirteen stars. There was print on the white stripes: *A well-regulated militia is necessary for the security of a free state, and the right of the people to keep and bear arms shall not be infringed upon.* On the table were similar T-shirts for sale as well as caps saying *Take America Back.* The handshakes of both men were firm.

McKnight invited Mark to sit down. "Names McKnight. And you are?"

"Mark Perry."

"Mark. Good to meet you in person. Glad you decided to come. How was the trip?"

"Easy. No problem."

"Glad to hear it. Remind me. Where you from?"

"West Haven. Connecticut."

Mark was surprised when McKnight said, "You drove all the way up here for the show?"

"Yeah. Sure. Mostly curious about…"

McKnight laughed. "I know. The Defenders. Good. Let me tell you a bit about us. Have a seat."

That's when McKnight went into his spiel. There were thirteen points, one for every original colony. Every point expressed a grievance of one kind or another. They ranged from attempts to limit the "Constitutionally guaranteed right to bear arms" to the FBI spying on true patriots. Included were the horrible ways in which diversity, equity, and inclusion efforts in the workplace gave positions of power to incompetents and froze out white men. McKnight's bottom line was that true patriots like the Defenders had to take back the country from the woke liberals who were destroying it.

Mark agreed with everything McKnight had to say. He didn't just listen; he elaborated on many of the points McKnight was making, especially the way vets didn't get what they deserved. Most of the points McKnight made Mark had thought about, and the minute McKnight said them, Mark agreed, especially about the invasion of foreigners who were replacing true Americans in jobs and positions of authority. One of Mark's supervisors at Hennessy Landscaping had been from Jamaica.

He told McKnight, "The spade was a fucking idiot. He thought he was some kind of king shit because he'd been to a goddamn community college. I had seniority, but still, Hennessy gave him the job."

"You got screwed. That's the kind of stuff I'm talking about. We have to put an end to that bullshit."

The Camp Liberty situation McKnight described to Mark was more elaborate than what they had discussed during their phone call and more appealing. McKnight said, "You understand, I've got to be careful with what I put up on the website or talk about on the phone. I don't want the FBI or State Police getting curious about us. There are lots of survival training camps around the country. One more won't attract any attention. And, some weekends, that's what we'll be doing."

"And the other weekends?"

"What I said. The Defenders are about taking the country back, Mark. Are you up for that?"

"That's why I'm here."

"Good. Cause we're about action, not bullshit."

McKnight asked Mark about his military background, his tours in Afghanistan, and what he'd been doing since he was discharged. Mark talked quickly about his service time. McKnight kept slowing him down. He wanted to know specifics, down to the weapons Mark was familiar with. However, McKnight had to push to get Mark to talk about the last few years. When he thought he had gotten as much information as he was going to get, McKnight said, "Sounds to me like you're ready for a change."

"Absolutely."

"Could you leave with me at the end of the show?"

The question took Mark by surprise. "I, I suppose I could. Sure. Why not? I only packed for the weekend, though."

"Not a problem. We'll provide you with everything you'll need."

"I'll need some clothes. I didn't pack much."

"Of course. This is not a fly-by-night operation. We are well-funded, and we mean business. Tomorrow morning, I'll give you a credit card. Twenty-five hundred dollar limit. Go on up to L.L.Bean and get whatever you need."

"Seriously?"

"Do you think you'll need more than that?"

"No, no. That's really generous."

"I told you. We're well-funded. Are you sure you're ready to do something and not just talk about it?"

Mark whispered, "Absolutely. What are the plans? You know. What's our mission?"

"Not here. Plans are being formulated. If you want to be involved, it will require absolute secrecy. Can you handle that?"

"Hell, yeah."

"And it means joining up now, even though Christmas is in a week. You'll be missing Christmas. Can you handle that?"

"I've missed Christmases before."

"And not letting anyone know where you are, at least for now? It would be a new life."

Mark thought for a second before saying, "Yeah. I can do this. A new life sounds good."

***

McKnight took Mark and another recruit, Leonard Pratt, to dinner that night. Pratt had driven up from New Jersey. An ex-seal, Pratt was shorter than Mark, younger, wiry, and intense. He reminded Mark of one of his buddies in Afghanistan.

After an evening of castigating both political parties and agreeing on the need for a new wave of patriotism, McKnight gave each a copy of the *Field Manual of the Free Militia* and said, "Study this tonight. It's important. If it makes sense to you, we'll leave after the show ends tomorrow afternoon. Remember, though, you talk to no one – no family, no friends. No one."

That night, Mark studied the seventy-three pages of the *Manual*. He was surprised by the opening pages devoted to a biblical rationale for the legitimacy of militias and violence. He took some time to jot down answers to the discussion questions that followed this section. Three of the questions – *Can you describe the difference between acting out of revenge and acting on behalf of justice? Why is the one right and the other wrong? What is your definition of authority that must be obeyed?* – caused him to go back and review the textual material. He was surprised by the Christian principles that supported the militia movement. Mark had never paid any attention to religion. His parents never belonged to any church. Reading the manual, he concluded that what little he did know about Christianity was erroneous. Both the Old and New Testaments supported and demanded violence to redress wrongs: *As we have seen, Jesus Christ was not a pacifist and it is sometimes necessary to respond to evil with force. But why and when is force right and when is it wrong? Through the Bible there are several key principles to answer this question.*

He read and re-read the section in the manual titled *The Heritage of Arming and Organizing*. When he read the statement, "*If you become convinced that the federal government is bent on systematic violations of our personal liberties, it is your moral duty and obligation to join with others so convinced to restore true liberty for all Americans,*" he did a fist pump and out loud said, "Yes."

Mark had never thought of himself as a student. Still, he found himself reading and studying sections and taking notes: *The right to arm and organize; The reasons to arm and organize; Who and what is the free militia?; Equipping yourself for the free militia; General organization of the free militia; and Secrecy and security in the free militia*. Reading about the cellular structure of militias, he wondered whether the Defenders of Liberty had more than one cell. He knew from the reading about the separation of cells that McKnight would probably not tell him even if it did. He wondered where McKnight fell in the hierarchy of the militia movement.

When Mark finally got to sleep, it was three o'clock in the morning. He was exhausted and excited. He had found a home where he was needed and welcome. Above all, he felt alive. God, it was good to feel alive again.

***

Leonard Pratt, Lenny, the other recruit at dinner, was staying at the same hotel. When Mark came down for breakfast, he saw Pratt; he went over to him. "Mind if I join you?"

"No. I was hoping to bump into you. Go and grab some food."

"Want anything?"

"No. I'm good."

Supplied with what the hotel advertised as "breakfast," Mark returned to the table where Pratt ate his sausage, scrambled eggs, and "do it yourself" waffles.

"What do you think?" Mark asked.

"About?"

"The manual."

"Didn't get all the way through it. Religious stuff bored me out of my mind. Fell asleep. You?"

"Yeah. I had to read that section a couple of times. Religion's not my thing."

"Me neither. You gonna join?"

"Yeah. You?"

"Not sure. I've got a bunch of questions for McKnight. Money mostly. How much? When do we get paid? Stuff like that. Insurance. You know, health, life. We covered? I got to treat it like a job. I also want to know where his money's coming from for this."

"Think he'll tell you?"

"Probably not, but I'm going to ask."

"You ever do anything like this before?"

"You mean private merc stuff?"

"Merc?"

Lenny looked from his food. "You know, mercenary. No, I haven't, but one of my brothers does. Vic. He's worked in Iraq and Kenya for a company called Unified Protection. He made some big bucks, but UP's dissolved. Vic works for another group now, in Argentina."

"No shit." Mark focused on his scrambled eggs. Then he said, "I don't think we're going to get paid much. This is more of a patriotic thing. It's about taking America back from the fucking liberal elite snowflakes."

"Yeah. Sure. But someone's putting a lot of money into this. We should be paid well for putting our butts on the line."

"I suppose."

"You don't?"

"Don't what?"

"Think we should get paid top dollar?"

"Yeah. I guess."

"McKnight said they're well-funded, right? Well? We should get paid. At the end of the day, you know someone's going to wind up wealthy with a lot of power. It's always about money and power. Right?"

"I don't know. I mean, sure, it's about taking control again."

"Yeah. And giving it to who?"

***

Mark spent the rest of the morning and afternoon at the show. He had planned on selling one or more guns from his collection to help him get through the winter. McKnight had told him he wouldn't have to do that, so he spent the morning going from booth to booth. He was surprised at the variety of weapons that were for sale and started to think about the armaments that would be essential if the Defenders were to be an actual

57

fighting force. He spent a lot of time at the displays from manufacturers. Bushmaster Firearms was well represented. Bushmaster, based in Nevada, was able to get nine thousand guns a month to market, most of them assault rifles.

Some of the displays were small, sponsored by men his father's age who were trying to sell antique weapons or their "favorite" hunting rifles because their wives didn't want them out in the woods anymore. Their prices were usually ridiculously high, and it was clear they were there to hang out with friends and probably get away from their wives.

There had to be five hundred tables, at least. Everything related to guns was sold, and some things that weren't. At one table, a man and his wife were selling steak rub. Multiple tables and display booths were set up for holsters, gun cases, slings, knives, T-shirts, books, parts, ammo magazines, gear bags, and safety equipment. There were also professional service vendors who could repair or modify your weapons. Every special interest group associated with the shooting sports was represented. Political tables gave you the opportunity to sign petitions and learn about the progress of gun control legislation and efforts to defeat it. You could even buy local honey and jerky.

Mark noted that there weren't many women. It didn't surprise him. Ages were distributed across a bell curve, with the bulge being in their forties and fifties. It was Maine. He didn't see any Black or Brown faces except for two members of the facility's janitorial staff.

Mark wandered from table to table. At times, he stopped to talk to vendors about their wares; at other times, he listened to the conversations between vendors and prospective buyers. Using his mobile phone, he started taking pictures of items he wanted to buy, a wish list. He became serious about comparing products and prices even though he knew he didn't have the funds to purchase anything. "Right now," he told himself. "Soon." He thought about Lenny's brother. Argentina. What was Argentina like? What was Lenny's brother doing there? Being a mercenary must pay a hell of a lot more than mowing lawns. Maybe after Camp Liberty.

He ate lunch by himself and made a list of what he would need to equip himself to live at Camp Liberty. In the afternoon, he drove up to Freeport and started shopping. With all of the discount stores, he didn't have any trouble getting everything on his list. When he returned to the gun show, the Defender credit card McKnight had given him still had $800 on it. McKnight had said, "Whatever he needed." Mark went over to one of the knife vendors he had visited in the morning. He spent $110 for a Revenge Combat Knife.

Chapter Six: Sally Gwynn

Luke, Mark's brother, told me about "the girlfriend." I was a bit surprised Sally Gwynn was willing to talk to me. Calls to Mark's friends began and ended with, "I don't know where he is." Maybe Sally, like his mother, was worried about Mark. Sally said she didn't know anything but come over anyway. Come for coffee at nine, right after she got her son off to his Christmas break swim team practice at the YMCA.

Sally's house was a few blocks from the beach in West Haven. It was a neighborhood of small houses on small lots, a quarter of an acre at most. Some houses were boxes with gambrel roofs and concrete stoops with iron banisters. Some were Capes. Every house had a driveway, but only a few had garages. There were no sidewalks.

Sally Gwynn lived in one of the smaller Cape Cods. Painted a bright blue with white shutters, it was hard to miss. A white vinyl picket fence circumnavigated the front yard. I pulled in behind what I assumed was her car, an older Toyota Corolla, also blue.

Sally was not what I expected. She was very high-energy, the kind you wondered if she was on something high-energy. She led me through the living room and into the kitchen and invited me to sit down. The house was neat, clean, and orderly. White walls were covered with family pictures and prints depicting scenes of the Southwest. In one corner was a small white Christmas tree with all blue ornaments. Under the tree were a couple of Christmas presents still unopened.

Sally had short, dyed blond hair and several ear piercings. Tattoos covered her left hand and wrist and continued until they disappeared into her sleeve. She wore jeans with holes and a red hoodie. I couldn't tell how much she weighed, but my guess was her physician had advised her to put on some weight.

"Morning's only time I got to myself. I usually work lunch and dinner shifts at Savin's."

"The restaurant. I've eaten there. Thanks for seeing me."

"As I told ya, I got no idea where he is. He just ups and goes. All he tells me is he's going to some gun show in Portland. I tell him ta call me when he gets there. Does he? No! We've been together for six months, and then nothing. Talk about ghosting. Pretty shitty, ya ask me. Don't ya think? Especially at Christmas. Merry Christmas."

"Sounds like it came as a surprise."

"Ya bet your fuckin' ass. Pardon my French."

"Not a problem. Six months. Quite a while. How did you and Mark meet?"

"At work. Came in for dinner with his ex. I waited on them. He flirted with me, right in front of her. Found out later they were celebrating just getting divorced. How's that for weird?"

"Unusual."

"Weird. Turns out she wanted to move back to Oklahoma to be close to her family. He didn't want to go. So they split. Later, I found out they was only married for two years. No kids. So, I guess no big deal for either one of them. No idea why they got married in the first place. Didn't have to. It was her idea, too. Not his. Then she decides to go back home. Nuts, huh?"

"Why, do you suppose?"

"I dunno. Homesick? She was young. Just a kid. Twenty. Twenty-one. Somethin' like that."

"Why do you think Mark married her?"

"He said he needed to settle down. Bullshit. Like marriage is supposed to take care of that, sure."

"Why do you think?"

"She was young. Pretty. Started off idolizing him is my guess. You know. Older guy. Thought he'd take care of her."

"And then…"

"Life happened. Good old reality set in. Poof. There goes the romance."

"How'd you and Mark get together?"

"He started coming back to the restaurant. He'd sit at the bar. We'd chat when it got slow. He asked me out. I didn't have much time with work and taking care of Wally. That's my son." She held out her tattooed hand and showed me the initials "WLG."

"What's the 'L' stand for?"

"Lawrence. My dad's name."

"How old is Wally?"

"Just turned fifteen. Thinks he's eighteen and should be able to do whatever he wants to do. Can be a real handful."

"I'll bet. I have two children. Adults now. Teen years can be tough."

"Tell me about it. 'Specially being a single mom. Me and his father split when Wally was two. I mean took off. His father took off. Somewhere. Who knows? Mark, though, Mark was good with Wally. Played computer games with him. Paid attention to him. It helped. And now he takes off. Men. Can't believe he did that to Wally. You know, Christmas and everything. Wally even bought him a present. Still under the tree."

"You were surprised then, when Mark left."

"Honestly, yes and no. I knew something was up. He had some new friends, and, you know, they were talking all sorts of stuff. You know, I'd hear them, and they… I'd rather not say anything. I don't want to get him in any trouble. Who knows? He still may show up. Maybe New Year's. Who knows?"

"You don't want to get him in trouble?"

"Nah. He wasn't supposed to tell me nothin'."

"Look, Sally. I don't want him to get into any trouble, either. His parents are concerned, especially his mother. They just want to know he's okay. That's it. Nothing more."

"Me, too. I'd like to know he's okay."

"Has he been in touch with you?"

"No. I told you. Not since he left."

"You did say he had ghosted you."

"Well, not really. To be fair, he said, ya know, he wouldn't be in touch for a while. I thought he meant a few days. Maybe a week. So, it's not really ghosting."

"Did he say how long before he'd be in touch?"

"No."

"So, you two were on good terms when he left?"

"I didn't want him to go, but yeah. We were okay. I mean, I hoped he'd be right back."

"Do you have any idea where he might be? His parents told me about the gun show in Portland."

"He told them that?"

"Yes. You seem surprised."

"Hell, yeah. He told me not to tell anyone where he was going."

"Did he say anything about after the show? Any idea where he might have gone?"

Sally didn't say anything, but I could see there was more.

"Anything would be helpful. His parents….."

"I know. They're worried. I get it. He'd be real mad if I told you anything, though."

"I understand. How about I tell you what I think? You can then tell me whether I'm on the right track. Would that be okay?"

"Maybe."

"Good. I think Mark went to meet up with, possibly to join, some group that would be at the gun show. He's probably still in Maine. Maybe living with members of that group. Am I on the right track?"

"Maybe."

"Maybe?"

"I don't want to say no more."

"I understand. You feel very protective of Mark. How about one last thing? Defenders of Liberty or the Maine Militia?"

I didn't think she'd give me an answer. I hoped to pick up a non-verbal response by tossing two possibilities. I was right. It was small, but I was sure I saw a quick breath when I said Defenders of Liberty.

"I told you. I don't want to say nothin'."

"I know. I'm sorry. But you see, I'm caught in a bind. His parents are worried, especially his mom, and I told them I would try to find Mark to make sure he's okay. At the same time, I don't want to ask you to do something you don't want to do because of your commitment to Mark. Maybe you can help me out another way."

"What's that?"

"I don't know much about Mark. Tell me about him. You mentioned he was good with Wally."

I was trying to establish a safe ground for her to let her guard down and build our relationship so I could return with more probing questions. It worked.

"Yeah, he was. He talked to him, played video games with him, and spent a lot of time doin' that. He was going to put up a basketball net in the driveway but didn't get around to it before he left."

"Wally must miss him."

"I guess. He doesn't say nothin' to me about it."

"Teenagers."

"No shit. Mark was like some kind of action hero to Wally. You know. Special forces. Fought in Afghanistan. Mark's big. Real tall. Six foot three or something. Strong, too. Wally's going to be tall, too. His dad was tall. Not as tall as Mark, but tall."

"Sounds like Wally might have identified with Mark."

"Yeah. I guess."

"What else can you tell me?"

"What else da you want to know?"

"I don't know. Anything. I'm just trying to get a sense of him. How did he spend his time?"

"Besides work?"

"Tell me about his work."

"He did okay. Worked for a landscaping business. I also helped him get a job as a valet at the restaurant. He picked up a couple of shifts every Friday and Saturday night. Between the two, he did okay. This winter's been tough, though. A real bitch. No snow until now. No plowing."

"Yeah. Until now."

"I know. Crazy, huh. Maybe if this blizzard happened in December, he wouldn't have gone."

"Hard to tell. Maybe. How'd he spend his time when he wasn't working?"

"Dude's a gym rat. Even though he's workin' labor. Spends a lot of time in the gym. He's big on MMA stuff."

"He's into mixed martial arts."

"Big time. So are his new friends. All they talk about. That and politics. All the freakin' time. All he cares about. MMA and politics. Talked about competing. Wanting to go into training. No money, though. It costs. A lot."

"You said politics, too."

"Hell yeah. Watches that OAN TV station – all the time."

"Conservative, huh."

"Hey. I am, too. Mark, though, he's real conservative. He even has a short-wave radio. Listens to some station up in Maine. Sounds a little fringy to me. Conspiracy stuff."

"His mom mentioned something similar. She said he's changed."

"She did?" Again, she sounded surprised that Mark's mother had shared this kind of information with me.

"Yes."

"Yeah. I guess." She thought for a moment. "Yeah, I guess you could say he changed."

"In what way?"

"I dunno how to put it. When he's watching the news, he gets all mad. Saying the country's going to shit. Talked about all this woke bullshit, immigrants takin' over. Things like that."

"Was this the change you mentioned?"

"No, no. He always complained about that stuff. Lately, he's talking about how things are going to be different. There are people who are goin' to change things. New people."

"Interesting. He tell you who?"

"I dunno. Just people."

She pulled her knees up to her chest and wrapped her arms around them, protecting and closing down. I decided to try anyway. " Did he mention any names? That might help me find him."

"No."

One word response. Still, I asked, "Anything else?"

"Like what?"

"I don't know. I'm trying to understand what Mark was thinking when he left. Did he say anything specific about how things were going to change?"

"I said enough."

I had gone too far, and now she shut down verbally. She got up from the small kitchen table where we had been sitting and walked over to pour herself another cup of coffee. She asked me, "Want some?"

"No thanks. I'm good." I had trod into a forbidden area but had nothing to lose by continuing.

"What did he say about these people?"

"Said they'd never have pulled punches in Afghanistan like Goodman did. Hated Goodman for that."

"I know Mark was in Special Forces. Did he serve in Afghanistan?"

"I told ya. Five or six tours. Said it was the best time of his life. Wished he'd never left the military. Missed it."

"What did he miss?"

"Always talked 'bout his friends. Called 'em his brothers."

"He doesn't have that now, brothers."

"Maybe at the gym. These new friends."

"Not at work?"

"At work? You kiddin'? Cutting grass and plowing with a bunch of wet backs can't speak English? No way. Thought they were idiots.

Should never have been allowed into the country."

"Why didn't he get a different job?"

"And do what? He dropped out of high school and joined up when he turned seventeen. End of his junior year. Army didn't teach him nothin' but how to shoot a gun."

"Seventeen. That's young. Big decision for someone that age. Did he ever tell you why he enlisted?"

"Said he couldn't stand school and being with that bunch of losers. Phonies. Hated them. Got suspended once for fighting."

"He say how his parents took that?"

"Dad backed him up. Dad's got a temper, too."

"He get along with his father?"

"Yeah, pretty much. Thinks his dad is more talk than action, though. Pisses him off. Thinks he's a phony. A lot of talk. Bullshit artist."

"About what?" I prodded.

"I guess everything."

"Mark is more of an action person."

"You bet he is."

"I'm curious: as an adult, did he get into arguments with people? Fights?"

She hesitated. "No one was going to push him around if that's what you mean."

"Well, I was wondering. I understand his ex-wife filed a complaint against him, and yet you said that when you met him, they were celebrating their divorce."

"That thing with his ex was all bullshit. He told me she threw something at him, so he slapped her. She called the cops. She over-reacted. Not a big deal."

"Were you ever scared when you were with him?"

"You mean of him hittin' me?"

"Or Wally?"

"Hell no! I'd never tolerate that kind of bullshit. Hit my son. You kiddin' me?"

"So, you felt safe with him?"

"Damned straight. Sometimes, I'd tell him to calm down when he was watching television and going on about politics. I think it scared Wally. He could get really worked up. One time, when I told him to calm down, he stormed out of the house and slammed the door. Came back later, though. Apologized. Said it'd never happen again."

"Did it?"

"No way."

I kept asking questions, trying to get a better understanding of Mark Perry. The change his mother had mentioned appeared to hinge on two events. The first was the United States' withdrawal from Afghanistan. The second and most recent event was knowing about some vague people who would change things. Mark's response to this possibility seemed to have moved him from rage to hope.

Sally Gwynn and I talked for about an hour. When I felt I was getting no new information, I said, "If you hear from Mark, please tell him to call his parents. They are concerned. If you get worried and change your mind about telling me what you know, please give me a call." I handed her my business card. "Call me any time, even if you just want to chat. Okay?"

"Yeah." She looked down at the card. "What's the PhD?"

"Doctorate in Criminology. I used to be a teacher. I mostly taught police and people wanting to be police."

"Seriously?"

"Yeah. A lot of years."

"And now you do this."

"Yeah."

"You like it?"

"Yeah. I do. Thanks for your time and the coffee."

She walked me to the door.

Back in the car, I said to Blackie, "What do you think?" He was used to me asking him questions, but he just stared at me.

Eve texted: *Molly and I are going to an 11 class at Takuma's. See you there. I have your stuff with me. Let's have a late lunch at the diner.* Of course, she would sign up for an eleven o'clock class, and of course, she would bring my workout clothes with her. I was to get back to work. It was time for some rust removal.

Having Molly join us was a treat. I didn't get to see much of my daughter these days. With her recently minted Ph.D. in computer science from Yale, Molly had stayed on working on a hush-hush project with one of the senior faculty members. Eve and I were convinced she worked for the CIA or another federal alphabet agency. Whatever it was, I knew we would never know the agency or the project.

*** *

Every town along the Connecticut seashore has one or more Greek diners. The Blue Sky in Stratford is our favorite. One reason is its location. It's across the street from the Safe Harbor Marina, where our boat sits in its cradle, "shrink-wrapped" for the winter. When Eve texted "*late lunch at the diner,*" I knew precisely what diner she meant. It would also mean a quick after-lunch drive into the boat yard to gaze upon our shrouded thirty-six-foot sailboat, *Álainn*. Of course, there was no reason to check on *Álainn*. If anything had been wrong, the boat yard would have called, but I don't know any boat owners who don't do winter checks – just to be sure.

I love diners. I love the big menus even though I usually order the same thing. I love the familiarity. If you're alone, you sit at the counter. Most of the time, you wind up talking to the person sitting next to you. The diner, for me, represents the idea of America. Everyone can eat at a diner. The food is not exceptional, but you can rely on it.

My 'remove the rust' plan was to alternate between cardio-strength exercises three days a week and working with Takuma on alternate days. Sunday would be a day off. Today was a cardio-strength day. Unlike some gym rats, I don't slow down once I start. No chatting, checking my phone, sitting down on a machine. I keep my heart rate up from when I get on the elliptical machine until I finish with the free weights. It is an hour of pure work. Stamina. Keeping my stamina up at my age takes a lot of work, and I have not been working. Today, I finished right on time.

We had three cars. I arrived at Blue Sky a few minutes before Eve. I settled into a booth and sat so I could catch her attention when she came in the door. She saw me right away and started walking towards me. I love looking at my wife. Eve is slim, graceful, and very Mediterranean. She has black hair, an olive complexion, and dark brown eyes – the complete opposite of me.

Molly walked in a minute after Eve. As always, she was full of energy, with red hair pulled back into a ponytail and a long L.L.Bean coat – her Christmas present from us.

Eve settled in next to me; Molly took the seat opposite us. Sissy appeared. Sissy was the daughter of the owner, and she knew all three of us. "Hi, guys. Whatcha want? Got a couple of specials today. Selzers with lime for you two? Whatchawant Molly?"

While we were waiting for our lunches – spanakopita and salad for Eve, chicken souvlaki for me, BLT for Molly – Eve told me to bring Molly up to date on the disappearance of Mark Perry. When I finished Molly said, "You sure you want to do this? These people are crazy. Certifiable. I mean, out to breakfast, lunch, and dinner. Eve, are you…"

"Okay with this? Of course not, but he's promised not to take risks."

"Dad!"

"Molly!"

"Okay. I'll shut up, but…"

"I'll be fine. I'm just finding someone."

"Yeah, but…"

Over the years, I've mastered a look. Directing it at my children it means, "I'm not going to talk about this." Most of the time, they respect it.

Eve changed the topic and asked me how my interview with Sally Gwynn had gone.

"I liked her. Single mom doing her best. Working her butt off. Taking care of business. Taking care of her son. The house was neat as a pin. I think she cares about Mark Perry. Probably wanted more from him than he was prepared to give. Not sure. She seemed bothered by his absence but not freaked out."

"Did you learn anything useful?"

"Only a couple of things. He did tell her he was going to Portland to the gun show, and I think quite a bit more. She was surprised he had told his mother as much as he had. He was told, or at least felt the need, to be very secretive about where he was going and what he was doing. It sounds like he was following a page out of the *Militia Handbook*. My guess is he was told to be secretive."

Molly said, "*Militia Handbook*? That freaks me out: there's actually a *Militia Handbook*."

"There is. A guidebook on how to overthrow the government of the United States of America. Bizarre, but true."

"Sally?" Eve got me back on track.

"Yes, Sally. I also discovered that he was friends with some buddies at some gym where they taught MMA. The way Sally described them, they sounded like they were far right, maybe members themselves of some extremist group."

Eve said, "It wasn't Takuma's was it? I can't imagine Takuma…"

"Sally didn't say, but no. Not Takuma's. Probably someplace in New Haven or West Haven. That's where he lived. My guess is there are several places in and around New Haven."

Expert on all things New Haven, Molly said, "Probably twenty or thirty."

I nodded. "I asked Sally whether he joined up with the Maine Militia or the Defenders of Liberty."

"She told you?" Eve asked.

"Not verbally."

"You and your non-verbal's," Molly said.

"Hey. Sometimes it works."

"So?" Eve asked.

"Defenders of Liberty."

"You're sure?"

"I'm sure."

"Which means?"

"I want to do a little more digging and learn some more. Jackie's working on it. Maybe Mark'll get in touch with his parents or Sally. If so, that'll be it. In the best of worlds, Mark Perry will announce that he's alive and well and living in Sparta, Maine. He also owes some pretty big apologies for blowing Christmas off."

"And if not?"

"Blackie and I may be making a trip to Maine."

Molly said, "You're kidding. Right? Knowing he may be hanging with a bunch of militia types, and you're…"

"Only going to see if I can find him and report back to his parents. Nothing more."

"Gees, Dad."

Chapter Seven: Heng Pho

Thursday afternoon, when we got back home after lunch and three – might as well do them while we're out – chores, I texted Jackie to see if she'd learned anything new about Mark Perry, the Defenders of Liberty, or anything at all that might help find Mark. Her answer was cryptic: *Not since I talked to you when you left Sally Gwynn's house.* When I read the text to Eve, she said, "You do know that Jackie only works miracles once in a while, not hourly." I knew better than to offer a comment.

Eve continued, "Do you think Jackie might enjoy coming with us this evening?"

Why didn't I think of that? Of course she would. A few text exchanges later, it was arranged. Jackie would meet us at our condo in Milford, and the three of us would drive to Hartford together to meet Henry Gore and Heng Pho at Salute.

Jackie was early. While we waited for Eve, Jackie said, "I can't wait to meet Heng. She's really got her act together." Of course, Jackie had googled Heng Pho and knew whatever one could know about a rising young academic from information on the internet.

When we got in the car, Jackie said, "Frank, she's a superstar. Did you know she's Cambodian? Graduated with distinction from the University of Chicago. Dissertation will probably become a book. I'm surprised she's doing her postdoc at UConn rather than someplace like Harvard or Stanford."

I responded, "You do remember Eve got her doctorate at UConn and that's where Henry teaches?"

"Oh, come on. You know what I mean."

"We do," Eve answered.

I was not going to let Jackie off the hook. "I'm not sure I do. Would you care to elaborate?"

Eve said, "You don't have to. He's just baiting you."

"Into revealing her penchant for academic elitism."

"Leave her alone," Eve cautioned.

"Okay. So, what has impressed you so much about the young Dr. Pho, who should be at Harvard rather than UConn?"

"I'm sorry. I…" Jackie started.

"It's okay. However, I dare you to say anything disparaging about the City University of New York and its illustrious John Jay College of Criminal Justice."

"I wouldn't dare."

"Good. So. Heng Pho?"

"She spent two whole years interviewing right-wing extremists all over this country and in Sweden. She wanted to know what, if any, differences existed between the two countries."

"And?"

"Strong similarities. White males, twenties and thirties. Military backgrounds. Some had religious backgrounds, but they were not religious themselves. Authoritarian personalities. Problems with relationships. They felt like they were getting shafted by society. They are convinced their current government cannot be trusted. Also, a strong sense of wanting to protect their homeland from invaders. aka immigrants."

"Some of that fits Mark Perry. I wonder if he thinks he got shafted. You know, personally. What else?"

"They believe their government is not interested in their needs but only concerned with the needs of others."

"Like?"

"You name it: immigrants, Blacks, Jews. The elites have theirs, so they can be generous to the marginalized and screw everyone else."

"Like them."

"Yep."

"How about Mark Perry? Did you learn anything more about him?"

"No. Not since…"

"This morning. I know. You told me."

I always know when Eve is giving me "the look." Even though I was driving and focused on the road ahead, I knew I was getting "the look." It reminded me, "Jackie doesn't work miracles every hour."

Salute was decorated for Christmas. As we entered, we had to walk around a giant Christmas tree to get to the hostess's desk. Christmas wreaths hung on the walls, and our hostess was adorned with a Santa Claus hat. I was struck by the contrast between the sparseness of Sally Gwynn's decorations and the lushness at Salute.

Henry and Heng Pho were waiting for us. They both stood as we approached the table. I found myself staring at this young woman. Heng Pho was exotic. I had never formally met a Cambodian woman or man before. Her skin color was truly brown. She was short and a bit chunky. She had an infectious smile that was warm and welcoming. A younger, single me might have flirted with her awkwardly but persistently. Nothing was threatening about her. I could easily understand why men with extremist views were willing to grant her interviews for her research.

I watched my beautiful, brilliant wife instantly bond with the young woman when Henry made introductions, and we did a round of hand-shaking. Jackie seemed starstruck. Henry beamed with delight at his role, bringing us together. Although I, or rather Nutmeg Security and Investigations, was paying the bill for dinner, Henry was clearly the host for the gathering, a role he enjoyed immensely and performed very well. Henry, for all his hyperbole, was a delightful raconteur. It was a somewhat deceptive facade. Henry was both a brilliant academician and a cunning politician.

Once settled at the table, we ordered drinks. Heng and Eve ordered glasses of chardonnay, and Jackie ordered her "signature" drink, a Frank

Sinatra – two fingers of scotch, two of water, and two ice cubes. I had introduced Henry to the Vesper, named after James Bond's love, Vesper Lynd, in *Casino Royale*. Henry insisted we both order them. "As we embark upon a new adventure, we must bond with Bond, the greatest male fantasy hero of all time."

"What about the Lone Ranger or Superman?" Eve asked.

"They neither drank, ate well, nor enjoyed the company of beautiful women. Lois Lane doesn't count. Never consummated."

"As far as we know," Heng added.

"Off-screen does not count. And what kind of name is Lois Lane? She is Midwestern white bread. One cannot imagine Lois Lane emerging from the ocean in a bikini like Ursula Andress did as Honey Rider or Halle Berry as Jinx."

Eve interrupted the direction of the conversation. "If you haven't discovered it already, Heng, in real life, Henry is a feminist. In his fantasy life, he is trapped in the misogyny of the 1970s."

"Is the student offering a critique of the teacher?" Henry asked.

"Former student. Order your dinner."

Henry ordered Giobatto for his entré and gave it a five-star recommendation. Heng and Jackie followed suit. Eve and I, not as susceptible to Henry's enthusiasm as the others, ordered a Pomodoro for Eve and a Ragu Bolognese for me. While waiting for dinner, Henry, Eve, and Heng talked about the comings and goings of people and projects in the Political Science Department at UConn.

The arrival of dinner marked a transition. Henry said, "Okay. Shall we proceed to the task at hand?"

Eve asked, "Are you referring to dinner or why you brought us together?"

"Both, of course." Henry turned to me, "Frank, context, please."

I updated the group on my conversations with the Perrys and Sally Gwynn. Jackie presented the information she had gathered online. When we finished, Heng asked, "How can I help?"

Henry answered for us, actually for me. "Our heroic sleuth, here, is one of the most curious men I have ever had the pleasure to know. The criminologist in him always wants to know not only what evil lurks in the heart of man but how it got there. I told him you were an expert on these destroyers of democracy."

Heng demurred. "Oh, wow! How to set me up, Henry. Frank, I do not consider myself an expert."

Henry insisted. "Nonsense. You are. I have read your dissertation."

"You mean someone read it besides my committee? I'm flattered." Heng turned her attention to me. "Frank, I can tell you what I learned from my reading and the interviews I did. Unfortunately, I also have some personal family experience with extremism – in Cambodia. Both of my parents had to escape from the Khmer Rouge when they were children. Families turned on families. It's one of the reasons I became interested in how people, ordinary people, turn to violence. Millions of people were put to death."

I said, "I did see the movie *The Killing Fields*, but that's the extent of my familiarity."

"The film barely scratched the surface. It would have been hard, though, to show the terror and the extent of the inhumanity. Genocide and the conversion of ordinary people into mass murderers is, unfortunately, not unique."

Eve started reciting a litany. "Armenia, Rwanda, Germany, Rohingya, Darfur, Bosnia…"

Jackie quickly added, "The Cherokee, Osage, Pequots."

"America has a history of it as well," Henry added.

I asked Heng, "Do you think that America is currently at risk of…"

"No. Not in the way you're probably thinking. But many of the dynamics are similar."

Henry interjected, "As I said. She is an expert. Heng, please hold forth."

"Hold forth? Really? Okay. But stop me if I start boring you. This has been my life for the past five years, and I am fascinated by these people."

"Please," I said. "Assume I know nothing."

"Okay. Here goes. Understand, though, that there is a lot we don't know about the dynamics that lead to extremist ways of seeing the world and possibly to violence. Family, cultural influences, education, success, peer pressure, and personality play a role. And where does extremism lead? Does it always lead to violence, to terrorism, to genocide? Are there developmental stages? Is there some line that an extremist crosses when they become violent, and what is it?"

Jackie chimed in, "How do you discriminate between a terrorist and a freedom fighter?"

"It's a great question. And, depending on your point of view, who are the victims and who are the oppressors?"

Eve said, "The victim-oppressor distinction never captures the nuances of complicated histories and turbulent political situations. Palestinians, Hamas, Hezbollah, Israelis. The biblical stories of Sarah, Hagar, Ishmael, and Isaac."

Henry said to Heng, "Eve is Lebanese. She knows terrorism first hand."

"I left Lebanon as a teenager, so I have memories. I still have family there."

Heng said, "I didn't know you were Lebanese. So, you know this ancient history. Jews trace their heritage to Isaac, Palestinians to Ishmael. Ancient divisions. Separation."

"Who is the 'other' and why is the 'other' an 'other?'" Eve added.

Henry contributed, somewhat gratuitously, "I love it when my former students practically quote me."

I was becoming impatient and wanted to move beyond academic dissections. "What have you learned in your work?" I directed my question to Heng.

"Honestly, much of what I've learned supports the work of Professor Lane Crothers.

Eve explained, "Crothers teaches at Illinois State. American Political Culture."

"You know his work?" Heng asked Eve. Bonding again.

"I would say I know more about it than I know it," Eve answered – my always scrupulously honest wife.

Heng said, "His work is the most salient to understand what is taking place today. His book *Rage on the Right* is, I believe, one of the definitive works to understanding what is happening with the militia movements you're interested in."

Eve said to me, "I'll get it for you from the library at school."

Heng continued, "According to Crothers, people drawn to militias want a heroic character to lead them, someone they see as larger than life – a billionaire or a general – as long as they're larger than life. It's all part of the authoritarian mindset. Some current militia groups appear to be adopting a new heroic character, a former Army general, John Pope."

We were getting closer to what I was interested in, but we still weren't there. I said, "Tell me more about the work of this Lane Crothers."

"Yes. Crothers. He points out that there is a militia myth, which is part of the DNA of the United States from its beginning. Militias always have 'Right' on their side in this myth. It has been reinforced over the years in books and films. Crothers points to Mel Gibson's film *The Patriot* and John Milius's *Red Dawn* as examples of Hollywood perpetuating the myth. What the militia extremists want is to embody the myth, to bring about a return to the 'Good Life' the 'Right Way.' They see themselves as protectors. They will bring this about through heroic action as it was in the past – our American Revolution. They believe that's what's needed today."

Henry jumped on her comment. "A good life for white, heterosexual, Christian males whose ancestors have been here for a few hundred years."

Jackie asked, "Isn't that who has the power now?"

"Aha, my inquisitive friend," Henry continued. "Obviously so. But a Black man from Chicago got elected to the White House – twice. That scared the shit out of them. They didn't understand how we could have a Black president of the United States. To make it worse, he went to Harvard. The only thing that would have been worse in their minds was if he'd been a Jew. They felt he had no business being president. How could it happen?"

"How about because we elected him?" Jackie answered.

"So true. But only because, in their minds, the elites and the Jews who control the media and the money got him elected." Henry took on a deep Southern drawl. "He's a god damned towel head, for Christ's sake." Returning to his normal voice, he continued, "The Council of Conservative Citizens gained a lot of members after that election." Back to the Southern accent, "We oppose all efforts to mix the races of mankind." Back to normal, "Do you have any idea how many white male Southern politicians belong to that group? The damned CCC is the progeny of the White Citizens Councils, who are the progeny of the KKK. They believe they know the mind of God." Back to the drawl. "God is the author of racism. God is the One who divided mankind into different types. Mixing the races is rebelliousness against God."

Heng took back control of the conversation, and Henry let her. "It is race. But it is not just race. All populist social movements, left and right, blame elite groups for not caring about the common man."

"Isn't that a false equivalency?" I asked. "Putting liberal populists in the same bed with the right-wing nutcases?"

"Yes and no. Both see a similar problem – elites rigging the system for their own benefit. They differ on how to solve it. For example, how do you get the power to change things? The Left wants to expand voting and make it more inclusive. The Right wants to restrict voting to make it more exclusive."

Henry had to comment. "Viva la difference."

Heng ignored him. "Let me come back to Crothers for a minute. He says there are five characteristics of the groups you are interested in. The Right and the Left do not share these characteristics."

"Can you wait a minute?" Jackie asked. "I want to take notes." No one said a word as she reached into the small backpack on the floor next to her chair and took out her iPad. "Thanks. Okay. Go."

Heng easily shifted into lecture mode. Although her tone was conversational, she was clearly in familiar territory and had led others through these points. I started to pay close attention. This was what I wanted to know.

"Are you sure you want to go into the weeds on this?" Heng asked.

"Absolutely," I replied.

"Told you he was a curious one," Henry added.

"Okay. You asked for it. Number one," Heng said, "there is a chosen people mentality. Only certain people are entitled to have rights. For the extremists on the Right, these are the 'natives.' Not indigenous people, oh no. White people who have been here for a few generations. No people of color or recent immigrants need apply.

"Two. Our American national identity, who we are as a country, comes from this nativist group of people. Only members of this group are real Americans, and they are the backbone of America. They have made America great, and they will make America great again.

"Three. Engagements outside our national borders through trade, wars, or treaties are suspect."

"Why?" I asked.

"Because they can bring in foreign ideas, dangerous ideas that will corrupt our way of life and our way of thinking. For example, socialist and globalist thinking are corrupting influences. They will dilute that which makes us unique and great."

Henry added, "It's American exceptionalism on steroids."

"That's crazy," Jackie said.

Eve said, "Maybe, but it's pretty common. Look at the way religions often work hard to keep their children from intermarrying with people from other faiths or ethnic groups. The foreigner is always suspect, isn't he or she? However you define the foreigner, they are to be walled out, prohibited from entering the chosen society."

"Exactly," Heng said. "And that leads us to Crothers's fourth characteristic. There is a nostalgia for an idealized past when everybody knew their place and stayed there. That's when America was truly great and seen that way around the globe.

"Finally, the fifth, and this is the one that drives most liberals a bit bonkers, there is a conspiracy mindset. Our corrupt state of affairs, the downfall of the way things are supposed to be, is because dark forces – primarily elites, Jews, and the 'Deep State' – have conspired together. They have a plan, which they are currently executing, to change the very nature of America. Above all, a group of globalist elites pose an existential threat to their way of life."

Henry said, "Thou shall not distribute wealth and power to those people who shouldn't have any. Affirmative action, multilingual signage, men in drag reading to kids in the library – it's terrible, terrible, terrible according to these people. They believe we are falling apart as a country, and it is all because of these elites and their wokeness."

"Interesting," I said. "His girlfriend said Mark Perry was listening to a lot of conspiracy stuff on his short-wave radio."

"What?" Henry exclaimed. "Short-wave radio. You've got to be kidding me."

"She didn't say Maine, by any chance?" Heng asked.

"Wait a sec." I pulled out my phone and went to my notes page. "WBCQ. I looked it up. Monticello, Maine."

Heng said, "It is one of the strongest, if not the strongest, short-wave radio stations in the world and caters to extreme right-wing broadcasting. He probably listened to the Hal Turner show."

"Short-wave radio?" Henry said. "Why?"

"Because you can always track someone's internet usage. You can't track what they listen to on the radio, and the FCC does not monitor short-wave content. It's the Wild West. WBCQ should be called conspiracy and hate international. You can buy time for thirty dollars an hour, and you get to say whatever you want to anyone listening."

"Short-wave, though. God, these people hate us," Jackie said.

Heng said, "In some ways, it might be easier if it was hate. I think it's worse. It's contempt."

"Contempt?" Jackie asked.

"Yes. Contempt. Think of all of the mocking and the name-calling. Libtard, sheep, snowflake, woke. You aren't worthy of being hated. You are so stupid; hate would be wasted on you. Watch the right-wing commentators on television."

"Faux News," Henry said. "Their leader and his collection of perverse prevaricators stirring the proverbial pot."

Heng Pho ignored him and continued, "Or listen to right-wing newscasters on the radio. They are all filled with contempt for anybody who doesn't measure up. If you're not Republican enough, you're a RINO, Republican in name only. They divide the world into us and them, and the 'them' are contemptible."

I asked, "Is this new? Is there anything qualitatively different about what is taking place now? I am remembering the sixties, the extremists on the Left. Weren't they equally contemptuous of 'the man,' 'the system,' and often their parents?"

Henry answered. "It's different. The political parties were not as divided as they are today. Back then, you did not have party leaders expressing their contempt for the other side at the drop of a hat. There was at least a veneer of civility."

"The Republicans seem to have mastered contempt," Jackie said.

"Let's not forget our less than stellar candidate, Hilary Rodham Clinton, and her use of the word 'deplorables' to describe those who did not support her," Henry added.

"Are you still obsessing over that?" Eve asked.

"Yes. That one word contributed to making the right legitimate in American politics. Remember that bar. You know the pizza place."

Eve answered, "Henry is referring to a pizza restaurant right off the UConn campus. After Hilary Clinton made that statement, a sign went up over the bar that said: "Deplorables welcome here.""

Henry continued, "Back to the sleuth's question. One big difference between the sixties and now is how people get information. The number of channels for information, disinformation, and misinformation has exploded. There is no common core of information, and with so much competition for attention, whoever screams the loudest and is the most outrageous gets the audience and the money. The algorithms of the social media giants accelerate the spread. They feed you what they think you want to read and hear."

Heng added, "Today, there is an acceptance and expectation of violence. There was violence then, but it was limited and not accepted by the general public. It was seen as an aberration. Guns were not as available, certainly not assault weapons. Violence is expected today. That is new."

"Expected? You sound like you think we're headed for a civil war?" Jackie said. "Talk about depressing."

"Another researcher, Professor Barbara Walter, would say we are on our way," Heng said.

"Who's that?" I asked.

Eve said, "U.C. San Diego. Expert on contemporary civil wars. She thinks we are headed in that direction. She sees signs we are moving from a democracy to an anocracy."

"What's an anocracy?" Jackie asked.

Henry answered, "It's when people elect their dictator."

Eve said, "It's sort of halfway between a democracy and an autocracy. Checks and balances go out the window. The elected autocrat can then control elections so they retain power or refuse to yield power."

"Like Putin or Erdoğan?" Jackie asked.

"Among others," Eve added. "Look at Netanyahu's attempt to change the Israeli judiciary."

"Anocracy is typically what militias want," Heng said. "It usually involves absolute control over all governmental functions. Militias want their heroic strong man to have all the levers of power."

Henry added, "Autocrats want to abolish the civil service so they can have the power to appoint people at all levels of government."

"Why now? Why's this happening now?" Jackie asked. There was a plaintive tone in her voice.

"So many reasons," Heng answered. "Demographic shift is a big one. The coloring of America. 2045. That's the projected date when whites are no longer in the majority in the United States. Women. Look who's graduating from college and graduate schools. Women are increasingly dominating the professional class. Women now outnumber men in the college-educated labor force. Harvard's class of 2027 is 53 percent women. These demographic shifts are immense, and they have consequences."

"For women, it's about time," Jackie said.

Henry said, "Ahh, tis true. Sleuth and I have had a long run of…"

"Running things," Eve said.

"Well, yes."

Heng got us back on track. "There's another new dynamic. If you are a young, non-college-educated white male, you now see yourself as having a unique identity. That is a big change. Until recently, white men didn't think of themselves as a group, and certainly not as a minority group."

"Are they the backbone of the militia movement?" I asked.

"More like the muscle. They are the foot soldiers – men like your Mark Perry. It is the generation above them who are the leaders: the right-wing politicians who incite them, along with the right-wing media," Heng said.

"Are you saying they're pawns?" Jackie asked.

"Followers, yes. Pawns, no. They are ready, willing, and able."

"It has always been the case," Henry said. "We send our young off to wars declared by their parents. *Dulce et decorum est pro patria mori*."

"It is sweet and fitting to die for one's country," Eve translated.

"Poem by Wilfred Owen written during the big one, the war to end all wars," Henry added.

"Wait a minute," Jackie said. "These militia types aren't soldiers going off to war."

"I have to disagree with you," Heng said. "That's exactly how they think of themselves."

Henry added, "And we, the woke, are the enemy they want to defeat."

We continued through dinner and dessert. As we were leaving, Henry asked, "Are you going to go to Maine in search of this young man and this Defender group?"

"If he hasn't been heard from by tomorrow morning, I'll have to. It'll be two weeks, and being gone with no word over Christmas is troubling."

Heng said, "If you do..."

Henry interrupted, "Take Heng with you. She's still collecting interviews. She knows these people. I am sure she would be helpful."

"I don't know that I'm going yet. But sure. Yes. I'd love to have the company if you'd like to join me."

***

At nine o'clock at night, route 91 from Hartford to New Haven might as well be reserved for trucks. Route 95 from New Haven to Milford is the same way. My Subaru Outback is not a light car, but an eighteen-wheeler driving past me, going seventy miles an hour when I am doing the speed limit, will buffet the car. I always do the speed limit when driving with Eve. In some areas of her life, she remains the goody-two-shoes nun. Fortunately, it is only in some areas of her life.

Jackie had dozed off in the back seat. I said to Eve, "I like her."

"Heng? So do I. I'm glad Henry introduced us. Did you get the information you wanted?"

"Some. I feel like I have a reading list, though."

"Not a bad thing."

"No. Never is."

We drove silently for a while before I said, "I had an idea that has nothing to do with work. I was thinking about Ben and..."

"Hmm. I think I know where you're going."

"Well? Why not?"

"Because he might not appreciate you trying to fix him up."

"She's smart. Pretty. Right age."

"And she might..."

86

"I know. Have a boyfriend."

"Or a girlfriend."

"I suppose."

My son Benjamin, now approaching thirty, remains unattached. Working for the high-pressure law firm of Lawton, Chase, and Harrison does not, he continually reminds us, allow much time for meeting women. Meanwhile, his kid sister Molly was recently affianced to her longtime boyfriend, "Stan the Man." If my son doesn't have time to survey the field of potential mates, I don't see anything wrong with his father, on occasion, noticing an attractive, possibly available woman. As the wiser of the two of us, Eve thinks my matchmaking ambitions are quite humorous. Being the good sport she is, she said, "Do you want me to ask Henry about Heng's relationship status?"

"Do you mind?"

"No. Of course not."

Jackie heard us talking, woke up, and joined the conversation from the back seat. "I think she'd like Ben."

"You do, do you?"

"Yeah. Ben's a hottie."

"As an employee of Nutmeg Security and Investigations, I would prefer you not refer to my son as a hottie."

"He is, though."

Eve said, "I think we should probably change subjects."

Jackie did as she was told. "You going up to Maine. To Sparta?"

"I don't know. Maybe."

"If you go, can I come with you and Heng?"

"No. Two is more than enough. I don't want to overwhelm them."

Eve said, "I'm more concerned about them overwhelming you. Someone else from Nutmeg should be going with you, someone like Pat Brady or Butch Stofani or Archie Webber – maybe all three."

"I can't afford to take another staff member. There is barely enough in the budget for me to go."

Jackie knew enough to stay out of this conversation.

Chapter Eight: Intrusion

When I called Friday morning, the Perrys had not heard from Mark. I told the couple I would drive up to Sparta to see if I could find their son. Mom sounded relieved. Dad didn't complain about the cost.

I was alone as I left the office in New Haven and headed north. A year ago, before he retired, Sam would have been sitting next to me in the car. He would have wanted to come; he would have insisted upon it. The detective in him would want to know how and where this young man had disappeared. As an owner, he wouldn't be worried about his billable time. If he wanted to do something, he just did it. Meg, though, hearing the possibility that militias were involved, would have forbidden him to go. After I got shot, she insisted it was time for Sam to retire. Her exact words, as reported to me by Sam, were, "You're going to stop this cops and robbers stuff right now or I am walking out the door."

I could have asked one of our staff members to accompany me. Butch Stofani or Pat Brady would have been glad to go. Still, as the new one hundred percent owner of Nutmeg Security and Investigations, I felt responsible for our bottom line, and there was no way in hell the Perrys would pay for two of us to go. The cap we had agreed upon, $3,000, was low as it was. So I swallowed whatever anxiety I had, reiterated to Eve that there was no danger, and started driving up Route 91 to Maine. I had Blackie with me. Blackie was not billable, although perhaps he should have been. He had saved my butt twice.

I was surprised when, at dinner with Henry, Heng Pho had asked if she could tag along. I welcomed her company as a traveling companion, although as a backup, if there were trouble, she would make things more difficult. I'd have to worry about her. I was already wishing I'd said "no."

I hadn't though. After I talked to the Perrys, I called her and asked if she still wanted to go. I was hoping she would have plans and couldn't make it. She said she was free. Sensing my concern, she said, "I've interviewed over a hundred of these guys, Frank. Believe me, most of them are nothing but talk." I was worried about those who weren't, like Mark Perry, an angry ex-Special Forces guy who worked out, was into mixed martial arts, and had a big chip on his shoulder.

I was armed. I was wearing my Glock 23 and had a Glock 21 locked in my glove compartment, along with extra magazines for each. I hadn't been to the shooting range in months. More rust that I hadn't gotten rid of. Rusty and old. I was heading towards sixty, although I still had a few years before arriving. Was I still a good shot? I used to be. What the hell? I was only trying to find this kid, not drag him kicking and screaming from some band of bloodthirsty militia weirdoes.

In Hartford, I left Route 91 and went on to Route 84, leading to Sturbridge. I was early to pick Heng up in Storrs and was hungry, so I stopped for lunch in Vernon, Connecticut, at Rein's Delicatessen. It is the best Jewish delicatessen outside of New York City, and I always stop there when headed this way. It was jammed as usual, but I was able to find a spot in the bar at the back. A Pastrami Reuben with an egg cream brought back memories of being a graduate student at John Jay in Manhattan. That was a long time ago, and now I was on my way to pick up a member of the next generation of graduate students.

Even though it was below freezing, Heng was waiting for me in front of the apartment building where she lived – Oaks on the Square – right off the UConn Storrs campus. She put her overnight bag in the back of my Subaru Outback. Blackie got up, stretched, ignored her, and returned to his place right behind my seat.

"You're right on time," Heng said.

"It's too cold to wait outside. I could've texted you when I got here."

"This is fine. Remember: I lived in Chicago for the last five years."

89

I started driving towards Route 84, which would take us out of Connecticut and into Massachusetts. We chit-chatted about the weather for a few miles before Heng said, "I appreciate you taking me with you."

"I'm glad to have the company. I'm not sure you will have anyone to interview, though. We don't know that Perry's in Sparta."

"There might be others at the camp. Who knows how many this McKnight may have recruited?"

"True. And you think some of these people will be willing to talk to you?"

"Probably."

"That surprises me."

"In some ways, their willingness to be interviewed is a big part of the picture. They don't feel like anyone cares about them or what they think."

"What about all this privacy stuff I've been reading about in the Militia Handbook?"

"I know. It seems contradictory: bravado on the one hand and secret conspiratorial plans to overthrow the government on the other. They're marching around in hoods while handing out pamphlets and driving their own cars so any government agency can quickly figure out who they are. Consistency of thought and action isn't exactly a strength for most of these groups."

I didn't say anything in response. She continued. "By the way, I looked up this Defenders of Liberty group that may have recruited Mark. They have a low profile and are fairly new. SPLC. Are you familiar with them? Southern Poverty Law Center? They don't have them listed as a terrorist group yet."

"Maybe they're not. Jackie found some stuff, though, that suggests that they are."

"I didn't find anything that would suggest that."

"Jackie searches in places I don't know about. She does a fair amount of hacking."

"Oh."

"She is convinced the people associated with the Defenders are, in her words, 'Wack jobs.' Especially McKnight."

"I wouldn't have picked that up from their website. They emphasize training people in survival skills. It all sounds pretty benign. Strange, maybe, but not crazy violent."

"Maybe. By the way, Jackie says a group of heavy hitters have their own candidate for the presidency, and McKnight is involved with them. His older brother, Douglas, is part of the group."

"Seriously? A presidential candidate?"

"Apparently."

"Let me guess. Pope?"

"Yep."

"That makes sense. He's the new hero for these groups."

"You know of him?"

"Yes. He's pushing the theory of the 'Unitary Presidency.' If it were up to him, the president would control the entire executive branch, including the DOJ. No Civil Service. Actually, I think he would do away with Congress."

"Anocracy?"

"Anocracy."

After our first hour in the car, we listened to the radio, and Heng dozed off for almost two hours. There was no more serious conversation.

***

Claire Church, our "all-purpose person" at Nutmeg, had made reservations for us at the Independence Inn in Dover-Foxcroft, Maine, on the banks of the Piscataquis River. Claire told me, "Sparta doesn't have any places to stay. Dover-Foxcroft sounds interesting. It's the home of the Whoopie Pie Festival. If you were there in June, you could go."

The Independence Inn was old, 1800's old. It had been built as a farmhouse, and as is true of many New England farmhouses, it had been added on to several times over the years. Eve would call it a New England rambler. It was late afternoon when we arrived, and the lights

91

on the outside Christmas tree were on as we drove up to the front of the inn.

Inside, Christmas decorations were everywhere. A fire was going in the parlor, and the assortment of cookies along with coffee, tea, and lemonade made one feel welcome. Sadly, the innkeeper, Miranda, wasn't available, according to Harper, the teenaged young lady who welcomed us and gave us our keys. Harper told us Miranda was at the hospital in Bangor with her husband, who had been there for a few days while recovering from a back operation. Miranda would see us at breakfast, though. I gathered I was to be disappointed by Miranda's absence.

After unpacking, I met Heng in the parlor. On the coffee table were menus for local restaurants. I started looking through them. "We don't have a lot of choices for dinner."

"How about the pizza place? I'm a grad student. It's the cuisine of necessity."

"Joe's it is."

Joe's Pizza was one of those "only in Maine" places. It's pizza. But someone at Joe's, probably the owner, got it in his head that in Dover Foxcroft, there were wine lovers willing to fork out up to $200 for a bottle of Antinori Tignanello chianti. There were over twenty varieties of Italian wines, from $15 to $200. I was curious, but not $200 worth of curious. After we agreed we would drink a red, I did fork over $25 for a nice Sangiovese. I ordered a "Super Italiano Calzone," and Heng had a "Joe's Special" pizza.

After our server poured our wine, I said, "I was surprised last night when you compared what happened with the Khmer Rouge in Cambodia to what is happening in the United States today."

"I bet it seems impossible to you. It's not a replica, but some of the dynamics are similar. For example, the Khmer Rouge saw the educated class as oppressive and did everything it could to get rid of them. My grandfather was a dentist. Because he was an educated professional, they sent him into the country to plant rice. A dentist had to go plant rice. Who was going to fix people's teeth? My grandfather, the dentist, a big threat?

How insane was that? Fortunately, he got my grandmother, mother, and two uncles out of the country just in time. He never made it. We have all been back to look for some marker of his passing. Nothing. It's like he never existed."

"I'm sorry."

"Two million. The Khmer Rouge killed at least two million Cambodians in the space of four years. That's all it took – four years."

"Unbelievable."

"No. Believable. It happened. Americans have their head in the sand. Look at the disdain the Right has for science and scientists. Look at what happened during the Pandemic. The Right claimed the scientists were all lying and shouldn't be listened to. How is it different? Now, the right is attacking colleges and universities as the root of evil. The Khmer Rouge saw the cities as evil. So does the Right in this country. Why? Because cities are where education, culture, and economic power occur. Education and culture are not exactly high on the Right's value system. Economic power is a whole other thing. Revolution is almost always seen as a 'taking back' from some group. We deserve it; they don't."

"I see what you're saying."

"Do you?" I was surprised by the vehemence of her question. It was a clear challenge.

"I think so. Or at least I'm beginning to."

"I'm sorry. That was rude of me."

"No. It's okay. Really."

"You sure? I can be pretty obnoxious when I get going."

"You weren't being obnoxious. I'm curious, though, how do you get these people to talk to you?"

"Oh, they never see this side of me. To them, I am this sweet little, non-threatening Asian thing who wouldn't hurt a fly. They love teaching me about everything wrong with America and how to fix it."

***

We agreed upon a time to meet for breakfast the following morning. I called Eve to say good night when I got to my room. I told her about the conversation with Heng and the intensity.

"It's personal with her; it's her family. You know how I get when I talk about Lebanon."

"You're right. With Heng sometimes I don't know whether I'm talking to an objective researcher or a family survivor."

"Both."

I was still thinking about the conversation with Heng when I finally got to sleep.

***

Breakfast was at eight o'clock. I love breakfast. Usually, I discipline myself to be a minimalist at breakfast, but it is a discipline that I am delighted to forgo when staying at an inn that includes a 'farmer's breakfast.' I wonder if many farmers ever ate so well. Heng's yogurt, fruit, and tea did not make me feel guilty as I indulged myself with an omelet, sausage, hash browns, and a curated collection of pastries.

Innkeeper Miranda fussed over us. Her husband was doing well and would be home in a few days. When she asked what brought us to Dover-Foxcroft, I said, "We're going up to Sparta to check out a place called Camp Liberty. Ever hear of it?"

"No. Can't say I have."

"It used to be a camp for kids, Camp Nebizun."

"Oh, sure. Once in a while, parents would stay here if they were visiting their children. I heard it closed down."

"New owners. I understand it's now a place to teach survival skills to adults."

"Sorry. Don't know anything about it. Would you like some more coffee?"

When we got in the car and were on the road headed to Sparta, I said, "What do you think? Do people around here know about Camp Liberty?"

"No idea. She sure wasn't curious."

"Or she didn't want to say something that might offend us."

Heng became thoughtful. "My guess is she doesn't know and doesn't want to know."

***

Sparta is a small town. The main street, Lake Street, contains the general store that sells gas, a small library open on Wednesday evenings and Saturday mornings, a town garage that houses the volunteer fire department, and an automotive garage with a single bay. According to the Wicki I had read, the population had risen to over one thousand people only once, and that was in 1860.

We had an address for Camp Nebizun but didn't see any signs for the camp, either Nebizun or Liberty. We drove by a dirt driveway, which we thought was probably the correct address, a couple of times before deciding this had to be it. There was a mailbox, but it didn't have a number.

We went up and down hills and could see the lake as we came over the top of one hill, but we had to stop. A metal gate blocked the road. A small wooden shed stood next to it. It was painted bright red and looked new. As we approached the gate, a man came out of the shed. He was dressed in hunting garb – camouflage pants, jacket, and hat. He carried what I recognized as an AR-15 assault rifle.

We stopped. As he approached the car, he pulled up a scarf to cover the lower half of his face. When I started to get out, he shouted, "Please remain in your vehicle and roll down your window." I did as I was told.

"This is private property. Do you have business here?" he asked.

At breakfast Heng and I had discussed how best to inquire about Mark Perry. I said, "My name's Frank Kelly. This is Heng Pho. We would like to speak to Colonel McKnight."

"Do you have an appointment?"

"No, we don't. We've seen the information about Camp Liberty on the website, and we'd like to speak with the Colonel about signing up for some classes."

"We don't have any classes over the holidays."

"Oh, well, can we speak with the Colonel, anyway? We're interested in all of the camp's activities."

My response surprised and confused him. "Wait here." He stepped back from the car and returned to the shed. A minute later, he came out and walked over to the car. "The Colonel's busy right now. If you want to come back in an hour, he will see you then."

Heng and I exchanged glances and nodded to one another. I turned back to the armed guard. "Please thank the Colonel for us. We will see you in an hour."

I turned the car around and drove back towards Sparta. When we reached the main road, we turned left and went for more than a mile before pulling into a parking place in front of the Sparta General Store.

Inside, the store was a "general" store. It included a small café area in addition to shelves of paper goods, canned goods, a refrigerator section, and freezers for frozen dinners, ice cream, and vegetables.

Heng and I approached the counter used for everything from ordering to checking out. I ordered a coffee. When Heng ordered tea, the older man behind the counter reached down, took out two boxes containing a variety of teas, and put them on the counter. "Pick your poison." Behind him, we saw a woman talking on the telephone. She looked at us while she spoke.

We collected our coffee and tea and sat down. "What do you think?" I asked Heng.

"Looks like someone has announced our presence in the community."

"I agree."

"Are you going to show them your photographs of Mark Perry?"

"Not now. I want to avoid alerting them about who we're looking for. We'll see how it goes with McKnight. Maybe we'll come back later."

We spent the next hour nursing our drinks and chatting about our backgrounds and families. I learned more about her grandmother's exodus from Cambodia and the journey on foot to Thailand with young children. I learned about the Cambodian migration to the United States and the enclaves that developed in Long Beach, California and Lowell, Massachusetts. As she recounted her story, I also learned that she had never been married, was not in a relationship, and her parents were worried that she would be single forever because she worked so hard. It was an excellent opening to let her know that I understood her parents' concern because I just happened to have a single lawyer son who also worked too hard.

***

Precisely an hour later, we were back in front of the gate to Camp Liberty. This time, the guard pushed in numbers on a keypad, the gate swung open, and we drove through.

After a half mile, the road started to descend, and around the next curve, we saw the camp. There were several buildings of various sizes arranged around a central area. We didn't see anyone walking around, and there was no sign of people living there except for two trucks and three cars parked behind a large barn. I was surprised at the sight of a tower with three large satellite dishes attached. I said to Heng, "Look at that thing. It looks industrial. It must have cost a fortune."

"Frank, this isn't …"

"A camp to teach survival skills to city dwellers on the weekend. No way. Something else is going on here."

We drove another quarter mile into the center of the camp and stopped in front of a building with the sign "office" over the door. The door opened, and a middle-aged man came out. He was also dressed in camouflage. I asked Heng, "Why don't you stay here until I see if McKnight will talk to us? That's him. I recognize him from a picture Jackie showed me."

I walked around the car and approached him, hand out. "Colonel McKnight, I'm Frank Kelly."

He shook my hand, "What can I do for you and Dr. Pho?"

"You know who we are?"

"You gave us your names."

He had used the hour to Google us. So much for being circumspect.

Heng got out of the car and walked over to where we were standing. McKnight shook hands with her, "Dr. Pho."

Heng replied formally, "I am delighted to meet you, Colonel

McKnight. Thank you for agreeing to speak with us."

"I haven't agreed to anything. I'm just curious about why you're here."

"Well, we're interested in Camp Liberty and…"

"No, you're not. Now cut the bullshit. Why are you here?"

I chose to be direct. He already knew who we were. I responded, "There is a young man who's missing. His name is Mark Perry. His parents have asked me to try to locate him. Mark has shown an interest in your group, and we know he went to the gun show in Portland, where you had representatives. We thought you might have met him and know where he is. His parents just want to know that he is well."

"I've never heard of him; he certainly isn't here. How do you know he went to Portland?"

"He told his parents he was going to the gun show."

"So you don't know he actually went."

"No, we don't, but we think it's highly likely based on what he said to his parents and his girlfriend."

McKnight paused for a second before he said, "So he told several people where he was going, and that's why you're here. And that's the only reason you're here. Has it occurred to you that he may have gone somewhere else and that telling people he was going to Portland was just a way of hiding where he was going or what he was doing? There are thousands of possibilities."

"Yes, I know."

"And you, Dr. Pho? Why are you here?"

"I hoped to interview you and perhaps some members of the Defenders of Liberty."

"For what reason?"

"I'm trying to understand what attracts people to groups like the Defenders. I want to give them a voice."

"No, you don't! You want to create inaccurate stereotypes as you have in the past."

"Colonel, I don't…"

"Yes, you do. I've read your bullshit."

"You know my research?"

"I've read enough about it to know you're a fraud who couldn't tell the difference between a patriot and a terrorist if your life depended upon it."

"Colonel, I…"

"Are you both satisfied? I've answered both of you – no and no. I want you to leave. As of right now, you are trespassing."

"Colonel," I started, "there are parents who are worried about their son. Surely…"

"Now. Get back in your car and leave now. You're trespassing."

"Okay. We're going. Before we go, could I walk my dog? We've got a long drive ahead of us."

"No. Now move."

"Yes, sir." I couldn't restrain my sarcasm.

We got back in the car. I whispered to Heng, "Remember the back of the barn where the trucks and the cars were parked? I'll act as though I don't know where I'm going. I'm going to drive over there. Use your phone and take pictures of the trucks. Mark drives a pickup. Try to get the license plate numbers. One of them might be his. Let me know when you get them, and I'll get us out of here. I don't think he'll do anything more than shout."

"Are you sure?"

"Pretty sure. This guy's starting to piss me off."

I started the car, slowly weaved, and circled like I didn't know where to go. When I started heading for the barn where I had seen the vehicles, McKnight shouted something I couldn't hear. I kept going, went between two smaller buildings, and then drove around behind the barn.

"I got them," Heng said as we drove past the trucks. One has a Connecticut license plate."

"Good. Now let's get out of here." I drove back around the building to the center area where McKnight was pointing towards the road. I smiled and saluted.

A few minutes later, we were back at the general store. First, I checked Heng's picture of the Connecticut license plate number against the number in the information folder I had on Mark Perry. It was Mark Perry's truck. Then we showed our pictures of Mark Perry to the owner, the man who had waited on us, and an older couple who were seated at one of the tables. No one had seen him.

Back in the car, I dialed the number for the Perry household and gave them the news. "I suspect Mark has joined up with a militia group called the Defenders of Liberty in Sparta, Maine. I didn't see Mark, but his truck is at their camp. The man who directs the camp said he had never heard of Mark, but there is no question that it's Mark's truck."

"Wait a minute." I could hear James Perry talking to his wife. I assumed he was relaying the news to her.

Perry asked, "What do you suggest we do?"

"Well, you could have the Sheriff's Department visit the camp. We took a picture of the truck. The picture would give the sheriff enough cause to visit. He could call it a 'wellness' visit. I don't know. He might want you to file a missing person, as well."

"We don't want to do that. We already talked about that."

"If you wanted me to, I could knock on some doors and show Mark's picture around."

Again, "Wait a minute." Another conference with his wife. "No, that's going to cost too much."

"I'm already here. Won't cost much more."

"No. Now that we know where he is, we'll take it from here."

Chapter Nine: Ambush

Gordon had promised his brother that the Defenders of Liberty would be ready when the time came to mobilize into action. When the call came, it was Doug who stated, "A problem with the campaign has developed, and I think you might be able to help us with it"

"What's wrong?" Gordon asked.

"It's Montana. The governor. Our people have repeatedly talked to her about dropping out of the race. She isn't budging. The last time, we flew someone out there to meet with her face-to-face. We tried to impress upon her that now is the time for her to withdraw her candidacy."

"What happened?"

"The dumb bitch thinks this is politics as usual. Told our person to get lost. She's clueless."

"How can I help?"

"I think she may need a visit from the Defenders of Liberty. She needs a different kind of message, apparently."

"We can arrange that."

"No violence, but scare the shit out of her. You have people who can do that?"

"Absolutely."

"No names. No identifying any group. And no one can get caught."

"I understand."

"They can't fuck this up. This can't be like Watergate. I mean it. They have to understand that."

"Don't worry. We're ready. I have just the person to lead it. Seasoned professional. He understands what's at stake."

"How much time will you need?"

"A week. No more."

"Good. I don't want to know anything. I'll see the results."

***

Governor Mary Olson told the captain in charge of her state police detail that they would not be needed once they dropped her off at her country place. She and her husband would be there for three days, and they had her husband's car if they needed to get something from the nearest town, Patience, Montana. The Guv, as she was referred to by the citizens of Patience, needed time away from the affairs of Montana. She also needed some time with just her husband to consider what to do about her struggling primary campaign for the presidency of the United States of America.

Only four candidates remained and had met the party's qualifications for the New Hampshire debate. Originally, there were seven in the race. Three had dropped due to a lack of traction or money. As much as the remaining candidates shouted at one another and spent money, no one was breaking loose from the pack. According to national polls, she was polling in the fourth position and had been stuck there for weeks. Mary Olson didn't like being stuck. She had never been stuck before. She had gone from being a state representative to a state senator to a state attorney general to the governor without ever being stuck.

She was mid-way through her second term and couldn't run again because of term limits. Making a run for the presidency made sense. Her keynote at the last convention had been well received. She had won both gubernatorial elections with wide margins. She had a national following because of her conservative stances – she had just signed into law a ban on drag shows in public places – and she was a woman. It was time for a conservative woman to try for the White House. "Mary Olson is the United States' version of Margaret Thatcher," proclaimed more than one Montana newspaper.

But she was stuck in low double digits. Double digits, but low double digits. She and Edward had some serious talking to do. One option was dropping out and letting everyone know that she would be open to a role as a vice-presidential candidate. Another option was to go on a mad dog attack directed at the three top candidates. Her campaign staff wanted that one. She had lots of options. Edward was always her best sounding board. Besides, they hadn't had much time for intimacy recently, and they had their best sex at their country retreat.

Thirty miles north of Helena, Mary's grandparents had built the retreat in the 1950s. They named it Sokináápi to honor the Blackfeet people who had first settled there. Loosely translated, the word meant to fix something or someone, as in doctoring them or healing them. Being governor and campaigning was exhausting. She was also exhausted from the family's Christmas at the governor's mansion in Helena. With Christmas on a Monday, it had turned into a three-day affair. As much as she enjoyed it, she needed some "doctoring." With its two hundred and thirty rugged acres of the Lewis Mountain Range, Sokináápi provided privacy. In combination with the abutting National Forest, Mary and Edward had miles of trails to ride horses or snowmobiles, depending upon the season.

She loved Sokináápi. It was part of her life. She had been going there since she was an infant. It was the place for family reunions and weddings, and, most of all, a place to retreat to and find comfort in the familiar, a haven from the world's tribulations. It was hers now, all hers. She had bought out her brother's interest. For the next three days, there would be no campaigning, no children, grandchildren, family, friends, or staff. Just the two of them. Perfect, she thought as she watched the limousine assigned to her turn down the driveway and head back to Helena. Edward should be arriving any minute with the groceries for their getaway. "I want to bake bread," she had told him. "When was the last time I had the time to make bread?"

Four miles away, Mark Perry, Lenny Pratt, and Barry Stark were trying to keep warm in a Toyota Rav 4 stolen from a long-term parking lot outside the SeaTac airport in Seattle, Washington. The stolen car had Montana license plates on it. The plates had been stolen from a different car, a car in the long-term parking lot at the Missoula, Montana airport. Perry, Pratt, and Stark had nothing to do with these thefts; they were all arranged by the Freedom Frontier, a 600-member Militia group that claimed to be the "Backbone of the Constitution." Colonel Gordon McKnight had asked for help, and the Frontier were pleased to provide it.

After three days of driving from Sparta, Maine, the three Defenders of Liberty had picked up the stolen Toyota when they arrived in Helena. Barry Stark's car, which had taken them to Montana, was now parked out of sight in the garage of the leader of the Montana Patriots, a local militia group.

Although McKnight had made the arrangements with these groups, his second in command at Camp Liberty, Barry Stark, organized the mission and was in charge of the three-man team. In his mid-fifties, Stark was a Massachusetts State Police retiree. His had a career devoid of distinction. He did nothing heroic during his thirty years. He was never injured in the line of duty. Any civilian complaints about his "unwarranted aggressive behavior" were dismissed as without foundation. He was always available for extra duty, and with his sergeant's salary during the final five years of his employment, he made close to $200,000 a year.

His retirement was celebrated by his second wife, Cindy, and seven friends from the Belchertown State Police Barracks at the Grapevine Grill in Belchertown, Massachusetts, a small town northeast of Springfield. Only Cindy and two of their friends were aware of his fascination with fascism and his commitment to the Defenders of Liberty. She didn't like the idea of his being away for weeks at a time, especially over Christmas, but it was a sacrifice she was willing to make to "Take America Back."

Stark had been dozing when his cell phone rang. "This could be it," he said to Perry and Pratt as he slid the phone's answer image from left to right. He listened as one of the Montana Patriots told him that they had just seen the governor's limousine leave with two state police in it, and the governor's husband had just entered the driveway and was heading towards the house.

"Got it," Stark responded. He put his phone away and took in a deep breath. He let it out slowly and said, "We're up. You ready?"

Pratt answered for both of them, "Let's rock and roll."

The three men got out of their vehicle. The door and trunk lights had been dismantled as McKnight had instructed. They put on ski masks to hide their faces. They retrieved their equipment from the car's cargo area. They each had night vision glasses, a Kevlar vest, a headset with a microphone, and a single earpiece.

"Comm check," Stark requested.

The three of them spoke a few words quietly into their microphones. Satisfied their communication system was operative, they removed their weapons from the back of the vehicle: SA80 assault rifles and Sig Sauer P320 pistols that were chambered for .40 S&W ammunition. They also had cans of bear spray. "It shoots farther than pepper spray and works just as well," Stark had told them.

They were parked on a rough dirt access road in the National Forest. Leaving the car behind, they would have to hike cross country to reach their destination. The hiking would not be challenging. It was mountainous, but they would pick up a trail used by hikers, horseback riders, and snowmobilers most of the way. The trail they planned to use would lead them right to Sokináápi. The December weather, though, was a concern. It was below freezing in an icy fog, and snow was always possible.

It was dark when the three men entered the barn through the side door. "We'll wait here until one or two, depending on when we see the lights go out," Stark told the others. "I want them in bed and sound asleep when we enter the house. We'll take turns resting and keeping watch until then. No talking unless it's absolutely necessary. There aren't supposed to be any dogs, but I don't want to take a chance."

"What about alarms?" Pratt asked.

"If they set them, and they go off, we'll have them turn them off, call the alarm company, and report them as false alarms. If the alarm company sends anyone, it will take at least forty-five minutes before they can get here. They'll be recalled. Don't worry about alarms. Now, get some rest. I'll take first watch."

***

At two-thirty in the morning, the three men opened the kitchen door of the ranch house and turned on their night-vision goggles. There were no sounds from inside, and no alarms went off. Stark stopped as they entered and looked for the alarm display. Finding it, he saw that it had not been turned on.

The three of them were familiar with the house's layout because of an article in Montana Magazine on *Sokináápi* from years before, when Olson first ran for state representative. The three men made their way through the dining room and living room to the far end of the house, where they assumed Mary and Edward Olson were sound asleep. The bedroom door was open. The three entered and took positions around the bed.

Stark flipped up his night goggles and turned on the lamp on the governor's side of the bed. Perry and Pratt also flipped up their goggles so the light would not blind them. Pratt turned on the light next to Edward.

"Shock," Stark had told Pratt and Perry. "We want maximum shock." The three of them pointed their weapons at the bed. Stark reached down and pulled the bedclothes off of the naked bodies of the sleeping couple. "Well, look at that!" Pratt said.

Startled by feeling cold and hearing Pratt's voice. Edward rolled over, looked up, and screamed, "What…"

"Quiet," Stark admonished.

Hearing the noise, Mary woke up. Seeing a man in a mask with a rifle pointed at her, "Who…" Mary shouted.

"Both of you. Shut up. Don't say a word, and no one will get hurt. Take a look around. Look carefully. Take a moment. Look at your situation and do what you are told; we don't want to hurt you if we can avoid it. Just do what you're told. Shake your heads if you understand."

"I..." Mary started.

Edward grabbed her hand and squeezed it. She stopped.

"Good," Stark said. I am going to read you something. They are instructions. Governor, I want you to listen to them very, very carefully. I will read them to you twice. Then, I will ask you to repeat the instructions to make sure you understand. Nod your head if you understand."

"Who the hell are you to....." Mary started.

Mark Perry turned his rifle around and raised it, prepared to slam the butt end into the woman.

Edward shouted, "Don't. Mary, shut the fuck up."

Mary looked at her husband and nodded.

Mary said, "I'm freezing. Can I..."

"Yes," Stark replied.

Edward grabbed for the sheet and blankets and pulled them up to their chins, covering their nakedness.

"Listen closely." Stark took off one of his gloves and reached into the breast pocket of his jacket. He pulled out a piece of paper and began reading:

"We do not intend to harm you. Please do nothing that would mean we might have to. You will, though, do exactly as we say. Pay attention to how easily we have put you in this situation. We can do it again and again. Our reach and power is national, and we will never hesitate to use it.

"First, you will call your campaign manager tomorrow morning and tell her to arrange a press conference tomorrow at noon. You will not tell her the topic. Tomorrow, you will drive to Helena, and you will announce to the press that you are ending your campaign. You will thank your supporters and your staff. You will tell them you are not endorsing any other candidates at this time.

"Second, you will continue to conduct business as usual. When you are asked about future plans, you will tell people that you will focus on the business of Montana and nothing else. You will say the future you will leave for the future.

"Third, when your party's candidate does emerge, you will do whatever you are asked to ensure he is elected president of the United States." Stark paused and said, "Do you understand what I have said? Nod your head if you do."

Mary spoke, "Are you serious?"

"Deadly serious." Stark read the instructions again.

When he finished, Mary said, "You don't really think you can get away with this, do you?"

Edward said, "Mary!"

"Don't Mary me." To Stark, she said, "Who the hell do you think you are, telling me what to do?"

Stark didn't raise his voice. McKnight and Stark had role played how Stark would respond. "That is an excellent question. We are people who have just entered your home while you were asleep. We are well armed. Understand this. We are a national organization. We can do the same thing with your children, grandchildren, parents, and anyone you love. We can kill you, maim you, or torture you or any of them. We are patriots who are willing to do whatever is necessary to take back the United States. We don't see you as our enemy but as someone who is potentially supportive but who must step aside right now as a candidate. You cannot win the primary. Even if nominated, you could not win the general election. We must win this election, and you will help us make that possible. That's who we are, and we are telling you what to do. We are not negotiating."

"Jesus Christ," Edward said. "You're crazy."

"No, sir. We are committed. And we are not taking any chances. We are not trusting politics as usual."

"And if we don't?"

"Which of your grandchildren would you like to see in a hospital

108

first? And how will you explain your choice to your children? You already know you are not going to win the primary. We are just accelerating the timeline and keeping your supporters from spending money that can best be used by a winning candidate in the future. Do you question our commitment or ability to do what we say we will do? Do you want to risk finding out?"

Mary said, "You won't get away with this."

"I am going to hand you a piece of paper. I want you to study it closely. Then hand it back to me. Do you understand?"

Mary didn't say anything.

Edward said, "Give it to me."

Stark did. The names and addresses of the Olson's children and grandchildren were on the paper. Next to the names were details about work, school, and travel schedules. Edward read over the paper and handed it to his wife.

Mary read it. "You bastard."

Stark ignored her. "Do you want me to repeat my instructions?"

"No."

"Good. Now get dressed."

"I'm not getting dressed in front of you."

"Fine. Don't." Stark nodded to Pratt, who yanked the covers off the governor and her husband.

"You! You!" Mary screamed.

Stark ignored her. Edward got off the bed and started to walk towards the bathroom. Mark Perry got in his way. Edward said, "I've got to take a leak."

Stark nodded 'okay' to Perry. "Leave the door open."

Fifteen minutes later, Stark escorted a now-dressed for travel governor and her husband into the living room to wait for morning. He had them sit at opposite ends of the room. He told them, "Feel free to read, sleep, or just sit. There will be no talking."

At 7:45, Governor Mary Olson and her husband Edward left their weekend retreat in Edward's Land Rover and headed for the Governor's

Residence in Helena. As they reached the end of the driveway, four men in ski masks with rifles were on either side of the entrance, an exclamation point to the conversation that had recently concluded.

Stark, Pratt, and Perry left when the Land Rover was out of site. Without sleep, they took their time returning to their car.

"I'm famished," Pratt said. "Let's get something to eat."

"Me, too," Perry added.

"Not until we've switched cars and are on the road and have some miles between us and Helena. The sooner we get out of here, the better."

"Why?" Perry said.

"Just in case they decide to be heroes."

"Are you kidding?" answered Pratt. "They're both scared shitless. Who'd believe them, anyway? They've got no proof. It would look like they were trying to get sympathy for pulling out of the race."

"Or, they'd come up with something so they can say, 'Look at us. See how courageous we are,'" Stark said. "Fucking politicians."

"Not going to happen. Food," Perry said. "They're not going to say anything to anyone. Let's go get something to eat."

"Jesus Christ," Stark said. "How the fuck old are you?"

"Old enough to know I'm hungry."

"I second that," Pratt said.

"Okay. Let's go get my car. Maybe we can get something to take with us from the group in Helena. I'll give them a call. Some breakfast sandwiches and coffee enough for you adolescents?"

"That works for me," Pratt said.

They walked silently the rest of the way to the car. They loaded their gear into the back, Stark got behind the wheel, and they drove towards Helena. "Turn the radio on," Stark said. "Find a news station."

Sitting next to him in the passenger seat, Pratt did as he had been asked. "You think she will have made the announcement already? You told her noon."

"Just leave it on."

***

110

Like Barry Stark, Gordon McKnight and his brother Doug were also tuned in to news channels. At 12:20 AM Rocky Mountain Time, the major news outlets reported that Mary Olson was ending her campaign but would not be endorsing any candidate at this time. She pledged to support whoever the party's candidate turned out to be.

In Washington, Doug called members of the Committee to inform them of her decision in case they hadn't heard.

Chapter Ten: The Committee

Nine were invited, but only seven members of The Committee responded that they could make it to the dinner following Mary Olson's press conference. They were not surprised when she announced her withdrawal from the Republican primary. Still, Douglas was disappointed that two members would be missing. That was unusual. Attendance had been good since the group started meeting halfway through President Goodman's first term. A few hours' notice was unusual, though. And it was the week after Christmas.

The group was to meet in their usual place, a private dining room in Tony Vecchi's Saloon on K Street in Washington, D.C. The restaurant strived to recapture the ambiance of a 1920s' steakhouse, and Douglas McKnight loved the feel of the place. Banquettes along the walls were covered in dark red leather as were the cushioned chairs. The walls were covered in black wallpaper with streaks of gold. A New York strip steak would set customers back fifty dollars and a martini fifteen. Such prices did not faze members of The Committee. They would charge their meals to expense accounts of various corporations, consulting companies, and ultra-conservative foundations. Nineteen-twenties jazz played discreetly throughout the restaurant except in the private room where the members of The Committee had requested that the speakers be turned off.

Douglas McKnight was the first to arrive. Upon entering the restaurant, he called Tony Vecchi aside and said, "Thanks for setting this up on such short notice, Tony. I appreciate it."

"No problem, Mr. McKnight. We're delighted to serve your group.

I'm glad the room was free. Let me know if there's anything you need."

"Just privacy, Tony, just privacy. Will Earl be available to serve us?"

"As you requested."

"Great. Thank you for being so accommodating."

"Anytime."

Doug knew Earl Mason would be discreet. When The Committee first came together the previous year, Doug emphasized the need for discretion to Tony. Tony assured Doug of Earl's sensitivities to the needs of a group such as Doug's, "The real decision-makers in the country." Reliable tips of thirty percent assured that Earl always knocked before entering to take orders, deliver drinks and food, and clear the table once the meal was complete.

Doug went up the stairs to the private room. It looked barren with no one in it. Four tables had been brought together so eight could comfortably hold a conversation. Earl entered the room from a service entrance, said, "Good evening, Mr. McKnight," and began spreading a white tablecloth across the tables.

"Evening, Earl. There'll just be seven of us tonight, and we need the conference phone if that's not too much trouble."

"No trouble at all. sir."

Doug both expected and appreciated service. He liked getting to know the people who served him. From previous conversations, he knew Earl came from a long line of people who knew how to provide service. His great-grandfather had been a Pullman Porter when that was an elite position for a Black man in America. His grandfather had been a waiter at Justine's in Memphis, and his father had been a chauffeur for a United States Senator.

"Thank you, Earl. People should be arriving in about twenty minutes. We have some critical issues to discuss, so we may skip cocktails and appetizers. We'll see how others feel about that when they get here. However, when you're through setting up, please bring me a Lime Rickey with bourbon.

"Certainly, sir."

Doug liked to drink but did not like it when people got drunk. He was a disciplined drinker; he told his wife this whenever she suggested that he was drinking too much. "Have you ever seen me get sloppy or maudlin?" he'd ask her.

"No. You just get quiet and don't say anything to anyone. Including me. I'm the only one who knows."

"Bullshit," he'd answer and walk away to end the discussion.

Doug preferred drinking bourbon in multiple forms: sours, rickeys, and Manhattans. He even preferred bourbon in his bloody marys. The lime rickey was a Washington, D.C. drink, and Doug was nothing if not an inside-the-beltway man.

Douglas McKnight had lived and worked in Washington, D.C. since he graduated from George Washington University's School of Law in 1981. His father wanted him to go to law school at Vanderbilt, where Doug had earned his bachelor's degree. The paternal plan was for Douglas to join the Memphis law firm bearing his grandfather's and father's name. A summer intern position in the office of the representative from his congressional district gave Doug his first taste of Beltway power. Returning to Vanderbilt and Nashville after that summer felt like a letdown. "Nashville's a hick town with a bunch of singers pretending they're cowboys, and Memphis is even worse," he told his father.

Washington, D.C., was good to Doug. Although he maintained his license, he never practiced law. On the other hand, he knew all of the legal structures that would affect the various corporations he represented as a lobbyist and, before then, as a staff member of different federal agencies that employed him to represent their interests to congressional committees. His was a "policy-adjacent" world of influence. It was a world of monied interests eagerly shaping and using the levers of power to create the world that would get them what they wanted. And ultimately, they all wanted the same things: freedom from regulations, freedom from investigations, and freedom to gorge themselves at the federal trough of tax breaks and contracts.

Eight years of a somewhat liberal administration, though, turned things in the wrong direction. Eight years was a long time in Washington, D.C. A culture shift had started, and Douglas McKnight didn't like it. That was followed by the one-term presidency of Burkhart. That moved it slightly back to where Doug wanted it, but then Burkhart lost, and Goodman, the current occupant of the White House, was even more keen on regulations.

Looking out the restaurant's upstairs windows onto K Street, Douglas smiled. The Committee would ensure that this time change in the right direction would be lasting, long-lasting. The goal was a minimum of twenty years of righteous government, a government that would restore Christendom and capitalism to their rightful places in America. Twenty years would guarantee a righteous Supreme Court. Righteous. Doug loved the word. Virtuous. Honorable. The United States surrendered its virtue and honor to the amorality of secular liberalism, where an "anything goes" ethos gained traction. Control the presidency, and you control SCOTUS. Control the presidency long enough, and you will control SCOTUS for decades. Congress would become an afterthought. It was so simple. Ridiculously simple.

Josh Whitman was the first to arrive. Doug was always surprised by what a diminutive figure Whitman was. Five-foot-six and thin with a shaved head, an unknowing person would never suspect that this forty-one-year-old was a billionaire, not once, but several times over. A graduate of MIT, Whitman's wealth began when he and his father made a lucky acquisition of a start-up software company with a robust product and failed management. That led to investments and acquisitions of a complex array of technology companies in the United States and Europe. Whitman hated regulation, any regulation, any where, any time, any place. He fervently believed innovators should be given free rein to develop products and influence markets.

Douglas often teased, "Josh, you believe in the divine right of innovation and want to be the king."

Whitman would respond, "No. Just get your goddamn government boot off my neck and I'll be happy." Whitman went far beyond that. Like a host of Silicon Valley entrepreneurs, he believed democracy was an outmoded form of government. He wanted a government run like a corporation with a strong CEO and a clear-cut chain of command. He saw the entrenched bureaucratic state in Washington, D.C. as anti-innovation and anti-democratic. "Who elected those morons?" he'd complain. According to Whitman, Congress and the separation of powers were intellectual fantasies that had never worked. He would point to FDR and his consolidation of power during World War II as proof of what was needed. "We are at war with the Chinese, and these idiots have their heads buried in the sand."

Carmen Ciemny and her brother Jan arrived together. In some ways, Douglas felt closer to them than other members of the Committee. Carmen and Jan were devout Catholics and had lobbied Burkhart hard to add Catholics to the Supreme Court when he had the chance. They were successful. The six conservatives on the court were either Catholic or Anglican. Carmen and Jan's Catholicism was that of Pope Benedict rather than Pope Francis, whom they considered an apostate from the true Catholic faith. The Ciemnys attended Mass said in Latin and funneled some of their millions to conservative Catholic Bishops.

Admiral Nathaniel Darlan, United States Navy, Ret. commanded the room when he entered. Doug could never figure out quite how he did it. Somehow, though, Darlan conveyed he was the most important and intelligent man in the room. Darlan had initially been a strong supporter of Burkhart and encouraged like-minded flag officers of all service branches to do the same. However, he became disenchanted with Burkhart and his followers when they appeared to be more concerned with combatting immigrants, gays, and transgender people than the country's implementation of a coherent political philosophy. Darlan came to see Burkhart as nothing more than another politician with no vision, willing to shift positions daily to stay in power. Darlan was ecstatic when Burkhart realized he could not win a second term and was encouraged not to try. Among the members of The Committee, Darlan

116

spoke most frequently to John Pope. They sat together on three different boards of directors.

Darlan liked to feature himself as The Committee's intellectual-in-residence. It was Darlan who referred to the work of Patrick Deneen, a professor of political science at Notre Dame. Given an opening, Darlan would recite memorized passages from Deneen's *Why Liberalism Failed*. Darlan was fascinated by the political successes of Hungary's Victor Orbán. Doug appreciated Darlan's contribution to the group. He told his brother, "Nat is the real visionary in the group who keeps the big picture in front of us when we get bogged down in the minutia of the current campaign."

Joseph Conham's hedge fund, Fortress, made him the wealthiest member of The Committee. Although he tolerated Nat Darlan's bluster, Conham had the most significant sway in the group. He was the one with the money to influence elections and block legislation. He was the one with access to like-minded people of wealth. He was the one who was on the speed dials of people in Congress. Conham was also Doug's biggest client. Reserved, steady, polite, almost to a fault, Doug thought, Conham's passions were expressed in action rather than words. At times, he scared Doug because of his willingness to destroy people who got in his way or crossed him. When Conham acted, it was not done in anger; it was done out of necessity. One time, when Doug complained to Conham about a congressman from a purple district who had reversed himself on a vote he had promised Doug, Conham told Doug, "Don't worry about him. He's history." That was all: "He's history." In the next election, the congressman lost in a primary to an unknown young lawyer whose election was very well financed and whose oppositional research on his competitor was so brutal that the former congressman left politics in disgrace.

On The Committee, Peter Lind was the real politician. The Conservative Action Coalition (CAC) had awarded Senator Peter Lind of Indiana its highest rating every year for eighteen years – 100%. Only two other senators had scores close to Lind's for that long. In Indiana, people loved Lind. He railed against government spending, and Indiana received less federal money than two-thirds of the states. He believed in protectionist trade relations and wanted all "illegals" deported immediately. His contempt for liberal "snowflakes" and the "Woke folk" was well known. One time, he compared South Bend and Bloomington to Sodom and Gomorrah. Peter Lind assured members of The Committee of the silent support of many senators and congressmen. Doug could count on him to come late to meetings, be the last one to leave, and, once in a while, needed help walking down the stairs, having consumed more alcohol than any other member of the group. Doug worried about Lind's capacity to "Keep his big mouth shut."

The two who could not attend had valid reasons. Lawrence Hawley, Burkhart's vice president and now CEO of the Founders Foundation, spent Christmas in the hospital having his gallbladder removed. Hawley thought he should have been the party's nominee to run against Goodman after Burkhart withdrew in 2019. Hawley's rhetoric and policy positions were too extreme for funders, and he couldn't get his campaign off the ground. He was well connected, though, and people answered the telephone when he called, and he did call. He was "linked in," an essential cog in the behind-the-scenes life of the "New Right."

Angelica Wasserman, whom everyone called Angel, was the widow of Barney Wasserman, the "okay" Jew who created a conglomerate of disparate companies that was the subject of a Harvard case study on using data to make critical strategic decisions. Where Barney had played both sides of the political street depending on what his companies needed, Angel had only one interest. She wanted to destroy the liberal establishment that had never accepted her or her husband because of their perceived rough-shod beginnings.

The Wassermans were poor New Yorkers with accents – she was an Italian from Little Italy; he was a Jew from Flatbush. They had "made good." Rather than elite colleges, both attended the City University of New York part-time, which is where they met. Later, after Barney became successful beyond what either thought possible, they donated money generously through their family foundation. However, while a large donation to the Harvard Business School was accepted after the Business Review published the case study, the couple was not. Barney received a lovely letter expressing gratitude for the gift but no invitation to meet with the dean or any other member of the faculty or even alumni. Nothing. By contrast, Angel loved the attention she received from Douglas and the other members of The Committee. And they loved Angel. They loved her fervent hatred of liberals, the mouth that went with it, and her willingness to spend money to take the country back from "effete frauds." Angel loved the word "effete." She had texted Douglas her regrets that she could not attend the meeting. Her daughter was overdue to deliver her second child, and Angel had to stay in New York. They were hoping for a New Year's baby. Angel would call in to the meeting.

When all the members arrived, Doug suggested they forgo cocktails and appetizers. It was Senator Peter Lind who pushed back, saying, "I've had a shitty day. I want a drink."

"I'm with you, Peter." It was Admiral Nathaniel Darlan.

"So be it," Doug answered with a grin. Doug played many roles in the group. Of all his roles, "social oiler" was probably the most important. Not only did he not mind the role, he relished it. It enabled him to have the influence he would not have had otherwise. His wife said his theme song should be "Smooth Operator."

Doug was smooth. It had served him well. Although a multi-millionaire, his wealth was nothing compared to many others in the room. Doug's lobbying firm was highly profitable, but only some of his money came from consulting fees. Most of it came from insider information that allowed him to legally, and sometimes illegally, make investments and sell holdings at opportune times.

Members of The Committee appreciated his smoothness. He functioned as their chief of staff. He led their meetings, kept them in touch with one another, and had a fantastic memory for names, details, and dates. He did it in such a way that no one would ever call him the leader, but he made sure no one would call anyone else the leader either. Bending to graciously support cocktails for these two was easy peasy.

An hour and a half later, The Committee was ready to get to work. They conferenced Angel in, then Doug began, "As you know, Olson has withdrawn from the race and agreed to withhold any endorsement until we tell her what to do."

"Problems?" Darlan asked the question.

"None. The operation was completely successful. The Defenders took the lead. Four different groups were involved. Each did their part."

Angel spoke next: "Please express our appreciation to your brother for a job well done."

"I will do so. Shall we move our focus to the remaining three candidates?"

"It's too late to apply financial or persuasive pressures to get them to withdraw," Joseph Conham said. "The final debate is less than two weeks away. The three of them are neck and neck. I can't see us doing anything that wouldn't arouse undue suspicion."

Darlan said, "I agree."

"We have a plan," Doug said. "It involves some risk, but I am confident it will work. We have to up the stakes. People must see John Pope as the only candidate for president who can save the country. Nothing can be off the table in achieving that goal."

"You aren't suggesting we…" Peter Lind began.

"Take drastic measures? I am. It's risky, but I think it's our best shot if we are to get John drafted for the Iowa Caucus on January 15th."

Lind continued, "Are you sure we can even get him on the ballot."

"I'll come back to that."

Conham said, "Shall we go over the plan for the debate? Doug, do you want to lead us through what you and your brother have come up with? You said it upped the stakes."

"Glad to. The goal is to eliminate or neuter the remaining three candidates so Pope will have no significant competition once the caucus and the primaries begin. As you know, with Olson out of the picture, the only three left are Senator Juan Perez from Florida, former Governor Sidney Paxton of Texas, and Senator Terrence Manning of Kansas. The three are in a dead heat according to the polls, but Perez is the one who has climbed the most over the last two months to reach that position. Given his trajectory, he is the biggest threat to Pope's candidacy. Also, in temperament and policy direction, he is closest to Pope. We will eliminate him from the race just before the debate, two days before."

"What do you mean eliminate him?" Lind asked.

"You getting squeamish, Peter? It's a bit late for that."

"How?" Darlan asked.

"The Mara Salvatrucha gang will assassinate him."

"MS-13. How will that happen?"

"When Perez was Attorney General in Florida, he led an all-out war on MS-13. Although MS-13 had started as a street gang in Los Angeles, mostly Salvadorans, it had spread to other U.S. cities, including Miami. Perez pushed law enforcement to take a shoot-first approach to getting rid of them. If MS-13 members were caught alive, he immediately got them deported. Floridians were behind Perez. MS-13 are bad hombres. The machete is their preferred weapon. Anyway, Perez's anti MS-13 campaign was successful, and MS-13 has sworn revenge."

"You're not suggesting we go into business with MS-13?" Peter Lind asked.

"No. But we will make the death of Juan Perez look like a gang killing, and the weapon will be a machete. Everyone will blame MS-13. Internet chatter before and after the event will link the death to MS-13. There will be public outrage. People will blame Goodman for being soft on crime and not protecting the American people. People will call for a strong leader, someone like John Paul Pope."

"What about the other two?" Conham asked.

"If they don't drop out before the caucus, at some point Molotov cocktails will be thrown near their cars. The goal is to scare them rather than hurt them. We want to create a sense of chaos in America. No one is safe. Our way of life is under attack. We have to take America back."

"Security?" Conham asked. "All three are eligible for Secret Service."

"Perez declined. The other two have it."

"Who will be blamed for the firebombs?" Darlan asked.

"Antifa. Again, we will start the chatter before the event and continue it afterward. Thanks to Josh's influence, Pope is already scheduled to be an 'expert commentator' on CNN responding to the debate. We assume the debate will be canceled after the firebombs. However, the network will have to fill the air time. Pope will have ample time to discuss the need for a strong leader to defend the country and the American people. Any questions?"

There was silence around the table. Angel, listening in, didn't say anything.

"Good," Doug continued. "So we agree." Doug paused. No one said anything, so he continued, "The 'Draft John Pope Committee' will swing into action and flood Iowa with mail and social network messaging during the five days before the caucus begins. All we need coming out of Iowa is for John to have a good showing. He may actually beat the other two. We are confident that the Perez supporters will go to Pope."

Josh Whitman answered. "You're right. Iowa's not a problem."

"God bless the craziness of the Caucus system," Angel said. "What about New Hampshire? That's a week later."

"Write-ins. It's the only way. But it will work," Doug said.

Jan Ciemny spoke for the first time. "New Hampshire's small but proud. People are going to be furious after Perez is killed in their state. This chaos should cancel the debate, and I bet that will motivate at least three hundred thousand to show up to vote. People there are used to voting. Getting them to write in John Pope's name will not be difficult. We know who the likely voters are. All of them will be mailed instructions with a sample ballot showing them how to write in Pope's name. Again, social networks. Viral pictures from New Hampshire showing Perez."

Carmen added, "Paxton and Manning are low on cash. They'll never know what hit them. A win in New Hampshire and the party in South Carolina will have to have Pope on the ballot for the February 24th primary there. By Super Tuesday in March, Pope will be on the ballot in all the states and will be leading. I'd be surprised if either Paxton or Manning doesn't drop out and throw their support to Pope by then in hopes of a VP nod."

Angel spoke up, "And then the road to the White House."

"And a return to sanity," Doug added.

Chapter Eleven: Luke

Mark was exhausted from the long drive back from Montana. He was surprised when Gordon McKnight told him he was wanted in the office at Camp Liberty. Mark assumed that McKnight wished to congratulate the team on a successful mission. However, he was the only one there besides McKnight when he walked into the office.

McKnight pointed to a seat on the opposite side of the desk. He didn't get up or offer to shake Mark's hand. "Sit." It was a command.

Mark sat down and thought to himself, *What the fuck is going on?* It had been a long time since someone ordered him like that, and he didn't like it, especially after spending the last week in a car. Had something gone wrong that the crew didn't know about? If so, why was he the only one in the office unless McKnight was debriefing them individually? Nothing went wrong, though. Mark was sure nothing had gone wrong. They had listened to the news. Olson had resigned just the way she was supposed to. She had followed their script to the letter.

McKnight waited. When he began, his voice was distant, cold. "When we talked at the gun show, when you first came to Camp Liberty, before you left for Montana, what was the one thing that I emphasized over and over again?"

Mark didn't have to think about it. "Secrecy. The need for secrecy."

"And in the manual I gave you?"

"Same thing."

"What did you not understand?"

"Nothing."

"Then why did we receive a visit from a private investigator two days ago looking for you?"

"A what?"

"You heard me. A fucking P.I."

"You're kidding me. I dunno. How the hell should I know? Who was it?"

"Someone called Frank Kelly from Nutmeg Security and Investigations in New Haven."

"Never heard of him."

"Well, your parents did. They hired him."

"They did what? I don't know nothin' about that."

"Well, your parents sure as shit do. They hired him. How the hell did your parents know where to send him?"

"I dunno. I didn't tell 'em where I was goin'."

"And he had someone with him, a fuckin' gook writer."

"A writer?"

"Yes, a writer. She wanted to interview some 'members of the Defenders of Liberty.'"

"Why?"

"Why? Why do you think? So she could do a fucking hit job."

"What'd you tell them?"

"I told them I had no idea who the hell you were and to get lost."

"So there's no problem."

"Bullshit there's no problem. And this morning we had another visitor."

"Who?"

"He says he's your brother."

"My brother? Luke is here?"

"What did I just say? Give me your phone."

"My phone?"

"You heard me. Your fucking phone. I want to see who you've been calling."

"It's in my cabin. It's not even on. I haven't called anyone since I got here. You'll see. We didn't take our phones with us to Montana. We were told not to."

McKnight shouted into the next room, "Stark. Come here."

Barry Stark came into the office. "I want you to escort this asshole to his cabin, get his goddam phone, and then come back here with him and the damn phone."

"What the hell? You don't trust me now?" Mark protested.

"You're damn right I don't. You jeopardized months of planning. Just go get it."

"Alright, I will. Where's my brother?"

"None of your goddamn business. Now go get your motherfuckin' phone."

Mark didn't know what to think when he left the office and headed for his cabin with Barry Stark walking right behind him. Everything had been going so well. He liked living at the camp and the other men he was meeting. It was a small group; McKnight had only been able to sign up eight of them who lived there full-time. He had only been a Defender for a couple of weeks, but given their success in Montana, he was beginning to understand how much power the group could wield. And now this. His parents had hired a P.I. and sent Luke after him. What was that shit all about? Now McKnight didn't trust him. He hadn't contacted his parents even though it was Christmas. And Luke. What the fuck was Luke doing here?

Mark walked to his cabin, retrieved his phone, handed it to Stark, and returned to the camp office. Stark just walked behind him and said nothing until they reached the office. When he did, it was one word: "Inside." Stark turned around and walked away. Mark walked into the office. Luke was there, sitting by himself, facing McKnight's desk.

"Luke. What the hell are you doing here?"

Luke got up and turned around, "Looking for you."

"Why?"

"Why? Are you kidding? You haven't been in touch with anyone. Christmas. It was Christmas. You disappeared for Christmas. Mom and

Dad have been going crazy, especially Mom. They even hired a private investigator. That's how I knew where you were. He came here. He saw your truck. What are you doing here? You coming home? What is this place? Who are these people? They're treating me like I'm some kind of a prisoner. Am I? Let's get the hell out of here."

"Sit down. Just sit down and take it easy," Mark told him.

"No, I'm not going to take it easy."

"Luke, shut the fuck up and sit down. You have no idea what you've walked into. Now sit down."

Reluctantly, Luke did as his older brother instructed. Gordon McKnight entered the room. It was clear he had been listening from the room next door. He addressed Mark, "What a cluster fuck. I'll handle this." He then turned his attention to Luke. "Young man, right now, you're not going anywhere. Now do what your brother told you and settle down."

"I'll go any time I want to. You can't keep me here." Luke started to get up. McKnight didn't say anything, instead he slapped Luke across the head with such force that it knocked Luke out of his chair and sent him sprawling onto the floor. "I told you to settle down."

"Stop it," Mark shouted. "What do you think you're doing?"

"You. Get out of here. I'll deal with this," McKnight shouted at Mark.

Luke got up off the floor. He looked back and forth between his brother and McKnight before saying to his brother, "I'm alright."

Mark looked at McKnight then at his brother who was settling back in the chair. It was a decision point, and all three men in the room knew it. "Just do what he tells you and keep your mouth shut," Mark said, walking out of the room.

McKnight closed the door behind Mark and told Luke, "Just sit there. I'll be right back." McKnight left Luke sitting there and went next door to his personal quarters.

Mark walked across the center of the camp's parade ground and headed for his cabin. He needed to think. Halfway across, he changed his mind and headed for the waterfront. His brother. He had just watched

McKnight assault his brother, and he did nothing to stop it. But the mission. The mission was everything, and Luke had just shown up here, potentially screwing everything up.

While Mark was heading for the waterfront, Gordon McKnight called his brother Doug. "We've got a problem," he said.

"What?"

"Mark Perry. His fuckin' kid brother showed up. He's sitting in my office."

"How the hell?"

"The P.I., the one I told you about. He must have seen Mark's truck when he was here and told the family. So now the brother has come looking for Mark."

"Shit. So, what are you going to do?"

"I don't know. Maybe hold the kid here. I don't know."

"He's seen his brother?"

"Yeah. I couldn't very well deny it. He knew about the truck. I didn't want him running off to the sheriff's department and have them come nosing around."

"Okay. Let me think. I'll call you back." McKnight hung up the phone and went back into his office.

When he entered, Luke stood up. "Can I go now?"

"Sit down."

Luke didn't say anything and sat down.

When the phone rang, McNight left the room and went outside. It was Doug. "Alright. Here's what I want you to do. Have Mark tell his brother everything is okay and to go home. Have Mark call his parents and tell them the same thing."

"There's one complication."

"What?"

"The kid started mouthing off, and I slapped him."

"You did what?"

"I slapped him."

"Jesus, Gordon."

"I know."

"So, apologize. Give the brother some cash or something to pay him for driving up. Play extra nice. He hasn't seen or heard anything he shouldn't have, has he?"

"No, no. One of our guys has been with him since he showed up. All he's seen is the inside of the dining hall and my office."

"Jesus, you sure?"

"Yeah, I'm sure.

"Good. There's one other possibility. Might be a long shot. How old is the kid? He have any military experience? Do you think he'd have any interest in…"

"No way. Too young. Nothing like his brother. He's a college kid."

"Got it. We don't have a lot of options here. If we don't get it just right, we're fucked."

"Don't you think I know that?"

"Okay, so send him home. Apologize all over the place. More importantly, get Mark to make things okay with him. Have Mark call his parents. Tell them he has a new job and likes it but can't have visitors. I don't know. Come up with something. I know. Tell him that the people who come for the survival training don't always want people to know they are getting the training. You're just protecting their privacy."

"That might work."

"Have Mark deliver the message."

"Yeah."

"How the hell did the kid get past your guards?"

"I don't know. Someone fucked up and let him in. Don't worry. I'll take care of it."

"You'd better. No one can be allowed in for the next ten days. I mean it, no one."

"I know. I know. Don't worry about it."

"You shitting me? Given what's just happened, you bet your life I'll worry. Don't fuck this up. We're too close."

"I know. I'll take care of it."

"You damn well better."

Gordon McKnight inhaled deeply and slowly let his breath out, recalibrating his anxiety. He thought about his conversation with his brother. He wasn't sure that Mark could pull off the conversation that needed to happen, so he decided to take it on himself. He walked back into his office and sat down. Looking at Luke, he said, "Look, we got off on the wrong foot, and I want to apologize for what happened before. You see, we have clients who come here for survival training, and many of them are hesitant to let people know they are going through this kind of training. As you can imagine, in some quarters, it is frowned upon. We promise our clients absolute anonymity. And then you show up unannounced on New Year's Eve."

"I was just looking for my brother."

"I know, I know. I over-reacted."

"That doesn't give you the right to…"

"I know. You are absolutely right. I was upset that our security measures broke down, and I took it out on you. I never should have done that. I am truly sorry, especially since you are Mark's brother, and Mark is a very valued team member. I was concerned that he might have invited you. I jumped to conclusions. I shouldn't have done that. Let me try to make that up to you. You must be hungry from your drive up. Can I get you something to eat?"

"No. I just want to get going."

"Would you be okay with waiting here for a few more minutes? I want to find Mark and ask him to join us. Again, please accept my apologies for before. Also, and I know this won't make up for what happened, but I'd like to give you some cash to pay for your trip up here."

"I don't need your money."

"I just thought…"

"I want to talk to my brother."

"I understand. I'll be back in a couple of minutes."

It was ten minutes before McKnight returned with Mark. He checked in with Stark about Mark's telephone and learned that Mark had not communicated with anyone since he first arrived at Camp Liberty, including on Christmas. He looked for Mark and found him down at the waterfront, sitting on the lifeguard stand, which had been turned on its side for the winter. He sat beside Mark and said, "I talked to Stark. Sorry I questioned you about your phone and getting in touch with someone. I had to make sure."

Mark didn't say anything.

McKnight continued, "What we're doing here. It's dangerous as hell."

"Don't you think I know that?"

"I know you do. It's just, ya know, first that private detective and writer and now your brother."

"I know what it looked like. I get it. But why did you…"

"Hit your brother. I shouldn't have. I lost my cool. I apologized to him. I don't know if he accepted it, but I did apologize."

"Good."

"You're going to have to handle him. Get him to go home. I don't know what you're going to tell him. I was thinking maybe you should tell him that…"

"I can handle Luke. You don't have to program me."

"Sorry. I know. Look, we're getting ready for another mission. A big one. We can't mess this up."

"Don't you think I know that? I can handle my brother."

"Okay, and you'll call your parents?"

"Yes, I'll call my parents. My mother'll be upset, but my father will convince her everything's okay."

"You sure?"

"I'm sure."

"And your brother?"

"I told you. I can handle him."

"Okay. By the way, I offered him some money for driving up here. He wouldn't take it. You might want to convince him…"

"I'll get him to take it."

"What do you think? A hundred bucks?"

"Sounds right."

McKnight reached into his back pocket, pulled out his wallet, and gave Mark five twenty-dollar bills. "You sure he's going to be okay?"

"Yeah. He'll be okay."

McKnight walked away, and Mark entered the camp office to get his brother. "Get your coat on. We're going for a walk."

Luke did as his brother had requested. The two left the office and started walking towards the waterfront. The day was still, the woods quiet. Even though it was almost January, the temperature was just above freezing. The blizzard that had paralyzed the coast had swung out to sea, so central Maine had been spared. There were only a few inches of snow on the ground.

Mark offered his brother the money McKnight had given him. "Here, take this."

"I don't need his damn money."

"Don't be stupid. Take the money."

"You coming home with me?"

"No. I have a job here. This is where I work now. I can't leave."

"You can't. Why can't you? They making you stay?"

"No. No. I like it. What we're doing is important."

"What do you do?"

"We train people."

"Yeah. Sure. In what?"

"How to take care of themselves in the woods. Survival stuff. How to shoot. Some hand-to-hand combat. Stuff like that. Stuff I learned in the Army.

"I don't see anyone."

"It's the holidays, for Christ's sake. Of course they're not here. Schools are out. You're not in school."

"School! You're calling this a school."

"Yes. It's a school."

"To learn what? Survivalists are nutcases."

"No. They're not. It's important stuff in case…"

"In case what?"

132

"Waco. Ruby Ridge. The government. The government oversteps again. We got to be ready. People got to be ready."

"Jesus, Mark. Do you know how crazy you sound?"

"No, no. You just don't see it. It's coming."

"It's coming. What's coming? What the hell are you talking about?"

"Change. Big change. Taking our country back."

"Taking our country back. From who?"

"Liberals who are destroying it. Immigrants storming across our borders raping, killing…"

"Have you totally lost it?"

"No. You just don't get it. You'll see."

"See what?"

"The enemy isn't out there anymore. It's within. It's corrupting us. Slowly and surely. We've got to stop it."

Luke didn't respond to that. He kept walking. He could hear Mark continue to talk, but he wasn't listening. A stranger was walking next to him. This wasn't his brother. This was someone he didn't know. Luke stopped walking, turned, and looked at his brother. He shook his head slowly and said, "Why didn't you call home? It was Christmas."

"I couldn't. I was traveling. Didn't have my phone with me."

"Where were you?"

"Can't tell you. I was on a mission."

"A mission. What kind of mission?"

Mark had been thinking about what he could tell his brother that would not betray his promises of secrecy. He said, "Sometimes we do protection work for important people. I can't talk about it."

"Is that what those 'M's are about?"

"What 'M's? What are you talking about?"

"The calendar hanging in that asshole's office. The one that has the big red 'M's on specific dates. So, you were off on a mission, protecting someone? That was your mission."

"Yes. We do that kind of work."

Luke didn't respond, so Mark continued: "I'll call Mom and Dad. Let them know I'm fine and just have a new job."

"Jesus, Mark. Do you have any idea how bizarre this all sounds? You take off for a gun show and disappear over the Christmas holidays. Now you're telling me you have a new job. You have fucking missions. You're protecting important people, and you're training survivalists in this god-forsaken camp in the middle of fucking nowhere Maine, and you can't tell me where you've been, and your fucking boss womps me, and you stand there and do nothing about it. And the way you're talking. Bullshit! I'm your brother. What the hell's going on?"

"I've told you. You don't want to listen. I'm done trying. Now, I need you to get in your goddamn car and go home. I don't want you to say another word. Do you understand me? Just get in your car and go. Now. Don't ask any more questions. Just go."

"I don't understand you. What the hell is going on?"

"Nothing more than I've already told you. You have to trust me. I'm fine. I'm doing what I want to be doing. It's New Year's Eve. Go home. Go out tonight. Get drunk with your friends."

"What are you going to do?"

"Stay here. Have a nice dinner. Go to bed early. I don't know. You need to leave now. Smile. Wave goodbye if you see anyone. Just get going, Luke. No more questions."

Neither said a word as they walked back toward the office. When they reached the car, Luke turned to his brother and hugged him. "You're scaring me. I don't know what you're into, but it's not good. Please be careful."

"I'm fine. Now go."

Luke got in his car and slowly drove out of the Camp Liberty driveway. When he passed the guard post, he waved to the guard and sped up. As soon as he reached the main road, he got out his cell phone and called home.

Chapter Twelve: A New Year

Gordon McKnight was determined that his men would have a great New Year's Eve and New Year's Day. He had spent enough holidays away during his time in the Army to understand the impact of distance and confinement of such holidays on morale and, especially, on the perception of leadership and whether it cared or not.

Of the eleven men gathered at Camp Liberty, Gordon was the only one who had been an officer during his military service. He had fond memories of holidays at the officer's clubs when he first joined the service and hated the demise of the "O" clubs that took place during the years he served. Although he visited irregularly, Gordon maintained his Army and Navy Club membership on Washington, D.C.'s Farragut Square.

Given the importance of their work, he wanted the Defenders of Liberty to feel special during the holidays. He knew the dining hall kitchen was well equipped, but the cook he employed was not up to the task of providing the meals he envisioned. He gave the cook the holidays off and wanted a caterer who could provide four small feasts for the residents of Camp Liberty. He knew he'd have to pay the caterer a premium because it was the holidays, but he didn't mind. Although Doug had cautioned him about having outsiders visit the camp, Gordon didn't want his men to have to do any work over the holiday. They were to celebrate a New Year and the dawn of a new country.

He knew a caterer. Blanche Cartouche was the wife of one of the other instructors at the Portland shooting range where Gordon had worked, and he was familiar with her political sympathies. During several telephone calls making plans for what Gordon and Blanche now referred to as "the party," he emphasized the need for a discreet staff who would "not hear or see anything." She assured him that the people she would bring could be counted on. Like her, they were convinced the country was headed in the wrong direction and that drastic measures were needed to return it to a country they could be proud of. "One is my brother, and two are cousins," Blanche assured him.

Gordon wanted to serve only high-end liquors in addition to various beers. For himself, he wanted Maker's Mark bourbon. Gordon told her that whoever the bartender was would be important, and she assured him her brother was just the man. He said, "I want these guys to enjoy themselves, but if your bartender, or any staff member, thinks one of my men is getting too loaded or misbehaving, I want you to let me know. Okay?"

"Sure, but which way do you want me to lean? How sloppy is sloppy?"

"I don't want them to hurt themselves or anyone else."

"Okay. We can let you know, but I don't want my people to get into arguments with them. That's up to you."

They reached an agreement that any Defender would be shut off if the offender became "too" intoxicated. If this happened, Blanche's brother would report the offender to Gary Stark, and Stark, rather than the bartender, would address the problem with the Defender. As they discussed this, Blanche asked Gordon, "Why are you being so careful? No one else is going to be there. It's not like anyone's driving someplace."

"Lots of reasons. Decorum. We drank at the O clubs, but there was always some degree of decorum. I don't want any of these guys to be seen as a drunk, especially a nasty, belligerent drunk. They've got to trust one another. These guys are wired enough as it is."

"I suppose. You know what you're doing."

"I do. I also don't want them saying things they shouldn't be."

"Got it. Makes sense. Something big coming?"

Gordon ignored her question, and Blanche knew not to press.

The two of them decided upon the menus in less than an hour. They wrote down a schedule. New Year's Eve dinner would begin at 1800 with appetizers. The wait staff would serve chilled shrimp and ten different canapes. The staff with trays demonstrating "abundance" would mingle among the guests, as they were now referred to. At 1930, dinner would commence: a green salad would be followed by roast beef, American popovers, asparagus, and roasted fingerling potatoes. After dinner, the guests would be invited to select one or more desserts from a dessert tray that would be brought to the table. The guests would be invited to order whatever beverages they wanted throughout the meal, although bottles of cabernet sauvignon and chardonnay would be placed on the table and replenished whenever emptied.

Blanche and Gordon spent a great deal of time discussing the time between dinner and midnight. They finally decided that the most appropriate activity would be a movie and eventually settled on *The Patriot* with Mel Gibson as the most fitting title for the evening.

"Okay," Blanche said. "So, it's midnight – Champagne, for sure. Watch the ball drop. You make a toast, yada, yada, and then we feed them again. Something simple. How about doing a pasta bar? Four different pastas, four different sauces. Some good Italian bread. Maybe a New Year's cake. What do you think?"

"Sounds good."

"You think any of these guys ever had anything like this before? You know, treated this way?"

"That's the point. I want them to feel special as hell."

"If they don't with this spread, they never will. Okay, so now it's New Year's Day."

"Brunch at 1100. Dinner mid-afternoon, say 1600."

"Are you sure you want dinner? Why not just have a fancy, make-your-own sandwich bar and a couple of soups? They're going to be watching football games, sleeping, dozing. Brownies, ice cream. You know, real relaxed. Maybe some chili and cornbread. Wings. You got to have wings. Different dips."

"You're probably right. What about the brunch?"

"Typical. Omelet and carving stations, mimosas, salads, pancakes, waffles. Usual stuff. We set it up for 1100, leave it open 'til 1300. They come and go as they please."

"That works. Cost?"

"You know, you have to supply the liquor. We can serve it, but you have to buy it."

"Right."

"Good. Okay. I need a day to figure out the cost. Staff will be expensive, and they'll expect a big tip – holidays."

"Of course."

"The cake. Had a thought about what to put on the New Year's cake."

"What?"

"How about: To A New World in A New Year."

"Yeah. That's good. I like it. Perfect."

***

Anita Perry knew how long Luke would take to drive to Sparta, Maine. She added another thirty minutes for Luke to find Camp Liberty and talk to Mark. They had agreed that Luke would call home the minute he had any news, so she waited in the kitchen with her phone on the counter beside where she was stirring the ingredients for Toll House cookies. She always made Toll House cookies for New Year's Eve.

Although they were only in their mid-fifties, Jim and Anita Perry hadn't done much to celebrate the New Year since their youngest, Luke, became a teenager and wanted to be with his own friends on the holiday. For the last four or five years, whatever celebrating they did, they did alone, but Jim and her sons loved Toll House cookies, so she always made several batches on New Year's Eve. Even if it was just her and Jim on New Year's Eve, the cookies would be there for her sons the next day or whenever they showed up. She liked doing it; they seemed to like it, too. They were nothing more than chocolate chip cookies with walnuts, but it didn't seem to matter. It was a tradition, and the Perrys didn't have many traditions.

Jim and Anita Perry had moved to West Haven, Connecticut from Pittsburg, Pennsylvania right after Mark was born. Anita's mother had been diagnosed with cancer. Anita's parents had divorced when she was young, and with no siblings, the care of her mother was up to her. Besides, Anita wanted to get back to water and beaches. She missed the New Haven area where she had grown up. West Haven was on the water and was less expensive than Milford, Branford, or the other towns on the Connecticut shoreline.

Jim didn't care where they lived. He was rootless. An Army brat, he had lived in several places in the United States and even spent three years in Germany. They were only in Pittsburg because his cousin had gotten him a job in a large warehouse driving a forklift. Jim liked the work and, over time, came to think of himself as a "warehouse man." When it came time for them to move to West Haven, Jim had no trouble getting a job at Ikea in New Haven. Anita found work as a receptionist at a large orthopedic practice in nearby Branford and had dreams of Luke, who took after her, becoming a physician or a physician assistant. She was thrilled when he got accepted at Fairfield University and decided to major in biology. She never worried about Luke; it was Mark who she worried about. It had always been Mark. It was Mark who didn't like school. It was Mark who thought the world was out to get him, so he had no choice but to fight back, and fight back he did. And now it was Mark who had taken off without telling anyone where he was going – at Christmas. It was Mark who had joined some kind of para-military organization, according to the private investigator they had hired to find him. Mark scared her. "What now?" was a question that was never far from her mind.

Luke called when she was taking the first batch of Toll House cookies out of the oven. "Mom, he's there. I talked to him."

"Where?"

"The camp, Mom. The camp. I was just there."

"Wait. Let me get your father. He's in the basement."

Luke waited. Why couldn't he just talk to his mother? She could tell his father. He wasn't going to tell either one of them very much. He next heard his father's voice: "You're on speakerphone. Did you talk to him? What'd he say?"

"Yeah, I talked to him. He said he's got a new job and he's going to call you and tell you all about it. He said he was away on a project over Christmas; it was all very hush-hush, so he couldn't say anything."

Anita asked, "When is he coming home?"

"I don't know. You'll have to ask him that when he calls."

"When's he going to call?"

"I don't know, Mom. He said he'd call."

"Is he all right?" his mother asked.

Luke was tempted to say no but had to figure things out first. He needed time to think. He needed to talk to Gwen. He hoped Mark would call immediately so he wouldn't be in the middle of things. He just wanted to get out of the conversation and pick up Gwen.

"Yeah, Mom, he's okay. He said he'd call. Look. I'm in the car. I'm going to head for Bridgeport and pick Gwen up at the ferry. I'll see you guys tomorrow. We can talk about it then."

It was his mother again, "You said he's going to call?"

"He said he's going to call. I need to get going. I'll see you tomorrow."

"You be safe now. It's New Year's Eve. There's going to be drunks…"

"I know, Mom. Don't worry. Gwen and I aren't going anywhere but Toby's."

Mark didn't call that evening. Jim Perry went out to pick up the pizza and salad they had ordered at Zuppardi's for their traditional New Year's Eve dinner. Anita had asked him to wait in case Mark called, but Jim answered, "Who knows when he'll call? Two weeks, and he hasn't called."

"But Luke said…"

"Luke said. That doesn't mean he's going to call. Who knows when he'll call? Could be another week. Why don't you come with me."

"No. I'm staying here. Leave your phone in case he calls you. I want to talk to him."

"He's not going to call today."

"Please."

"Okay. Here." Jim gave his wife his phone and left.

Mark didn't call. Jim came back with dinner. Eating pizza, they watched reruns of NCIS. Jim went to bed around eleven. Anita stayed up with the phone beside her. She dozed intermittently and eventually crawled into bed next to her husband at one o'clock in the morning.

The call came at noon the next day. Anita picked up her phone, saw the caller I.D., and said, "Mark?"

"Hi, Mom."

"Where are you? When are you coming home? I've been worried sick."

"Didn't Luke tell you?"

"Yes. I know you're in Maine at some camp. When are you coming home? Why haven't you answered our calls and texts?"

"Yeah. Look, I'm fine. I've got a new job. It involves a lot of secrecy and some travel. I wasn't allowed to tell you anything until now. Sorry about that. I'm fine, though."

"When are you coming home?"

"Don't know for sure. Be at least a few weeks. Maybe more."

"You're okay, though?"

"I keep telling you. I'm fine. You don't have to worry about me. Is it true? What I've heard? You hired a private detective to try to find me. Why on earth did you do that?"

"Why! You disappeared. We were scared stiff. I called the sheriff's department, too. I was afraid you were in an accident or the hospital or something. Why didn't you call us?"

"I told you. I couldn't. It's part of the job. I didn't know I was going to take it when I left, and then things happened real fast, and I couldn't."

"Luke said…"

"What'd Luke say?"

"He said you're okay."

"Good. I am. Nothing to worry about. Dad there?"

"No. Went out to get ribs and wings."

"Right. New Year's Day. Tell him I said hi. I got to go. I'll call you in a couple of weeks. Stop worrying. I'm fine."

"Wait. Tell me about this job."

"Not allowed to talk about it. Some of it's teaching."

"Teaching what?"

"Survival skills stuff to city people. Camping. Stuff like that. Got to go. Call you in a couple of weeks. Promise. Bye."

The line went dead. Anita sat at the kitchen table, staring at the telephone in her hand. She knew there was something very wrong. She always knew when Mark was in trouble. The call had increased her anxiety. She couldn't name what he had said that prompted it. She just knew. She always knew, and it was never good.

When Jim returned, she tried to relay the information Mark had provided as dispassionately as she could. His response was non-committal: "Good. He called. It sounds like he's okay."

That infuriated her. "He's not okay. He's involved in something he shouldn't be."

Jim didn't want to argue. He said, "We'll see what Luke thinks when he gets home." It was a finishing statement, a "we are through talking about this" statement. When it came to Mark, the two of them were used to non-discussions.

***

As she had done on more than one occasion, Eve interrupted me with, "Excuse me, Professor Kelly, but I believe you are using your lecture voice." It was New Year's Eve, and we were driving from our home in Milford, Connecticut, to Bay Ridge in Brooklyn, New York.

Of course, she was right. When I get fascinated with something, I tend to lecture, and I am fascinated with the process through which different immigrant groups settle after they leave the countries of their birth. Heng Pho was sitting right behind me, a Cambodian who had grown up on the east side of Long Beach, California. Locally, people called it Little Phnom Penh or Little Cambodia. Eve Karam sat next to me. My wife immigrated from Lebanon to Bay Ridge in Brooklyn as a teenager. Until the early 1970s, Bay Ridge was Norwegian. Today, it is Arab, Italian, Irish, Greek, and still changing.

Of course, the big draw is family, knowing people, people who can speak your language, feed you, and house you until you find your way and become independent. And then you stay for a generation, maybe two, before another diaspora begins, only this time within your adopted country. Sometimes, you retain your language and are bi-lingual; sometimes, it disappears.

The Karam family of Beirut, Lebanon, Eve's family, found a home in Brooklyn, New York, in a community that practiced the Catholic Maronite traditions they were familiar with during their life in Lebanon. Her parents found a place to live close to Our Lady of Lebanon, the Cathedral, and the home of the Maronite Bishop in the United States. That became the center of their social and religious life and remains so. Eve was more fortunate than many immigrants. She already spoke English in addition to French and Arabic. Still, the Roman Catholic school she and her siblings attended felt foreign. Songs, some elements of the Mass, and the emphasis on the Trinity rather than Christ were strange at first.

Eve and Heng are what the Gordon McKnights and Mark Perrys of America hate. These two women are from someplace else, a gook and a towelhead in their language. They're not only immigrants; they're women and successful – the trifecta to be hated. Growing up on opposite coasts, Heng and Eve had immigrated to communities that accepted and nurtured them. They had thrived. I am convinced that is what galls McKnight and Perry. Eve and Heng had thrived where neither McKnight nor Perry had. Resentment. According to them, McKnight and Perry were entitled to thrive; those two women were not. How could that be? It was wrong. Gordon and Mark saw themselves as victims in their own country.

143

I was holding forth with my analysis – or lecture, depending on your point of view – as Eve and I drove down Route #95 on our way to Bay Ridge for New Year's Eve with the Karam family. Heng had accepted our invitation to join us at the last minute. The graduate school New Year's Eve party Heng had planned on had fizzled, so she called to accept our invitation. In the back seat, next to her, sat my son Ben. My daughter, Molly, and her fiancé, Stan, were driving down separately. Heng and Ben were more tolerant of my wisdom than my spouse. Occasionally, they would add something to my monolog. That changed when we crossed over the Throgs Neck Bridge and entered Queens. Heng started asking Eve questions about Maronite Catholicism, the Karam family, and how we would celebrate the New Year.

It would be a two-day feast. Maronite Catholicism is more family-centered than Roman Catholicism, and hospitality is a virtue held in high regard. Like many American families, we would celebrate New Year's Eve and watch the ball drop from the top of One Times Square on television from the comfort of Eve's parent's living room.

Eve and I would spend the night with her parents in Eve's childhood room. Heng would get the guest room; Ben would be on the couch in the parlor – it was never called anything but the parlor. Molly and Stan would bunk in with Eve's oldest brother and his family.

New Year's Day would be a never-ending Mediterranean and Middle Eastern feast. It would be a family and neighborhood event, with people coming and going throughout the day. There would be börek with various stuffings of cheese and spinach, minced meats, pilaf, different kinds of kebabs, and omani shuwa. The food would keep coming and coming. Of course, there would be pita bread, various types of hummus, and falafel. Malabi and knafeh would be two of the many kinds of dessert.

Eve's two older brothers and younger sister would be there with their families. What neighbors and friends would drop by was unpredictable. Eve's parents would fuss over all of the youngsters as their children assembled, cooked, served, and cleaned. Eve and I had kebab duty. No, I had kebab duty, and no matter what the weather, I could be found outside in the postage-stamp backyard taking orders for kebabs and cooking them over the grill. Ben would be my waitperson and runner, taking orders and delivering my masterpieces to the assembled. Eve would be busy inside trying to get her mother to relax and let the younger people do all the work. She would be unsuccessful, but it was a necessary ritual that I watched year after year.

Several years ago, before my time, a negotiated peace was reached regarding New Year's Day football. The television could be on, but not the sound. It appeared to work on the surface, but the reality was different. So many people were coming and going in front of the set that only the die-hardest of fans would have the patience to follow the flickering images on the screen. There was an unspoken norm: "Thou shalt not ask people to move so you can see."

We stayed for cleanup and left a little before nine. Ben insisted on driving since I had driven down. This brought about a change in seating. Eve and I moved to the backseat. Heng sat up front next to Ben. Blackie was nested in the "way back." Being in the back seat with my son driving was unusual for me. I knew Ben was a good driver, but it was still strange. It reminded me of an old Peanuts cartoon. In frame one, Charlie Brown asks, "Lucy, what's security?" Frame two: Lucy responds, "Security is when you're driving with your parents and riding in the back seat, and your parents are upfront and whispering so you can fall asleep." Frame three: Charlie asks, "And what happens?" Frame four: Lucy answers, "You grow up and become an adult and have to ride in the front seat forever." Frame five: Charlie says, "Oh, Lucy, hold me. I'm scared."

Of course we got back to Milford safe and sound. It was eleven o'clock, though, when we got home. Getting Heng to spend the night in our guest room rather than drive back up to Storrs didn't take much convincing. Ben decided he might as well sleep on our couch in the living room rather than drive back to New Haven, even though it was only a fifteen-minute drive to his apartment. Neither Eve nor I commented on that decision.

When we were getting ready for bed, I nodded toward the living room where Ben and Heng were talking.

Eve said, "I think they'll talk most of the night."

"Just talk?"

"Just talk."

"And…"

"We'll see."

***

Fairfield University in Fairfield, Connecticut, has had a long, sometimes uncomfortable relationship with homeowners along Fairfield Beach, a stretch of barrier beach on Long Island Sound. A group of beach houses has always been available for winter rentals to Fairfield U. students. Where there are college students, there will be parties. "Things got out of hand" is a phrase associated with many of the parties. News of a party spreads quickly in a school of 5,000 students. Beach houses that comfortably accommodate twenty for a party may be asked to accommodate 200 or more. As a result, fully or partially inebriated students spill over onto nearby yards occupied by year-round residents. In addition, it was not uncommon for there to be several concurrent parties along the half-mile strip where most of the rental properties were.

Although the school was in recess for Christmas break, many students, like Luke Perry, day-hopped to the University, and some of their friends had already returned to their beach rentals – primarily to party. Luke's buddy Tobias, "Toby," and three others were living in the "Chill Out" beach house, and a "New Year's blast" with fireworks on the beach – not in front of their house – was a sure thing. Breaking his date with Gwen for New Year's Eve was unthinkable, regardless of his concerns about his brother. Besides, he needed to talk to someone about what was bothering him before speaking to his parents. Luke trusted Gwen. They had been together for over a year, and he was sure they would get married someday.

It was a jeans and sweater party where you brought your own refreshments and drugs – if that was "your thing." If you wanted to crash, you brought your sleeping bag and pillow. Because Luke had been away all day, Gwen had shopped for both of them.

Gwen Hunter lived on Long Island, in the hamlet of Wading River. While it is a three-hour drive to Fairfield in the best of traffic, Wading River is only a short distance from the Bridgeport and Port Jefferson Ferry that crosses Long Island Sound in forty-five minutes. When they were not in school, Luke and Gwen would take the ferry back and forth across the Sound to see one another. Luke was there to meet her when the ferry arrived at 8:15 PM New Year's Eve. When she came down the passenger ramp, she was wearing a big backpack and pulling a large suitcase. After hugging one another, Luke took the suitcase handle from her. "What's in here?" he asked.

"Let's see. Tequila, beer, nachos, and a bunch of other things Toby asked me to bring."

"Gummies?"

"Backpack. So, how'd it go?"

"Crazy. My brother's certifiable. Absolutely stark raving mad. I'll tell you on the drive over."

The drive from the ferry to Fairfield Beach only took them fifteen minutes. During that time, Luke took Gwen on his trip back and forth to Sparta, step by step. Gwen asked questions periodically but let Luke tell the story in his own way. They were pulling onto Fairfield Beach Road when she asked, "So what did your parents say when you told them?"

"I just told them I had seen him and talked to him."

"And they said…"

"Nothing."

"Nothing?"

"Well, not much. I don't think they know how to react. It's like they can't deal with it."

"Or don't want to."

"Probably both."

"Luke. Did you tell them everything?"

"No."

"About McKnight hitting you?"

"No."

"Luke, you were assaulted. This McKnight person hit you; your brother did nothing about it."

"I didn't tell them about that."

"Why not?"

"That would really freak them out. My father would lose it and do something stupid. Those fucking people up there have guns."

"So what are you going to do?"

"I don't know."

"I think you should tell the police, the FBI, or someone."

"What are they going to do? He wants to be there. He's one of them."

"You sure he wants to be there? Sounds like they've brainwashed him."

"No. Absolutely not. He likes it. You should have heard him."

"But what are they doing? You don't believe him that all they're doing is training people, do you?"

"And…"

"Protecting people? Bodyguards? Come on. Give me a break."

"What if they are?"

"You don't believe that, do you?"

"No. Not really."

"Maybe the police could raid the place. Find out what's going on."

"You've been watching too many movies."

"Luke, this is serious."

"I don't know what to do. Okay. Can we drop it?"

The legalization of marijuana in Connecticut didn't change much for college students who had never had difficulty obtaining it if they wanted to indulge. The black market was always available and was cheaper than the new retail outlets.

Luke and Gwen's group disapproved of other drugs. Toby was not about to risk his rent and made it plain that hard drugs were not welcome. Liquor, on the other hand, was matter-of-course, and a supply of various kinds and labels was readily available.

The food was haphazard. Guests brought a variety of chips and dips, which dominated until the midnight countdown when multiple bottles of champagne and prosecco appeared. Following hugs, kisses, and toasts, Toby and his girlfriend proudly produced three trays of lasagna they had cooked that afternoon. His two roommates brought out a big salad and loaves of Italian bread.

The party noise level dropped precipitously with the food. Small clusters of students engaged in earnest conversations could be found throughout the house. Around one-thirty, some people left, and others found quiet places to nest. Four, however, decided it was time to "polar bear." They stripped off their clothing, ran down the beach, and jumped into the cold waters of Long Island Sound. They didn't last long and were welcomed back with comments of, "You're out of your mind."

Gwen and Luke were not among the four. They were engaged in a heated discussion about the university president's stance on university neutrality. The president had said flying a Black Lives Matter flag was against university policy and had ordered the removal of a flag flying at the counseling center. Gwen and Luke thought taking the flag down was an insult to Black students and sent a clear message that the university did not have their backs.

Later, the two of them found some space under the dining room table to spread out the blankets Gwen had brought with her. All the beds and couches were taken. Nesting under the long table gave them some semblance of privacy.

Nothing more was said about the trip to Sparta until Luke drove Gwen to the ferry on New Year's Day. Gwen returned to the forbidden subject: "Are you going straight home?"

"Yeah."

"You going to talk to your parents about Mark?"

"Yeah."

"Good luck. Hope you figure something out."

"Yeah."

"You going to tell them about McKnight?"

"Probably."

"Remember. Your brother didn't defend you. He's been brainwashed. I'm telling you."

They hugged and kissed goodbye. Gwen said, "Love ya."

"Love ya back."

Luke waited until the ferry left the dock before driving home.

***

It was unseasonably warm in Bridgeport on New Year's Day when Luke watched Gwen walk on to the late afternoon ferry for Port Jefferson. Driving home, he thought about what to tell his parents about his trip to Sparta. He and Gwen had discussed it over bagels at Toby's house that morning. They decided he should be precise, telling them what had happened and what the different people had said, McKnight and his brother. In addition, he would voice his concerns. As Gwen had said, "What do you have to lose? If they ignore you, they ignore you." Gwen insisted that the family should contact the sheriff's office, maybe even the FBI or the ATF, the Bureau of Alcohol, Tobacco, and Firearms. Luke was reluctant to go in that direction. "He's my brother. I don't want him arrested. What if they arrest everyone?"

When he arrived home, his mother told him about her conversation with Mark. The telephone call had heightened her concerns rather than lessened them. After Luke gave his report, including the assault and Mark's response to it, she started to cry and pushed him to tell her more about Camp Liberty.

"Anita, let it go," Jim said.

"Dad, are you crazy? Mark's in trouble," Luke countered.

"So you say."

"Jesus. Dad. I know you don't want to believe it, but he's in deep shit. He's lost it. These people are nut jobs, and he's becoming one of them."

"So, Mr. Know-it-all, what do you suggest we do?"

"I've been thinking about it."

"No police."

150

"No, I know. No police."

"What then?"

"Gwen had an idea."

"You've been talking to Gwen about this?"

"Yes. Gwen and I talk, Dad. We actually talk."

Anita stopped crying and said, "Jim! Shut up! I want to hear what Luke has to say."

"Mom, he sounded like he's been brainwashed or something. It's like he's been programmed. You know, joined a cult."

"A cult? No, Mark would never join a cult," Anita protested.

"Yes, Mom, a fucking cult. We need to do a family intervention."

"A family what?" Jim asked.

"You know, just like with an alcoholic or someone addicted to drugs. A family intervention to get him away from that place before he gets in trouble."

Anita asked, "How would we do that?"

"We'd need help."

"Who?"

"I don't know. Maybe that P.I. could help. Maybe he knows someone."

"Frank Kelly?"

"That his name?"

Jim said, "Yes, his name's Frank Kelly. He costs, though, a lot."

"Jim," Anita said, "Enough. If you won't, I'll call him."

Chapter Thirteen: A New Normal

I was looking forward to a 'new normal' and committed to bringing it about. Usually, I'm not big on New Year's resolutions, but this year was different. Resolution number one: get the body back in 'before getting shot' condition. I had put on a few pounds with the hiatus from training and teaching; then I added holiday pounds. I had work to do. Resolution number two: Blackie, my trusted sidekick, also needed to return to his Shutzhund-champion best. I knew he'd get back in shape before I did, but what the hell, it wasn't a competition. Resolution number three: martial arts skills and weapons tune-up. My experience at Nutmeg taught me that if I was going to do this work, I needed both.

At work, the 'new normal' was wonderful. Vicki DeRosa was taking over as head of security. Sam reported that the week he and Meg had spent in St. Lucia was "invigorating." Apparently, in addition to spending time getting "invigorated," they talked about Vicki and Nutmeg and decided it was up to me and Vicki to decide on her employment. He quoted Meg: "It's his company. He can hire whoever he wants." Sam added, "We'll support you two in any way we can. Just let us know." I wasn't sure what that would look like, but it sounded like a positive step. Having Vicki onboard with the support of her parents was an immense relief. I still had to replace Meg as our financial officer, but Meg told me that her assistant, Irene Kenen, was capable and that I should consider her. I gave Irene the job.

I was looking forward to spending at least a month, maybe two, focused on training and teaching at Takuma's. Financially, Nutmeg was on solid footing. The income I brought in from investigations had always been to pay my overhead and a modest salary, which I really didn't need. So I planned to go on a two-month part-time sabbatical. In hindsight, I probably should have done that after I was shot.

Tuesday, January 2nd, arrived clear, crisp, and compelling. A good day to begin my New Year's commitments. Rather than simply walk Blackie, I took him for an early morning run around the harbor. It was four miles, modest by my old standards but long enough to make me feel like I was off to a good start for the new year.

On my way to Takuma's for my initial workout of the new year, I was listening to the news about the resignation of Claudine Gay, Harvard's first Black president, when my cell phone rang. I pushed the call accept button on my car's screen.

"Mr. Kelly, it's Anita Perry, Mark Perry's mother." Whoa. The first surprise of the new year. I had not forgotten about Mark Perry, but I had not been thinking about him either, not since his father said my services were no longer required.

I answered politely, "Yes, Mrs. Perry. How can I help you?"

"Could we come to your office and see you? We need your help. It's a bit complicated."

My 'uh oh' response kicked in, followed by an internal 'be careful' warning.

"Certainly. Is everything okay?" I answered – again politely.

"No. We don't think so. That's what we need to talk to you about."

"Sure. Has something changed?"

"We don't know. Please can we come talk to you? We need your advice. It shouldn't take long." Her tone was plaintive.

I noted that she was calling, not her husband, Jim. I didn't know if that was significant or not.

"Yes, of course. Would you like to come in today?"

"If possible."

"Would noon work?"

"Yes. That would be fine. Thank you."

I called the office and told Claire that the Perrys would be coming in at twelve. "Let's have some take-out menus ready. We may be ordering lunch if it looks like we'll be a while."

Jim Perry had told me I was done. Did they now regret it? Was I being rehired? I wondered if Harvard would regret firing Claudine Gay. I was sure they would.

I decided to call Heng and let her know about the call. She immediately responded, "Would it be okay if I came down? I'll just be a fly on the wall. I'm always curious about the families people like Mark come from."

"Sure, but feel free to participate however you want."

"Thank you. See you at noon."

***

When I got to the gym, Takuma was ready for me. He had prepared an hour's worth of 'age-appropriate' and 'fitness-appropriate' exercises for me to start with. "Slowly, my friend," he said. "We will start slowly."

The workout he had designed for me seemed ridiculously easy. "I'm not in that bad shape," I protested at the end of the hour, emphasizing the word 'that.'"

"I understand. I wanted to test your stamina as well as your flexibility and strength. I agree; we can push more. Still, you will recover more if we do this slowly. I do not want you to experience discomfort tomorrow. It can be a disincentive."

"You're saying I'm old."

"Experienced."

We then spent another hour doing some light sparring. When we began, my lack of skill was embarrassing. I was slow and did not anticipate Takuma's moves. Talk about rust! I felt foolish, like a beginner. By the end of the hour, it was coming back.

Takuma said, "You are reclaiming your skill. Your muscles are remembering. Give it time."

The last hour we spent with Blackie. He was excited to be back at work. Schutzhund was playtime for him: obedience, protection, tracking. For me, it was work. If Blackie was to perform perfectly, I had to as well. My commands had to be sharp, and I had to do almost as much running as Blackie. He only made one mistake. During obedience exercises, Takuma would try to distract him. He'd shout to me, call Blackie's name, or hit a can with a spoon. Blackie stayed on task. However, when Takuma fired the starter pistol we use, Blackie bolted. He came right back, but he had bolted. Of course, he did. He had seen me get shot. He had been kicked and hurt in the midst of gunfire. I calmed him down, and we did some more obedience exercises. Then we tried again. This time, the shot did not distract him, and he stayed right on task. We repeated it three times. He improved with every repetition.

Blackie was perfect, with Takuma as my "helper," during the protection trials. He had always loved the protection behaviors. To the untrained eye, Blackie looked like a ferocious, out-of-control dog when he was grabbing Takuma's arm or barking at him. Blackie could be scary as hell. I knew he was enjoying himself immensely.

When I left Takuma's, I called Molly. "You free this evening?"

"Could be. Stan's got a game tonight." Her exercise-addicted fiancé played basketball throughout the winter in the Connecticut Basketball League. It was hard-core, demanding, amateur basketball.

"Want to go to the range?"

"Sure. Seven?"

"Perfect."

Molly takes after me. She works out at Takuma's and is skilled in multiple martial arts. She is a better markswoman than I am a marksman, and I'm pretty damn good. I have to work at it. She's a natural. The fact that she is a PhD computer scientist at Yale astounds me.

My son, Ben, on the other hand, takes after Patricia, my deceased wife. He hates contact sports. Even as a kid, he preferred baseball and racket sports to football and hockey. He excels at tennis and squash. Where Molly is a math and science kid, Ben is the liberal arts maven who works absurd hours and has no time for anything other than the cases he is given at the law firm. However, he has recently become besotted by the charms of Heng Pho. As he left late on New Year's Day, he told me he was going to start making more time for non-work activities.

***

When I arrived at 11:45, Jim, Anita, and Luke Perry were waiting in the conference room. Claire had brought them coffee and water. I let them wait until Heng arrived, which she did five minutes later. When I opened the door, I interrupted whatever the Perrys were discussing.

"Hi, I'm Frank Kelly. It's good to meet you in person. This is my colleague Dr. Heng Pho, who will be joining us."

No one questioned Heng's presence, and we completed introductions, including getting everyone on a first-name basis.

Anita started right in before I had a chance to ask how I could help them. "We think this group in Maine is a cult. We hope you can refer us to someone who can help…"

"De-program him," Luke interrupted.

"De-program him?" I repeated.

"Yes," Luke continued. "He's caught up in a cult. We need someone to de-program him."

Heng and I looked at each other. I asked, "Why do you think he's joined a cult?"

"It's the only thing that makes sense," Anita said. "Why else would he not come home at Christmas and avoid us?"

"He called, though. Didn't he," Jim Perry said. "This cult stuff is nonsense."

"No, it's not, Dad. We've been over this. Gwen says it all fits – all of it. Charismatic leader, absolute control. Remember, Mark let that McKnight guy hit me and did nothing about it. Conspiracy nonsense. Yeah. It's all there. Dogmatic absurd beliefs. Isolation from friends and family. It's a cult. Gwen says there's no question."

I asked, "Who's Gwen?"

"She's my girlfriend. She's a psych major."

"Oh."

"Can you help us? "Anita asked. "You must know someone who knows how to de-program people like Mark."

"I'm sorry," I said. "But I don't. I know that the Defenders of Liberty is a militia group, but I'm not sure it's a cult in the way you are thinking about a cult."

I was in over my head, so I turned to Heng. "Heng, your thoughts."

"Militias are not cults," she began. "People join of their own free will because of their beliefs about the government, power, and their sense of victimhood. Anger drives them more than a lack of connectedness or a search for meaning. A militia is not interested in sex, religion, or the end of the world. Just because they believe in one or more conspiracies doesn't make them a cult. They are dangerous to others. They are terrorists." Her statement was forceful. There was no empathy in it.

I was shocked, and by the facial reactions of the Perrys, they were also shocked. She continued, "That isn't what you wanted to hear. You were hoping that somehow Mark wasn't responsible for joining up."

"But..." Luke began.

"She's right, damn it," Jim Perry said. "I told you this was a waste of time. You said it, Luke. He told you. He wants to be there. It's a job. He's getting paid. It's his choice. A lousy choice, maybe, but still, his choice."

"So, what do we do?" Anita pleaded.

"Nothing," her husband answered. "We don't do a damn thing. I told you this was a waste of time. Let's go." He got up, turned to me, and said, "Sorry to waste your time, Kelly."

It happened so quickly that I was caught off guard. Neither Luke nor Anita said another word. They got up and followed Jim Perry out of the conference room, leaving Heng and me to sit there looking at one another across the conference table.

"This is a new one for me. I've been discharged twice now by the same guy, and I wasn't even charging him this time. What the hell was that all about?"

"I'm sorry," Heng said. "I should have just been a fly on the wall."

"No. I'm talking about them, not you. Although I was a bit surprised by how, uh, clear you were with them."

"You mean harsh. They're just scared and looking for answers. It's just…"

"They need to know the truth. Whatever it is."

"Yes. To call these groups cults is misleading."

"I agree. You hungry? Claire has a bunch of take-out menus. We can order something."

"Uh. Sorry, but I can't. I texted Ben I was coming down. He asked if I would be free for lunch. I said I didn't know. Let me text him. If he's still available, do you want to join us?"

"No. No. You two go ahead. I've got some work I need to catch up on."

Ah, the sacrifices a parent makes for the happiness of their children.

Chapter Fourteen: Do Definitions Matter?

When Molly and I arrived, the shooting range was practically empty. I had three weapons with me, each with a different caliber and stopping power. Molly just had her pride and joy, the Magnum Research Desert Eagle 50 Action Express. It's a monster of a pistol. Please don't ask me how, but she can handle it. Because of its size and power, the range owners have nicknamed her Harry after the movie character Harry Callahan in the Clint Eastwood films. She loves it.

The Park City Gun Club in Bridgeport is more than just a shooting range. They offer over twenty classes and a host of different certifications. One of these is for the Utah permit. If you obtain a State of Utah permit, the permit is recognized in multiple states nationwide. Molly and I both have this permit as well as a Connecticut permit.

The range has ten stalls. The maximum length from the firing line to the target is seventy-five feet, which is a mile when trying to hit a small target with a pistol. Various targets are available and can be moved to different lengths along the firing line. Depending on the weapon I'm using, my accuracy varies quite a bit beyond fifty feet.

We unpacked our bags, put on our glasses and ear protection, and got down to business. We didn't talk. We fired, examined our targets, reloaded, and fired again. I switched back and forth between weapons. My Glock 23 is only seven inches long and fires the .40 Smith and Wesson shell. It's a small weapon, and I wear it when working. The

Glock 21 is an inch longer and heavier. It shoots a .45 shell. The third, a Glock 40, is a very different weapon. It is chambered for a .10 mm Auto shell, is 9.49 inches long, and weighs over 44 ounces. Glock classifies it as a 'hunting' pistol. Would it stop a bear? I hope I never have to find out.

Forty-five minutes later, I was ready to stop. Molly wasn't. I told her I'd meet her in the lounge. I was drinking a bottle of water and erasing email messages when she joined me.

"How'd you do?" she asked.

"Pretty good for not having practiced for several weeks. You?"

"Usual. I feel like I've hit a wall with this damn thing. I can't seem to get any better."

"Your wall is much better than most people's, especially with that monster you're firing."

"My pride and joy? Are you dissing my pride and joy, Father?"

"I would never do that."

"Okay. Changing subjects. Heng Pho. So, I met her at New Year's. Seems very nice. And now she's down here today and having lunch with Ben."

"How did you know that?"

"Ben. He texted me this afternoon. I've been trying to fix him up with a friend of mine. Always, and I mean always, he has a scheduling problem. So, this afternoon, he tells me he's not interested. I ask him why. He tells me he's just had lunch with Heng and really likes her."

"I think it may be mutual. They seemed to hit it off New Year's. They both stayed over into New Year's Day."

"As in spent the night?"

"Yep."

"And?"

"And what?"

"Don't be funny."

"Okay. Eve thinks they talked all night."

"That would be my brother. You think this is, like, for real – finally?"

"Who knows?"

"I sure hope so. It's about time."

"Leave him alone. If it happens, it happens."

"I know, but…"

"You want him to…"

"Meet someone, settle down, and have kids? I do. He's the oldest, after all."

"So?"

"Come on. You know what I'm saying."

"Okay. I do."

"How's work?"

"Good. Vicki's taking over security. Irene's moving into the financial management job, and I'm working part-time for a while."

"Good for you. Better than chasing off to Maine after a weirdo Militia type."

"Saw his family today."

"Oh no. You're not going to..."

"No. You have dinner?"

"No. You?"

"No. Oar and Oak?"

"Sure."

"I'll call Eve. See if she wants to join us."

When I called Eve, she said, "I was just going to text you. Ben just called. Apparently, he took the afternoon off and gave Heng Pho a tour of New Haven. He took her to Sally's for Pizza, the Yale Art Gallery, the Center for British Art, and walked her around Yale. The whole thing."

"Wait a minute. This is Benjamin Kelly we're talking about. He took the entire afternoon off?"

"Yes. And he asked if we wanted to get together for dinner."

"It's eight o'clock."

"I'm aware."

"Molly and I were just headed for the Oar and Oak."

"He's invited us for dinner at Zinc and says he is paying."

161

"Wait a sec. Let me check with Molly."

When I recounted the conversation to Molly, she said. "It's eight o'clock, and now he's thinking about dinner at Zinc. And he's paying. What's he celebrating? My guess is that my bro and Heng have been engaged in some activities besides touring, and I think she will not be returning to Storrs tonight. Way to go, Ben."

I didn't say anything to Molly. To Eve I responded, "We're in. Meet you there?"

She agreed and twenty minutes later the five of us were browsing through the menu at Zinc. I was reading from right to left. Ben makes decent money, but while the restaurant is lovely, it is not cheap.

It's in an old building on Chapel Street in downtown New Haven. It's the kind of place you go to celebrate special occasions. The fixed menu is small, and some would say exotic. Others call it eclectic. Zinc calls it "Modern American."

***

Ben and Heng were there when I arrived. When Ben greeted me, there was something different about him. He was anxious, excited, and happy all at once. Heng seemed reserved, certainly more reserved than when we met with the Perrys. Was she embarrassed about something? The two of them had a secret. I was sure I knew what it was, but they were not about to tell me.

Molly arrived next. She hugged Heng and then her brother. When she hugged Ben, she whispered something to him. I was sure he blushed. Molly was all smiles. She was enjoying herself as though she had just developed some new found power. I could imagine her teasing, "I know what you did."

Eve was the last to arrive. She hugged everyone at the table, planted a kiss on my cheek, then took her seat. Over drinks, she asked Heng, "How did you like your tour of New Haven?"

"I loved it, especially walking around Yale. The Sterling Library is amazing. The location in the center of the city is wonderful."

"Not like UConn."

"Not at all. UConn is its own city, which some planners dropped in the middle of a pasture. It feels isolated."

Molly said, "I just realized. I don't know where you did your undergraduate work."

Ben answered, "University of Chicago – undergrad and graduate." He turned to Heng and said, "Sorry."

She put her hand on his arm. "It's okay." To the rest of us she said, "The University's in Hyde Park. It's residential and, at one point, was quite lovely and affluent. It has had its ups and downs. Woodlawn, where I lived, and the campus are fine. Other neighborhoods are a bit dicey. It's only twenty minutes to downtown and The Loop, though, and it's easy to get there. I must admit, though, that after lunch at Sally's today, I will never brag about Chicago pizza again."

Molly smiled and said, "Sounds like you two had a delightful afternoon."

Ben gave her a brotherly "don't you dare" look.

Eve went on a rescue mission and asked me, "So, how did your meeting with the Perrys go?"

"I got fired again."

"I didn't realize they had rehired you."

"Well, I wasn't really on the clock yet."

"What did they want?"

"They wanted me – actually, I think it was Luke who wanted me – to find someone for them who could de-program Mark."

Molly asked, "De-program him? I thought you told me he was in a militia, not a cult."

"Exactly," Heng said. Any sense of embarrassment or discomfort was no longer present. "Luke's girlfriend is a psych major and thinks she knows a lot more than she does. She convinced Luke that Mark was in a cult. Which he's not. The Defenders of Liberty is a militia, not a cult."

"Why did she think he's in a cult?"

"Besides the fact she doesn't know what she's talking about?"

I knew this tone in Heng's voice. I had heard it when she talked to the Perrys. I wondered how much it was influenced by her experience with her brother and perhaps members of her family.

She continued, "Thinking it's a cult takes care of two things for a family that prefers denial. It absolves the so-called cult member of accountability for their choices, and it diminishes how dangerous militias are."

"Interestingly," I added, "the father, Jim Perry, coded it as Mark's just got a new job. How's that for letting your kid off the hook? They thought the problem would disappear if they simply used different labels for Mark's behavior."

Heng continued, "Militias want political power; they want to control the levers of power. They want to control access to resources. Cults, on the other hand, want to control their members. Cults look inward; militias look outward. Cult members are lost; militia members are angry. I'm sorry. I'm at it again."

Ben came to her defense. "No, it's interesting. What about gangs? Our New Haven office has defended several 'Exit 8' members. Everything from murder to drugs to theft. Since the gangs battle each other, if we defend Exit 8 members, we won't defend anyone from the Tre Bloods."

Now we were on my turf. I knew gangs. When I was teaching, I taught about gangs. The professor of criminology, AKA Frank Kelly, appeared on the scene in full lecture mode. "Gangs exist at opposite ends of the socio-economic scale. There are white-collar gangs who band together to suppress competition, buy politicians, and control markets. They are non-violent physically but economically punish people. They also demand allegiance. We usually don't refer to them as gangs, but in fundamental ways, they are civilized gangs, but still gangs. Think of the NFL owners and the Pharmaceutical Manufacturers Association. At the other end, you have gangs like the ones Ben is talking about. They also want to dominate markets, usually local markets, sometimes geographic turf. Discipline is always important in gangs. They exterminate opposition or make treaties to avoid extermination. Gangs are economic engines combined with protection and acceptance for members."

Eve came on board wearing her political science hat. "Gangs and militia exist in every Third World country. Look at the gangs in Haiti, the ELN in Colombia, and the cartels in Mexico. The militias in Sudan almost control the country. The same is true in Somalia. They make the creation of stable governments almost impossible. Absent stable governments, people come to rely on gangs or militia for survival. I can understand why belonging to a cult or having a new job are preferable explanations for the Perrys."

"Even if it means they are deluding themselves?" Molly asked. "Dad, I'm glad you aren't working for these people. They are whacko."

"That's one label. I'd prefer scared," I replied.

Ben asked, "So this Defenders of Liberty group, they're dangerous?"

Without thinking, I answered, "Yes."

Heng added, "Absolutely."

"So why don't the police do something, or the FBI, or the ATF?" Molly asked.

The lawyer answered, "On what grounds? What laws have they broken?"

"In addition, the local sheriff's office may be sympathetic to their view of the federal government," I said. "Every state bans private military activity. But little is done to stop it. And throughout the country law enforcement has been present and witnessed these militia groups marching in local parades dressed in militia uniforms and they typically do nothing."

"So?" Molly asked.

"It's against the law in at least seventeen states, including Maine, for private militias to wear uniforms in public that resemble those of the military."

"Are you kidding?" Molly asked.

"Not in the least," I answered.

"What's your plan?" Ben asked.

"Let it be."

"I have an idea," Molly said. "Why not send the family a copy of that *Militia Manual* you told me about?"

Chapter Fifteen: Let's Get This Done

The weather was all over the place. The week between Christmas and New Year's Day in Sparta, Maine saw six inches of snow and temperatures that varied between -3 and 38 degrees Fahrenheit.

In the early afternoon of New Year's Day, the temperature shot above freezing, and the snow started to melt. In their inebriated state, four Defenders decided it was time for a snowball fight.

Mark, Lenny, and their cabin mates, Pat Cavacco and Peter Donnell, left the dining hall's warmth, where everyone had gathered to feast and watch football games. Michigan was playing Alabama in the warmth of the Pasadena Rose Bowl, but for these four, it was a "who cares" game. So, the four of them took their shirts off, left the dining hall, stumbled out onto the parade ground, and started throwing snowballs at one another.

The fight ended when Gordon McKnight came out an hour later and hollered, "Get your sad asses back in here before someone gets hurt." None of the four complained. They were all freezing, but none would admit that an hour of getting pelted with snowballs on now-wet skin in the middle of January was more than enough.

Once inside, they were greeted with comments about their intelligence, sanity, and status as adults. One of their comrades who had remained inside adopted a Southern drawl and inquired of Lenny, "How'd you get grown, boy?" In response, Lenny took the snowball he had been hiding behind his back and heaved it at the questioner. The questioner, a large Maine lumberjack from Aroostook County who was significantly bigger than Lenny, took after him and chased Lenny out of the building and back into the cold.

Mark, Pat, and Peter put on their shirts and settled with the rest of the group to watch football. Hungover from New Year's Eve and satiated from the elaborate brunch, the dining hall occupants were quiet, except for an occasional groan or whoop in response to a fumble, pass completion, or long run.

Now fully dressed, Lenny returned from his banishment, collected his shirt, and joined Mark to watch the game. Forty-five minutes later, he told Mark, "I'm out of here. Can't keep my eyes open."

"Wait. Let's grab a couple of brewskis and sandwiches. I'll come with you."

When they walked out the door with their plunder, Barry Stark caught up with them. "Remember, we start training tomorrow right after breakfast. Make it an early night."

"Will do," Mark said.

Lenny just kept walking down the steps towards their cabin.

***

It was cold the following morning, bitter cold. The porch thermometer on the cabin Mark and Lenny shared with Pat and Peter read -5 degrees. The four of them got dressed in layers of the latest high-tech cold-weather clothing gear L.L.Bean had to offer. The outermost layer was colored in camouflage patterns. They went to the dining hall, where Gordon McKnight separated Mark and Lenny from the other two and guided them to a table where Barry Stark was already sitting. Mark noticed their bunk mates were guided to a different table to sit with someone they had not seen before at the camp.

McKnight told them to sit down and then sat down with them. "How you feeling this morning?" McKnight asked. It was clear the question was being asked of Mark and Lenny and did not include Stark.

"Good," Mark said.

Lenny smiled, "A little hung over." He adopted a faux Irish accent, "I would appreciate a wee bit of the dog that bit me if you don't mind."

"You've had the last alcohol you're going to see for a while," Stark said. "Get used to it." Stark was in command mode. Having been with him in Montana, Mark and Lenny knew better than to question his tone of voice.

"Good," McKnight said. "Let's get to it. You're going to spend the next week preparing for a mission that you'll execute on January 10th. When you were in Montana, the three of you seemed to work well together as a team. When I asked Barry who he wanted, he said the two of you."

Mark and Lenny looked at one another.

"Good," Mark said.

Lenny didn't say anything.

McKnight continued, "This is going to be different. Much more difficult. Greater chance of resistance. You won't be dealing with two people who were asleep in bed."

"All right. What do you want us to do?" Lenny asked.

"I'll get to that. Before I do, though, I want to remind you of the stakes we're dealing with here. I know you know this, but I will repeat it anyway. The country's been taken over by people who don't give a shit about it. They could care less about the values it was founded upon. At the rate we're going, the country will cease to exist if we don't take it back and restore it to its very foundations. We've got to do things that we wouldn't have dreamed of doing ten or twenty years ago. You know this, don't you?"

Mark didn't say anything.

Lenny sneered, "Things like scaring the shit out of that governor and her husband? That was fun."

McKnight glared at Lenny. "Lower your voice. Not even the others know about your last mission." He glanced at Stark as if to ask, *You sure you want this guy?*

168

Stark didn't say anything.

McKnight looked at Lenny, "Okay. You're right. That was child's play. It was necessary, and it worked. She dropped out, and there were no repercussions. That was just one step, though. One fucking step."

Taking the attention away from Lenny, Mark asked, "So what's next? What do you want us to do?"

"This time, you're going to create a shit load of chaos, and, in the process, you're going to remove someone else."

"Remove as in…?" Lenny asked.

McKnight's voice dropped, "Assassinate them." He didn't say anything more. He let the word assassinate sink in.

"Who?" Mark asked.

"I'll get to that. My question to both of you is, 'Are you good with that?' I want you to think about this very carefully. Think about the ramifications. If you're caught, you'll be charged with murder. If you try to say the Defenders ordered you to do it, we'll say you went rogue and that we had nothing to do with it. This isn't like being in a war, where you're killing an armed combatant. This person is a civilian and will be unarmed, although others around him might be. You hear what I'm saying?"

"Yeah," Lenny said. "If we're caught, we're fucked."

"Why you want us to kill this guy?" Mark asked. "What's he done?"

"He's a political hack, a middle-of-the-road prick, and he stands in our way. Right now, he leads in every single goddamn poll. With Olson out of the way, he's sure to get nominated. We've got to get rid of him. Understand? We not only have to get rid of him, we have to do it in a way that scares the shit out of people. They've got to start to realize how fucked this country is and see Pope as the only person who can get it back on track."

"Juan Perez," Lenny said. "You want us to kill Juan Perez?"

"Who's Juan Perez?" Mark asked.

"Senator from Florida," Lenny answered.

"Fucking wet back," Stark said. It was the first time he had said anything.

"Yes," McKnight said. "Senator Juan Perez from the great state of Florida. First viable spic candidate for president in history, and he's a goddamned Republican. Unbelievable."

"What's the plan?" Mark asked.

"You'll know more in a few days. For now, though, are you in or out?"

"I'm in," Mark said immediately.

Lenny was two or three beats behind Mark when he said, "Yeah. Me, too."

"Good. You start your training today."

***

Among themselves, The Defenders of Liberty called it the "Armory." No one had replaced the sign over the door. It read: "Equipment Shed." Since buying the property, Gordon McKnight had added a barnlike structure to the shed along with heating and cooling equipment. Where the original shed had open shelves and cubbies for sporting equipment, the Armory had locked closets containing a variety of firearms and assorted paraphernalia, from Kevlar vests to night vision goggles.

The new building contained a workout room with weights and cardio equipment and an open area with mats for martial arts practice. At 0830 on January 2, 2024, Gary Stark unlocked the door and ushered Mark and Lenny into the new part of the building and over to a table set against a wall. On the table were three machetes in their scabbards, three wooden instruments that looked like machetes, and three suits of protective clothing.

"What's this stuff?" Lenny asked.

"These are your weapons for the mission."

"Machetes?" Lenny asked. "You kidding me?"

"Nope. You're going to become an expert in the use of a machete."

"Are you?" Lenny asked.

"Am I what?"

"An expert?"

170

"Not yet. I'm just like you two. We're going to learn together."

"From who?"

"You'll meet him in a few minutes. First, we're going to go over the mission plan. When I do, you'll understand the reason for the machetes."

"Fuckin' machetes," Lenny laughed. "I don't believe it. Goddamn dark ages. Why not swords?" He picked up one of the wooden machetes, pointed it at Mark like a sword, and said, "En garde."

"Okay, wise ass. Put it down. Pull up those chairs, sit your butts down, and I will explain it to you."

When they did as they were told, Stark began. "Okay, here's the story. Perez. Cuban. His grandparents came to Florida to escape Castro. Perez's father got work as a laborer. Got married. Had a bunch of kids. Juan is the oldest and the one who made good. Goes to college. Goes to law school. Fresh out of law school, Juan began his career as an assistant prosecutor in Miami. Made his name prosecuting gangs. Had a real hard-on for the Mara Salvatrucha gang because they killed one of his investigators."

"The Mara who?" Mark asked.

"The MS-13, numb nuts," Lenny said.

"How the hell should I know?" Mark said.

"Jesus H. Christ. South American bad guys. Don't you read?"

Stark intervened. "Salvadoran. Started in Los Angeles. Spread out. Florida, especially South Florida, has a Salvadoran population. Lenny's right. This is a badass group. Anyway, Perez worked his way up the chain, eventually becoming attorney general in Florida before running for senate. All the time, he's focused on gangs, especially MS-13. It's like he's got a private war with them."

"They must have loved that," Mark said.

"Exactly. So, three years ago, MS-13 decides it's time for now Senator Juan Perez to leave the scene, permanently. They tried to kill him when he was speaking at a fundraiser in Miami. They fucked it up, though. Two MS-13 guys were killed, and another guy, their getaway driver, was arrested. You get the picture?"

"What the hell does that have to do with us?" Lenny asked.

"You're going to become MS-13."

"We're going to join the gang? If you haven't noticed, I'm not exactly a spic," Lenny said.

"By the time I get through with you, you'll pass."

"You're fucking kidding me."

"Do I sound like I'm kidding?"

"So, we blame killing Perez on MS-13," Mark said.

"You got it."

"So, what's with the machetes?" Lenny asked.

"Favorite weapon of MS-13. Sort of their signature. You're going to use machetes on this mission. And you're going to speak Spanish."

"What?" Lenny said. "I don't speak Spanish. Neither does he," pointing at Mark.

"It's okay. You're going to learn four or five phrases. Enough so any bystanders who also don't speak Spanish won't be able to tell the difference."

"This is going to be some fun and games," Lenny said.

"When we doing this?" Mark asked.

"January 10th. There's a primary debate that night at St. Lawrence University in Manchester, New Hampshire. We're going to make sure that debate never takes place. We're going to take care of Perez that morning."

"The three of us," Lenny said.

"Yes, the three of us. Any extra security will be for the debate that night. No one will be expecting anything to happen in the morning."

"You sure?" Lenny asked.

"Yeah. There's already been four other debates. No reason they'd change for this one."

"Do we know where he'll be?" Mark asked.

"Perez is scheduled to come in the day before to practice. We'll have his itinerary a couple of days before. We'll know exactly where he'll be."

"How?" Mark asked.

"Easy. His press guy gives out his itinerary to the media every morning. Nothing secret about it. Based on the last debates, he'll be heading for his hotel room after a morning campaign stop."

"So, we're going to hit him in his hotel room?" Lenny asked.

"Nope. Just before he goes into the lobby. We want everyone to see this and to hear us shouting at each other in Spanish."

"Jesus," Lenny said. "Sounds like a shitstorm. For us. How we going to get out of there?"

"I'm going to have a car ready and waiting. Don't worry. I've got it all figured out."

"You're going to be our driver?" Lenny asked.

"Yeah. You guys are younger, stronger, and faster. You got a problem with that?"

"No. Just asking."

The door opened between the original shed and what they now called the gym. A short, balding man in his late fifties walked over to where they were sitting. Stark told Mark and Lenny, "I want you to meet Louis Florez. He's going to teach you how to handle a machete. He's also going to teach you some Spanish. Good to have you with us, Lou."

"*Luis. Me llamo Luis.*"

"Right. Luis. Luis's with a brother organization in Orlando. He's also with the sheriff's department there. He's dealt with MS-13 since they came to Florida."

"Nasty guys you're going to be impersonating," Luis said. Although he had been in the United States since he was a teenager, he still had a touch of a Spanish accent. "We'll start on the language stuff tomorrow. Let's start by talking about your weapons."

Lenny said, "I get we're going to be using machetes. We're going to have guns with us, too, though, aren't we?"

Stark took a minute before answering, "No, you're not." He didn't explain himself; he just let his answer stand.

Luis said, "So you'd better get good with these things. You ready?"

Mark said, "Yeah."

173

Lenny didn't say anything.

"Okay. Pick up a scabbard and take your machete out. I want to tell you about these beauties."

Stark, Mark, and Lenny did as Luis instructed. "These beauties are made out of 5160 tri-tempered steel. The blade's a little under two feet long. These babies hold an edge. Feel that handle. It's Micarta. Strong as hell. With the finger grooves, it's not going to slip on you. Feel the weight. It's not too heavy, but it has enough bulk to do the job.

"Okay. I want you to separate. Go to different corners. Just swing your weapon around. Get used to the feel of it. Machetes are primarily chopping weapons, but they can also be used to stab, like a sword. But if you are stabbing in the chest, you've got to turn the blade and make sure it's on its side so it can slip between the ribs to get at the vital organs. Just play with it for a few minutes. By the end of the next couple of days, I want you to feel like your weapon is an extension of your arm."

Play they did – at least Mark and Lenny did. Barry Stark took it very seriously. In all of his years with the state police, Stark had never fired his weapon and had never been in an altercation that required physical action on his part. Although he was older than either Mark or Lenny by several years, when it came to combat, Mark and Lenny were the experienced ones.

After ten minutes of playing with their machetes, Luis called them to the table and said, "Get dressed. It's time to learn about combat with these darlings." All three men donned the protective clothing laid out on the table. It was similar to the kind of clothing used to train police dogs. Once they had it on, Luis inspected each one to make sure it was correctly fitted and securely fastened.

Luis picked up one of the wooden machetes and twirled it about. "These are a bit lighter than the real thing, but they're the same size as the ones you'll be using." He asked Mark to step forward. "Although you can stab with a machete, it is primarily a chopping weapon. That means you need room to swing it. There's nothing delicate about it. The blades you will be using are made of carbon steel. They're sharp, and they're not going to break when you hit something. They might bounce if you hit something hard, but they won't break. Think of using them in two beats: stop, then kill. You need to stop your adversary first, then kill him.

"Okay. Repeat that. Stop. Kill."

The three of them looked at him, not fully understanding his instructions. "I want you to say it. Out loud. Stop. Kill."

The three trainees repeated the words, and Luis had them repeat them again and again. "Right. You've got it. Let's start with the kill chop. You could hack the person to death and have them bleed out, but that takes time. What's fastest?"

"Head and neck," Lenny answered.

"Very good. One good clean chop to either, and the person's dead, but the head and neck are small compared with the rest of the body, and if the person's moving…"

"So, you've got to stop them from moving first," Mark said.

Stark smiled. "Stop, kill."

They spent the rest of the day in protective clothing, the three of them learning how to wield the wooden machetes. They learned how to chop at a thigh or shoulder, large targets, to stop an adversary. They learned how to chop across the neck or down onto the top of the head for a kill shot. They learned when to grasp the machete with two hands when chopping down to increase their leverage and power. "Think of it this way," Luis told them, "It's like an ax when you're trying to split an adversary's head open or chop into their shoulder so one side of their body is useless."

Late in the afternoon, with barely enough light to see, Luis took them outside into the woods and had them use their real machetes on tree branches. "Chop through," he'd shout at them. "Don't hold back, don't pull your punches. Chop as though you are absolutely sure that with a single chop, you can get through the branch."

An hour later, there was no light. Luis said, "Okay, that's enough. We'll pick this up in the morning."

The four of them sat together when they gathered for dinner that night. Gordon McKnight stopped at one point and asked, "How'd it go?"

"Fine," Luis said. "They'll be ready. We still have lots of time."

"Good," McKnight said. "Let's get this done."

When he left, Mark asked, "I wonder why we were never trained to use machetes when I was in Special Forces. Were you?"

"No way," Lenny said.

"Some military are," Luis said. "The United States Army used them in WWII when troops were in jungle areas. They're still available. The Brazilian Army uses them. They've been used in uprisings and..." Luis paused.

"And?" Mark asked.

"You know. Shitshows. Genocide. Rwanda, Cuba."

Everyone focused on eating.

Luis continued after a few bites. "It's a good weapon. Quiet. Better than a knife. Deadly as shit."

"That's for sure," Mark said.

"By the way. The ones you're using...made in El Salvador. We took them from an MS-13 house we raided."

"No shit," Lenny said.

"No shit."

Chapter Sixteen: Manchester

Juan Perez was exhausted and exhilarated. Although Mary Olson didn't endorse him when she dropped out of the primary race, Juan's campaign manager expected her followers to transfer their allegiance to him. He was right. Juan's poll numbers had shot up since Olson withdrew. The remaining two candidates were now long shots, and Juan wondered why they were still running unless they were trying for a vice-presidential slot on the ticket.

After tonight, Juan told his wife, "Paxton's money's going to evaporate. Poof. All gone, old man, and so are you. Sidney Paxton is just too damned old." So what if he had been governor of Texas? Juan was convinced he would drop out immediately after the debate. Paxton was a horrible debater. He alternated between mumbling and screaming.

Manning, the senator from Kansas, his other remaining opponent, was a nice enough guy but didn't understand that wearing his Christianity on his sleeve wasn't enough to get him the nomination. His sanctimonious little sermons were boring. He was still in the race because he had paid his dues to the party and assembled a steady cash stream from a few big Christian Nationalist donors. Manning had also assembled a group of pastors who told their flocks it was essential that a "good Christian" like Manning occupy the White House. The "good" was a not-so-subtle slam at Perez's Catholicism.

The Perez biography, at least the official one the campaign gave to the press, did not emphasize his religion. It mentioned it, but in passing. His service to his country in the United States Marines and tours of duty in Desert Storm and Iraq got much higher billing. Nothing, though, was as high as his professional life devoted to public safety as a prosecutor and Florida's AG. He was a warrior out to protect his fellow citizens from the scourges of gang-related violence, especially the notorious MS-13. What other candidate could boast they had a price on their head?

Juan had continued his crime-busting focus when he reached the United States Senate, only now the focus was on illegal immigration and the hordes of illegal immigrants subjecting United States citizens to rape and murder. The outgoing president, Goodman, had been an idiot opening the doors. More immigrants, legal and illegal, had entered the United States in three years than ever before in the history of the United States. At its peak in the 1850s, immigration never exceeded two hundred thousand a year. Now it was two million in a single year.

Given Juan's speeches, anyone would think that crime was on the rise throughout the land and that illegal immigrants were the cause. The crime statistics didn't support this contention, but that didn't matter as long as enough episodes could be used as absolute proof of the erroneous contention. Fortunately for Juan, there were plenty of these episodes so he always had something to talk about. He especially liked the story of the three illegals who raped children on the liberal bastion of the island of Nantucket in Blue Massachusetts.

At forty-eight, Juan was the right age to pull off his Batman-like persona. He had enough gray at his temples to convey experience and worked out sufficiently to have a bouncy step when he moved, always just this side of a light jog. His complexion was light, his height was tall, and his speech was educated. According to his campaign manager, he was the complete package. He even came with a pretty wife and two squeaky-clean teenage sons.

If his wife, Mirana, had been asked to write an honest campaign biography, a different image of the senator from Florida might have emerged. Mirana knew him as an insecure, closed-off man who had periodic bouts of depression and anxiety. She had known him since they were high school sweethearts; that history played well with the press.

178

A friend told her about his two short-lived "traveling affairs" on trips outside Florida and D.C. In both cases, they were with staff members of the people he was working with during these trips. In both cases, she knew he was lonely and scared, on the edge of an existential crisis. He constantly questioned how he could be a senator, the son of a sanitation worker and a hotel housekeeper. He had just gotten by in a third-rate high school and a second-rate college. He barely passed law school, and it took three tries to pass the bar. He was a fraud, an imposter, and would be discovered some day. In both affairs, the young women did an excellent job of validating Juan and his societal role. They were impressed that he had chosen them as objects of his attention and affection, no matter how fleeting. He was, after all, a United States senator.

Juan had been tempted to confess his affairs to Mirana but resisted. He was also tempted to maintain his traveling liaisons, but fear of being caught and his presidential ambition constrained him. Instead, he encouraged Mirana to travel with him whenever possible. When it was impossible, they used Facetime and other electronic means to stay in touch. He knew he was lucky that she understood his loneliness and doubt. He honestly didn't know what he'd do without her and told her so.

For her part, she did understand him. Her background had been similar to his, and she was also amazed at how her life had turned out. There was a difference, though. She didn't think of herself as an imposter. When Juan was elected to the senate, Mirana moved the family to Alexandria, Virginia. She had been trained as a librarian. She decided, though, that she was going to understand her new life. She went back to school. She took the required bachelor-level courses she needed to enter a master's program in public policy at Georgetown University. She not only excelled scholastically, but she also became his primary advisor.

It was still dark when Juan and Mirana left Manchester for Newington, New Hampshire, to meet workers on their way to work at Sig Sauer. A visit to a gun manufacturer with multiple contracts with federal, state, and local agencies was always a good photo opportunity.

Rain and warm weather had removed any snow remnants, and they easily made the hour-long trip. The morning of January 10th brought warm weather and only a slight drizzle, enough to put the hoods up on their jackets but not enough for an umbrella. The downside was that the Sig Sauer workers were not anxious to do more than shake his hand, mumble a few words – usually encouragement – and get inside the building. They were tired of being bombarded with television ads and candidates wanting to shake their hands. There was no press. "Too early and wet," Juan said to Mirana.

Forty-five minutes after arriving, Juan and Mirana were back in the car. In the front seat were their twenty-three-year-old volunteer driver, Paul Benson, and Delores Matthews, the Assistant Campaign Manager of New Hampshire for Perez.

On the outskirts of Manchester, Juan told Benson, "Let's stop at a Dunkin. I could use another cup of coffee."

"You sure you want to take the time?" Mirana asked.

"Yeah. We've got time. You worried about tonight?"

"No, not really."

"Good. After tonight, the primary is as good as over. Relax."

***

Barry Stark was sitting behind the wheel of the stolen Ford F150 pickup truck. He had pulled behind some bushes in a recreation area off Bridge Street in Manchester when he got word that Perez's car had left Newington. In the back of the truck, huddled under blankets and a tarp, Mark Perry and Lenny Pratt were stretched out so they could not be seen if someone drove through the park. A lone man sitting in his truck drinking coffee would not get the attention nor be as memorable as three men. "How long now?" Lenny asked through his communication headset.

"We'll leave in thirty minutes," Stark replied.

They were getting ready to leave when the driver of the car following Perez's car called. "They've pulled off to get coffee. Long line. I'll call you when they get back on route."

Fifteen minutes later, the call came, and Stark pulled out of their hiding place and drove down Bridge Street toward the center of Manchester. When they got downtown, he pulled into an alley alongside the New Hampshire Inn, where the Perez contingent was staying. Mark and Lenny climbed out of the truck. With the motor still on, Stark also got out, went to the back, and reached into the cab as though he were arranging packages or moving things around. He had his jacket hood up against the rain. His gray ski mask was pulled low over his forehead.

Lenny and Mark were dressed similarly. Their machetes were concealed beneath their closed, long jackets. They each wore earbuds that connected them to the car following Perez. They moved slowly. The timing had to be perfect.

When they got word the Perez car had arrived in front of the inn, Mark and Lenny pulled down their ski masks to cover their faces and communication devices. Mirana was the first out of the car. Perez was right behind her. In the front seat, Delores Matthews was gathering up papers she had placed on the floor. When Perez exited the car, he became aware of people moving to his side and turned towards them.

Mark and Lenny rushed at Perez, opening their jackets and grasping their machetes as they went. The two of them had rehearsed their actions repeatedly, turning them into a ballet of movement. Mark raised his machete over his head and chopped down as hard as he could on Juan Perez's left shoulder. Honed to a sharp edge, the blade cut through Perez's jacket and drove deep into the senator, severing the clavicle and the tendons and ligaments that held the shoulder together.

Lenny sliced from the side, cutting into thigh muscle, bone, and arteries. Perez buckled and started to fall. Mark raised his machete once more and, with all his strength, chopped down, cutting into the senator's head. He let go of the weapon, leaving the blade deep into Perez's skull. At the same time, Lenny used his machete to slice through the Senator's neck, cutting through the carotid artery and smashing into the spinal column.

Severed arteries spurt blood everywhere. Standing next to her husband, Mirana was covered in his blood, as were Lenny and Mark. Now on the ground, blood pooled around the senator, who had died instantly. Mirana looked down at her husband and then up at the backs of the two men running away. The three people coming out of the inn pulling suitcases behind them were voiceless in shock. Sitting in the car, Paul Benson and Delores Matthews didn't know something had happened until they heard someone shouting in Spanish. It was Mark Perry, "*¡Apúrate! ¡Apúrate!*"

Lenny shouted back, "*Detrás de ti!*"

Leaving their machetes behind, Mark and Lenny ran around the corner and into the alleyway where the truck awaited. Now, they could hear screams from in front of the hotel, but no one followed them. The two Defenders of Liberty jumped into the back of the truck and pulled the tarp and blankets over themselves. Stark had gotten into the driver's seat when he first saw the two emerge from the main street. Hearing Lenny bang on the back window, letting him know they were both aboard, he slowly drove out of the alley towards the back of the inn and away from the commotion that was taking place in front.

For the next thirty minutes, the truck wove its way along back roads and side streets heading north – just one middle-aged man driving five miles over the speed limit in the most popular vehicle in New Hampshire wasn't going to attract attention. Similar to the last mission, the vehicle was stolen from a long-term parking lot in Connecticut outside the Hartford Airport. The New Hampshire license plates were from another long-term parking lot – this one at the airport in Portsmouth. There were no traffic cameras along the pre-determined route.

Lenny and Mark huddled under the blankets and tarp in the back of the truck. For the first ten minutes, neither of them said anything. After a sharp turn jostled them into one another, Lenny pulled the tarp and blankets down off his face and said, "Got to get rid of this fucking mask. It's covered with blood. Stinks."

Mark didn't respond.

"You okay?" Lenny asked.

"Yeah, yeah." Mark pulled off his mask.

"That was some shit. He never knew what hit him."

Again, Mark didn't respond.

"You sure you're okay?"

"Yeah."

"You ever kill anyone before? Shit. This is your first. Christ, what a way to burst your cherry. With a fuckin'machete."

Mark said, "I got to get out of these clothes. I'm covered in blood."

"You and me both. What did Stark say it was to the farm? An hour?"

"I think less. Did you see her?"

"Who?"

"The wife."

"No. I was too busy. You looked at her?"

"Just for a second. She had blood on her face."

"No shit. It went everywhere. Arteries. I'm covered."

"Yeah. I wish someone had told me."

"It spurted all the way to her face. No shit."

Mark didn't respond.

When they reached New Durham, Stark pulled the truck into the barn of an abandoned dairy farm that had been for sale for over three years. Two cars were already parked behind the barn. While Stark closed the barn door, Mark and Lenny got out of the truck, removed their outer clothing, and put it in the back of the pickup. They put on the new clothing that had already been stashed there waiting for them. Stark removed the stolen license plates from the truck.

Next, they emptied two drums of gasoline over the truck and around the outside edges of the barn. With the accelerant in place, Stark set the timer on a simple electrical sparking device for thirty minutes. Powered by batteries, the device would emit sparks, more than enough to set off the gas fumes already accumulating in the barn.

Mark and Lenny got in Lenny's car and drove out first. They planned to take back roads through New Hampshire and Maine until they reached Sparta and Camp Liberty that evening.

Ten minutes later, Barry Stark left. He drove into Alton and the Bayside Diner. He sat at the bar with a cup of coffee, watching the news of the "Massacre of Juan Perez in broad daylight." When the alarms sounded, calling the volunteer fire department into action, Stark kept drinking his coffee. When he finished, he got in his car and started driving to his home in Massachusetts. He only stopped once to throw the stolen license plates into Wentworth Pond.

Chapter Seventeen: The News

Eve and I are predictable. If it's just the two of us, we eat dinner in front of the television set in the kitchen so we can watch the six o'clock news on our local PBS station. Regardless of which of us is cooking, dinner will be at six. Even though we had been receiving email and text messages about the assassination of Juan Perez all day long from our various news sources, tonight would be no different. We watched the six o'clock news.

The news was also predictable. There was the lineup of local and state police officials saying it was too early in the investigation to tell who the murderers were. Yes, the assassins had spoken Spanish words, and yes, Senator Perez had been threatened in the past by the Mara Salvatrucha gang, and yes, machetes had been used to kill the senator. No, Mara Salvatrucha had not claimed credit for the assassination. Yes, footage from security cameras in front of the hotel was being examined. No, no security cameras were covering the alleyway alongside the hotel where the assassins had escaped.

One of the three hotel guests who had witnessed the assassination was interviewed – she used the word murder. "It all happened so fast. And that poor woman. She had to see it, her husband, killed right in front of her by those monsters. There was blood everywhere. She was just covered."

David Brooks and Jonathan Capehart came on for commentary, even though it wasn't Friday, to talk about the consequences for the primary campaign and what the assassination said about political life in the

United States. After they finished, I said, "Brooks looked like he was in shock. Sometimes, he has difficulty grasping how low this country has sunk."

"So do I," Eve responded. "So do I."

When the station finished its coverage and shifted to other stories, Eve said something unusual. "I want to see what's going on with Fox."

"Seriously? You want to watch Fox?"

"Yes." And so we switched over to Fox, or Faux News, as I prefer to call it.

Already in New Hampshire to provide color commentary after the planned debate, Retired General John Pope was speaking:

> *The country is in chaos. No one is safe when a gang of thugs can assassinate a major candidate for office in broad daylight in front of his hotel. This was a decorated veteran who had served his country in wartime, fought crime at home, and then served in the United States Senate, and this is what happens to him? This is a travesty of immense proportions – open borders. Criminals come across at will and form gangs. He was killed with machetes. Machetes, for God's sake. In broad daylight in front of his hotel with people watching. Look at the pictures of his poor wife, covered in her husband's blood. And they got away. They came out of an alley, killed a candidate for United States President, ran back into an alley, and got away. Americans have had enough. The current administration has not fulfilled its most important job, protecting the citizens of the United States from all enemies, foreign and domestic. Instead, they have imported enemies, and this is the result.*

"He's going to run for president," Eve said. "Watch this. I guarantee it. Within five minutes, someone will ask him why he didn't throw his hat in the ring. He'll say something self-serving like he's not a politician. Then he'll be pushed again, and Eisenhower will be brought up as a successful president who was a former general. Watch."

Almost on cue, another panel member said, "You should run, John."

Again, as if planned, Pope said, "Don't be ridiculous. The Iowa caucus starts in five days."

"People know you, John. Come on. Name recognition is everything in politics, and you already have that."

"I'm flattered that you think I should run, but I'm not a politician. I'm not a gladhander."

Another panel member said, "Clearly, a 'gladhander' is not what the country needs, John."

Fifteen minutes later, Eve's cellphone announced she had a Facetime call coming in. It was Henry Gore. Henry doesn't believe in preliminaries. He launched right in: "John Pope. Can you believe it? That asshole is going to run, and he's going to be the Republican candidate for president, and he stands a damn good chance of winning the election."

Eve answered, "We know, we were just watching him on Fox."

"Frank there? Hi, Frank."

"Hi, Henry."

With my presence acknowledged, Henry continued. "Watch. With Perez out of the way, Tweedledee and Tweedledum are launching polls tonight and including Pope in the mix. One or both of them will drop out before Iowa. My bet's on Paxton. His 'unlikables' are in the stratosphere. Perez was going to crush him in the debate. Everyone knew that. That leaves the preacher, Manning. He'll drop out after Iowa if he doesn't croak before then."

Eve said, "Do you think Pope can put together a campaign in Iowa? He's only got four days."

"Come on. He's our new savior. He's going to get Perez's money and Olson's. Watch. Olson's going to endorse him tomorrow. You can bet she'll do some bartering. My guess is V.P. What a ticket. A retired general who has medals up the yin-yang and a Wild West female governor who is a great campaigner. She won in a landslide in her last election."

I butted in. "So, you think Pope can pull it off?"

"No question. Olson built a decent ground game in Iowa before she dropped out. She'll shift that over to Pope. He'll come out of Iowa with the party completely behind him."

"He's a right wing…" I started to say.

"Dictator wannabe. No shit. You can kiss the Constitution goodbye if he wins."

"That bad?" I asked.

"Worse. He makes Perez look like a liberal boy scout."

***

At Camp Liberty, Gordon McKnight knew the call would come. He sat in his office, waiting. The television set had been on all day. He had started watching CNN at eight in the morning. He had breakfast in front of the television. When the first news of the assassination was broadcast, he switched channels to see how all the major networks covered the news. He finally settled in on Fox News. An hour later, Stark called, "We've left the barn, and I'm heading home. Mark and Lenny are on their way back to Sparta. They're taking back roads, as we discussed. You should see them around four or five this afternoon. From what they told me, there were no problems. They were surprised with the amount of blood, but that was it."

"Good. I'll see you next Monday. Enjoy your time at home."

McKnight returned to watching television. It wasn't long before news organizations started to push the New Hampshire State Police to release the surveillance video covering the front of the hotel. The police said they would not do so because it was an ongoing investigation. They did not report that the FBI was now in charge of the investigation and had ordered them not to release the video.

Reporters from the various news organizations interviewed everyone they could find who was in Manchester that morning and within a block or two of the event. Their producers kept pushing them to add local color to the repetitive reports they generated to keep viewers interested. They told their reporters to spread the word they were willing to pay for any still or video images that anyone had of before, during, or after the assassination.

Biographical clips from Perez's public and private life began appearing on all the networks. Video archives were plumbed, and editors got busy creating extended tributes to the "fallen hero."

Lunchtime came and went. Gordon was anxious that he had not heard from his brother. This was precisely what "The Committee" had wanted. Why wasn't Doug calling with a well-deserved "attaboy?" The Defenders were taking all the risks. Where was the fucking credit?

When Mark and Lenny arrived, it was four in the afternoon. Gordon heard their vehicle enter the compound, opened the door, and waited for them on the small porch. As they approached, he waved at the two of them to come in. He left the door open for them and went to a file cabinet behind the desk. He opened the bottom drawer and took out a bottle of Maker's Mark Kentucky Bourbon. There were already three glasses on the desk.

When the two younger men entered, Gordon said, "Have a seat, you guys." Holding up the bottle, he said, "The good stuff. You earned it. Want some?"

Lenny said, "Damn straight."

Mark nodded his agreement.

Gordon poured drinks for the three of them. "Here's to a job well done." He offered his glass in a toast, and the three clinked glasses.

"I want you to tell me all about it. Every detail, but before you do, sit down. Take a few minutes to watch this." Gordon went over and turned the sound up on the television. "This is the biggest story of the day, the month, maybe the whole fucking year." Gordon changed channels, going from one to another. "See what I mean. Look at this. You changed history today. This is what we mean by taking back America. You two did this. You should be proud of yourselves. I talked to Barry. He said it went off without a hitch. Congratulations."

Lenny said, "Thanks."

Mark took a long drink of his bourbon.

189

The three of them watched television for twenty minutes. Gordon provided a running commentary on what the news organizations were reporting. He covered the biographical pieces of Perez, the descriptions of Mara Salvatrucha, and how certain everyone was that MS-13 was responsible for the "tragedy." He had recorded the panel discussion with Pope and played it for them. He also told him that several commentators had wondered if Pope would now enter the race.

When dinnertime came, Gordon said, "Why don't you guys go get something to eat? I'm going to hang out here. I'm waiting for a call. I'll have the kitchen bring me over a plate. I'll see you guys in the morning. Remember, this is a closed mission. Even though it's over as far as you two are concerned, you're not to discuss it with the others. There will probably be a lot of guessing going on. Just ignore it. Got it?"

They both nodded they understood.

After they left, Gordon called the kitchen phone and told them to make up a meal and bring it over with some ice and seltzer. He turned the television set to Fox News and settled in behind his desk.

One of the Defenders on kitchen duty delivered everything requested then left.

Gordon became anxious waiting for Doug's telephone call. He began to wonder if something had gone wrong. Had The Committee or one of its members been compromised? Why the hell hadn't Doug called? Finally, at nine o'clock the phone rang. "Where've you been? I expected to hear from you before now?" Gordon challenged his brother.

"Relax. We've been working our asses off getting a presidential campaign off the ground. What did you think we'd be doing? Twiddling our thumbs?"

"No. I just…"

"You guys did great. That what you want to hear? Job well done? Mission accomplished?"

"Yeah. Something like that."

"Well, you did. So, take it easy. You been watching the news?"

"Of course. All day."

"Good. Be sure to watch tomorrow morning – ten o'clock."

"Okay. What's happening?"

"Sidney Paxton will announce he is ending his campaign. Ten minutes later Josh Whitman will announce he's forming the committee to elect General John Pope, President of the United States. He will also announce that Governor Mary Olson will co-chair the committee."

"That quick?"

"Has to be. We only have four days."

"What about Pope?"

"He's traveling to Abilene as we speak. At noon tomorrow, he will hold a press conference in front of his boyhood home to announce his candidacy. Wife, children, grandchildren. The whole bit. He will then fly to Iowa City to meet with Olson's team there to start his campaign."

"I know this was the plan, but I've been listening to the news all day. A lot of the talking heads say he's going to run but that it's not realistic for him to do anything in Iowa. Maybe New Hampshire, but not Iowa."

"Bullshit! Perez was the only one who was competitive. We already got several of Paxton's big supporters to get him to drop out. Olson's supporters will go to Pope. They'd never go to Manning. Plus, she's got a good ground game in Iowa, and with the caucuses, that's critical. They have four days. Look who he's going to be competing against. Manning. Who the fuck wants an old bible-thumping has been when the country is in chaos? Pope will come out of Iowa not as the leading candidate but as the only candidate."

"You're sure?"

"Absolutely"

"What does Pope know about…?

"Nothing. Nothing at all. He's outraged that MS-13 assassinated Perez in broad daylight. He wants them brought to justice. He wants to round them all up, cut their balls off, stuff them in their mouths, and ship them back to El Salvador."

***

191

Luke was in class when his brother used all of his strength to cut into Juan Perez's head with his machete. Luke didn't see the blood flow onto Mark's hands and arms. He didn't hear Mark call out *"¡Apúrate! ¡Apúrate!"* to Lenny or see him leave his machete behind and run into the alley and jump into the back of the pickup truck driven by Barry Stark.

Luke was busily engaged in a class discussion of Kant's Categorical Imperative. He was taking the position that the presence of emotion in all human beings made the rationality called for in the Categorical Imperative a fantasy. He thought the idea of a common morality based on reason was absurd and that contemporary history was empirical proof of the fallacy in Kant's position.

The professor, a retired philosophy professor from Boston College who worked at Fairfield University as an adjunct, had heard the debate throughout years of teaching undergraduates. He said little until the temperature of the discussion began to rise, at which point he suggested that the participants state the positions of those with whom they were arguing. "Are you listening, or are you preparing your rebuttals?" That usually brought a respite from the "I am right and you are wrong" approach that the students were deploying – at least for a little while.

After class, Luke hurried to the library to meet Gwen in the café before his next class.

She saw him enter and left the table where she sat with two other people. She motioned to a free table, and Luke joined her there.

"Did you hear about Perez?" Gwen asked.

"Who?"

"Jesus, Luke. Juan Perez. Candidate for president. Republican Juan Perez."

"What about him?"

"He was assassinated this morning. It's all over the news."

"I had class."

"Some gang from Florida did it – with machetes. It's crazy. It's all over the news. Can you believe it? They practically chopped his head off. Right in front of his wife. Yuck."

"For real?"

"Just happened 'bout an hour ago. I'll bring it up." Gwen opened her iPad, went to CNN, and started the streaming news. The two of them watched for about five minutes before Gwen said, "Enough. It's horrible what they did to him – that poor woman standing right next to him."

Luke didn't say anything.

"Say something. Why are you being so quiet?"

"They have any pictures of the guys who did it?"

"They wore ski masks."

"Yeah, but do they have any pictures of them?"

"There was a security camera in front of the hotel, but they're not releasing the footage. Why?"

"Just wondering?"

"Why?"

"Nothing?"

"Luke?"

"What?"

Chapter Eighteen: A New Mission

On the day after the assassination of Juan Perez, the FBI released the security tape from the front of the Manchester Hotel. The actual slashing of the candidate was grayed out at the widow's request. The FBI's primary interest was in ascertaining if there was anything about the clothing or the size or movements of the men that might help with identification. The FBI said that because the men were fully clothed and wore gloves and masks, there were no DNA or fingerprint forensics to help identify them. They also reported, for the first time, that there was a video of the event recorded by a young woman standing opposite the entrance to the hotel. Hoping to glimpse the candidate and his wife, she started her phone camera as the two cars approached the hotel and recorded for ten minutes. Although the vehicles blocked her view of the actual assassination, she did record the shouts of the two men as they left the scene, as well as the two of them running towards the alley next to the hotel.

Watching the morning news in Washington, D.C., Douglas McKnight was comfortable with everything he saw and heard for five minutes. Then it all changed. He shouted, "Fuck!" which brought his wife into the living room.

"What's wrong," she asked.

"Nothing. I just realized I forgot to do something yesterday, and it's due today."

"When she left the room, Doug picked up his cell phone, went out onto the balcony of their condominium overlooking the Potomac, and called his brother in Maine.

Gordon picked up on the first ring. He knew the call would be coming. "Accents!" Doug whispered into the phone, concerned that his wife might open the door and overhear his conversation. "Fucking American accents. The FBI is now saying it may not have been Salvadorans after all. They're also talking about the size of one of the assassins. Too big for a Salvadoran. How big is a fucking Salvadoran? They've determined one of the men was six-foot-three. Are you fucking kidding me? Didn't you think about that? And accents. I thought you had these guys trained. Highly trained. Those are your words. They only said a few goddamned words, and they couldn't get that right."

"Take it easy," Gordon replied. "They're just speculating. There's nothing definitive."

"Stop it. The MS-13 is continuing to say they had nothing to do with it, and even the Ambassador from El Salvador is protesting that these were not Salvadorans, as anyone who heard the shouts would know. You've got to do something."

"What do you want me to do?"

"Get rid of them."

"Who?"

"That team."

"What are you saying?"

"Think about it. If this goes south and something happens with the governor and her husband, they can also talk about this goddamn giant who assaulted them in their fucking bedroom."

"Not going to happen. They're too scared."

"You've got to get rid of them."

"What are you suggesting? That I kill them? I'm not going to do that. So, stop it. None of this is going to make any difference. You heard what they said. No forensics. Nothing. They've got absolutely nothing."

"Nothing! You think this is nothing? You've got your head up your ass. It raises questions. There weren't supposed to be any questions."

"Okay. I get it. So, what do you want me to do? I'm not going to shoot my own men. You need to get clear about that."

195

"I know, I know. Something else has come up that may help. We may have another job for the Defenders. For now, consider it a possibility."

"What?"

"Easy. Take it easy. We'd need all your men on this."

"Everybody? What the hell is it?"

"Pope's going to decline Secret Service protection during the primaries. Once he gets the nomination, he may consider it."

"He's going to do what?"

"You heard me. He's going to decline Secret Service protection. Instead, he wants to be guarded by 'true Americans' who care about the country. He wants people he can count on. He doesn't trust the Secret Service. He wants his own people."

"Whose idea was this?"

"Nat Darlan originally, but everyone on The Committee thinks it's a great idea. I suggested The Defenders. Everyone agreed. You in?"

"Wait a minute. I thought you said it was just a possibility."

"Well, it is until you say yes."

"Jesus, Doug. Stop with the fucking mind games."

"Well?"

"You're kidding? Be the protection detail for Pope? Sure, but we need time to train people."

"There's no time. You have to send people out to Iowa today. This time I want you to go. Make sure no one fucks up. Recruit from some other groups if you have to."

"Like?"

"I don't know. American Warriors. Groups that helped you out in Montana."

"Are you kidding? We'd need people who are disciplined. Not just any..."

"Fine. You figure it out. Nat also had an idea about uniforms."

"Uniforms?" Gordon asked. "The Secret Service doesn't..."

"No shit. Simple. Off the shelf. Your guys already wear camo around the camp."

"Hunting camo, yeah."

"Doesn't matter. They won't look like fucking civilians."

Still wrestling with the idea of being Pope's protection team, Gordon asked, "What about things like gun permits and…"

"Given what's just happened and the mood of the country, do you think anyone is going to give a shit?"

"I don't know."

"Assault rifles and side arms. Both."

"And you're not worried about open carry?"

"We have lawyers who will take care of permits where we need them. In Iowa, it won't be an issue anyway, and we'll clear it up ahead of time in New Hampshire. So? Can I count on you?" Doug asked.

"Yeah. Sure."

"This time, no fuckups. Just get it done. Oh, and don't bring the team from the Perez hit. That's all we'd need. You understand. I don't want those fuck ups anywhere near this."

"Okay. Okay. They don't go."

"You'll be coordinating with Olin Matthews."

"Who's that?"

"As of two hours ago, he's Pope's campaign manager. He's been briefed about this and will make a statement to the press in an hour describing how security will be handled for the Pope campaign."

"We'll need money. How will we get…"

"You will bill the campaign for security services. You can start paying your guys the same salaries they'd make if they worked for a private security firm."

"They'll like that. How much?"

"Do I have to do everything for you, Gordon? Go online and fucking look it up."

"Alright. You don't have to shout."

"Can you handle this or should we give it to one of the other groups?"

"I'll handle it. I just hadn't expected it."

"And you take the lead. Have Stark stay behind with the other two."

"Yeah. I'll leave Barry Stark in charge."

"Oh, after the fuck up in Manchester, that's not very comforting."

"All right. Enough."

"Anything about the barn and the fire?"

"Nope. Just on the local radio station. Blaming the fire on faulty wiring and improper storage of gasoline. No investigation."

"That's it. No investigation."

"Volunteer fire department. And get this: the owner said nothing about the truck. Can you believe it? My guess is he wants the insurance and doesn't want to make any waves. Probably trying to collect on the truck that wasn't his as well as the fucking barn."

"How the hell can he do that? He doesn't have any paper on the truck?"

"No shit."

***

Everything went as scheduled. At noon in Abilene, Texas, General John Pope, Ret., declared his candidacy for the president of the United States of America. All of the major news channels were present for the announcement.

Pope, who had a love affair with public speaking and being in front of a camera, was a compelling figure. He used the words "strong" and "strength" twenty-two times throughout his fifteen-minute declaration. The other dominant constructions were "take back" and "return."

When he finished, he was swarmed by reporters. The only answers he gave to their questions were that Olin Matthews was to be his campaign manager and all of his focus was on winning the approval of the people of Iowa. He promised the reporters that he would answer questions over the next four days, but right now, he had to get on an airplane and fly to Iowa City to introduce himself to "the fine State of Iowa." No, he was not worried about security. His campaign manager would explain why.

When Pope got in the car waiting for him, reporters turned their attention to Matthews. The reporter from Fox News asked, "Given the assassination of Juan Perez, is General Pope afraid that somebody or some group will try to get him?"

The response surprised the reporters. Matthews reached into his pocket and withdrew a prepared statement:

> *Of course, we are concerned about the general's welfare. The violence in the United States is something that all Americans are concerned about, which is the reason the general is entering the race. He wants to bring an end to fear and violence in America. During the campaign, we will not rely on the Secret Service for protection. As we have seen time and again, they are incompetent. Think of all of the presidents who have been killed or shot. Kennedy. Ronald Reagan. And then candidates like Richard Buzhardt. Rather than protecting Obama, the Secret Service was off getting drunk and whoring. Seven times during the Obama Administration, they failed. No, we are hiring our own security. Patriots, not bureaucrats. Men and women who understand what it means to protect the future leader of the free world. Men and women who have served their country before and are choosing to do so again.*

"Who are these people?" shouted a reporter from the *New York Post*.

"They will be drawn from various patriotic groups that already exist. Members of a Maine group, The Defenders of Liberty, are already on their way to Iowa."

Chapter Nineteen: Worlds Collapsing

I hate paperwork and money. I like having enough money so I don't have to worry about it, but I hate thinking about it. But that's what I was doing Thursday afternoon. When I arrived at the office Thursday morning, Vicki DeRosa and Irene Kenen cornered me.

"Frank, we have to do this," Vicki insisted. "I'm new at this, and I need you and Irene to go through these end-of-year numbers with me so I understand what they mean."

"I'm sure Irene can help you more than I can," I answered.

Vicki has a look. It is a practiced look honed in years of getting her way from her father and probably her mother. It's hard to describe, and I am not sure anyone else could duplicate it in quite the same way. It says, "I am right. You know I am right. So why are we playing this game?" I got "the look."

"Okay," I relented. "This afternoon. Right after lunch. That work?"

"One o'clock. Conference room."

Of course, I was late, but I did show up. We spent two hours reviewing Irene's 2023 reports and projections for 2024. Financially, we were in excellent shape, and since this was Irene's first time doing this as our Chief Financial Officer, she went into exquisite detail. She was determined that Vicki and I would be knowledgeable, responsible managers. Her task with Vicki was much easier than it was with me. But I nodded 'I understood' at appropriate times, which seemed sufficient.

Vicki had been reviewing our sales tax policies and had a question. The State of Connecticut taxes everything it can lay its hands on. Vicki was wondering about 12-407, which states some of the services that must charge sales tax to its clients. It reads:

> *Private investigation, protection, patrol work, watchman, and armored car services, exclusive of these services provided by off-duty police officers and firefighters. Sales of coin and currency services provided to a financial services company by or through another financial services company are excluded from taxable private investigation, protection, patrol work, watchman, and armored car services;*

"I don't understand that second sentence," Vicki said. "When we provide security for a bank, do we charge them sales tax? We have been, but should we?"

Eve called as Irene began an explanation. The timing was perfect. I left the conference room and went to my office. Eve asked, "Have you been listening to the news?"

"No. I'm in a meeting with Vicki and Irene about money."

"Lucky you. Well, hold on to your hat. Pope just announced."

"Yeah. We knew that was coming."

"Olin Matthews is now the campaign manager."

"Who's that?"

"He's done other far-right campaigns, but that's not why I'm calling."

"Okay. You're burying the lead."

"Creating suspense."

"Okay, I'm suspended."

"Pope is refusing Secret Service protection and will use private security groups."

"You're not suggesting Nutmeg apply to protect this clown?"

"No. No."

"So?"

"He announced who they're hiring."

"Who?"

"Hold on tight."

"Come on."

"The Defenders of Liberty of Sparta, Maine."

"Oh, fuck. Are they out of their minds?"

"I'm just reporting," Eve said. "According to Matthews, they want patriots they can count on."

"You mean Brownshirts. God damned stormtroopers."

"Exactly. Pope is taking militias mainstream. He's making them a legitimate part of American society."

"Hitler. 1920s."

"Yep. Brownshirts? Weren't they the security people at Hitler's rallies?"

"Yes. And they beat the shit out of anybody who questioned the Fuhrer. Someone's going to get hurt."

"Lots of people are going to get hurt."

***

It didn't take Luke long to conclude that his brother was an assassin. It wasn't just Luke's memory of the red 'M' on the calendar in Gordon McKnight's office. It was watching over and over again the images of the assassins killing Juan Perez and then running away.

Luke knew his brother. He knew how he moved, how he ran, how he swung his arms when he ran, almost like he was climbing a rope as fast as he could. Mark pumped his arms when he ran. It was the arms. Luke didn't know anyone else who ran that way. Luke had played enough touch football games with his brother, chased after him when Mark had squirted him with a hose, and watched him run bases during baseball games to know his brother's run. He used to tease Mark, "You look like a weirdo when you run."

Then there was the conversation with Mark at Camp Liberty. His intensity about taking America back. How crazy he sounded. And the 'M' on the calendar. The goddamn "M" on the calendar. Luke was sure, absolutely sure. He was less sure what he should do. He didn't want to voice his beliefs to his parents. "What are they going to do?" he asked Gwen on the phone that night. "Dad'll deny it and say I'm just causing trouble. Mom'll be upset and start crying."

"You're right," Gwen replied. "You're sure about this? No possibility you're just reading into this because of what happened when you were at the camp?"

"I'm sure. Mark was one of those guys. He's lost it. Totally lost it."

"So, what are you going to do?"

"I've got to get him out of there."

"How? And where would he go?"

"Maybe he can go to Canada. Get out of the country."

"Canada? He can't go to Canada. He could get extradited from there."

"You're right."

"Luke, he hasn't been accused of anything. You're probably the only one in the whole world that thinks he did it."

"Not think. Know."

"Okay. You know. But you're still the only one. Why not wait and see what happens?"

"Because by then, it could be too late. I have to do something now. The safest thing is for him to disappear."

"Oh god, Luke. Can't you just stay out of it?"

"No. I've got to get him out of the country."

"Damn it, Luke. Oh shit. Give me a few minutes. I'll call you right back."

"What are you going to do?"

"Just give me a minute, will you? I'll call you right back. Promise." Gwen hung up.

Fifteen minutes later, Gwen called.

Luke started questioning her. "You didn't talk to someone, did you?"

"No. Of course not. Take it easy. I was doing some research. If you're dead serious about this, Ecuador has no extradition treaty with the U.S.

It's also pretty easy to set up citizenship. Mark wouldn't need a visa to get in, and applying for a visa once you're there sounds easy. Even citizenship isn't hard to get. But this is crazy. You know that. If you helped him, you would be an accessory to murder. Luke, you need to stop and think this through. Please. You don't know for sure Mark has done anything wrong."

"I do. For Christ's sake, Gwen. I know my own fucking brother."

"Stop it. I'm not your enemy. But you're sounding as crazy as you say he is."

"I'm not crazy. You've got to trust me on this. I know him. I saw the calendar. I know what he looks like when he's running."

"Please. Just don't do anything tonight. Please. Just sleep on it. Promise me?"

"Okay. I won't do anything tonight. But I want to learn more about Ecuador."

"Sure. But don't do anything."

"Okay."

At nine o'clock, Gwen called Luke. When he answered, Luke asked, "You checking on me?"

"No. I have news for you."

"What?"

"I was just going over my news alerts. Mark's group. You know, the Defenders of Liberty are going to be protecting Pope rather than the Secret Service. See. Maybe Mark was telling you the truth. All they're doing is training people and protecting big shots, just like he told you. Maybe you don't have anything to worry about."

"Unless this is all a big setup."

"What are you talking about?"

"They get rid of Perez so Pope can become president. Then they act like the good guys and protect Pope."

"Luke. You nuts? You're sounding like your brother. Do you honestly believe John Pope would have Perez killed to get him out of the way?"

"And inflame the country so he can ride in on a white horse? Why not? These people are crazy, Gwen. They're certifiable. I wouldn't put anything past them."

"You sound like a conspiracy nut. You know that, don't you?"

"If you had heard Mark, you wouldn't be saying that."

"I'm going to bed. You should do the same."

When they got off the phone, Luke started going through his emails and found the news alerts that Gwen had referenced. He opened them up and started reading. He also reviewed the download he had created of the assassination video. He was more certain than ever that there was a conspiracy and that his brother was caught up in the middle of it.

Next, he turned to information about Ecuador. He read official documents posted by the Ecuadorian government about visas and citizenship. He also looked at flight schedules out of Boston to Ecuador. Finally, he took a look at his credit card status. Yes, he could afford to buy a one-way ticket for Mark, if only Mark were willing. At one o'clock in the morning, he turned his computer off and tried to get to sleep.

He couldn't. Luke got up and went into his brother's room as quietly as he could. He was anxious about waking his parents and having them wonder why he was in Mark's room.

He went into Mark's closet and found his brother's big duffle bag from when he was in the army. He put the empty bag on Mark's bed, opened it, and started going through Mark's drawers, taking clothes out and putting them in the duffle. He knew Mark had only brought enough clothes with him for a weekend when he left for Portland.

Luke found Mark's passport in the drawer of the end table next to the bed. He slipped it into his back pocket. He kept thinking, "What will he need? I can't forget anything." He went over to Mark's desk, the one he had had since high school, and pulled out the drawer with files in it. There was a file named papers. Luke took it out and looked inside: discharge from the army, high school diploma, social security documents with the card missing – he must carry it with him. He'd have his driver's license and credit cards. What else would he have in his wallet?

When he was sure he had everything his brother would need, Luke turned off the light in the bedroom, picked up the duffle, and carried it downstairs and into the kitchen, trying to do so without making any noise. He didn't want to talk to his parents. Not tonight. No arguments. No explanations.

He put on his boots and coat, carried the duffle bag out to his car, and shoved it into the back seat. He started his car and backed out of the driveway without putting his lights on until he turned onto the road in front of the house and started heading to Maine. It was three o'clock in the morning. His dad wouldn't be up until six-thirty. When his father saw Luke's car missing, his dad would think Luke had to be at school for some early morning task or that he was meeting up with Gwen for some early morning sex. They had done that before.

Luke knew he had a five-hour drive ahead of him. He had no idea, yet what he would do when he reached Camp Liberty. He planned to stop in Portsmouth to call Gwen and let her know his plan to get Mark off to Ecuador. He'd text his mother and tell her he had a long day at school.

United Airlines had a 1:30 flight out of Logan Airport in Boston. If Mark didn't give him any crap, there was enough time to drive to Sparta, get Mark, and make it back to Logan in time for the flight. They would just make it. It was a strange flight. Mark would fly West to Houston, connecting to the flight to Quito. Luke called United from his car and learned there were available seats on both legs of the flight. He asked if he could buy a ticket at the last minute and was assured that it would not be a problem.

There was no traffic on the roads. Commuters were still asleep, and the long-haul truck drivers drove at a dependable speed of five to ten miles an hour over the speed limit. His drive would take him up to Hartford, then northeast across Connecticut into Massachusetts. Continuing, he would join Route 95 into New Hampshire. It gave him enough time to come up with a plan. Two hours later, he had one.

He would get into the camp by saying he knew Mark didn't have enough clothes with him and he had seen on the news that the Defenders would be protecting General Pope. Mark would need his passport for airports. He was sure his story was good enough to get him into see his brother. He was hoping Mark was still in Sparta and not out in Iowa. He had a hard time imagining that they would have sent Mark and the other assassin out to act like the Secret Service for Pope. That would be absurd.

In Portsmouth, New Hampshire, he left the interstate and pulled into the Circle Diner to call Gwen and get coffee and something to eat. The lack of sleep started getting to him, and he fought to stay awake. When he finished eating and was nursing his third cup of coffee, he called her.

It was six-thirty in the morning, and Gwen was awake. "You're up early," she said.

"Yeah. Been up for a while."

"Couldn't sleep?"

"Something like that."

"What do you mean?"

"I'm in Portsmouth."

"You're where?"

"Portsmouth. New Hampshire. Going to Sparta to get Mark and put him on a plane to Ecuador."

"Luke. That's crazy. Don't be silly. Come on home. Turn around and come back now. If you're right about Mark, these people are dangerous, and you're just going to get hurt. It'll be worse than last time. Please. Just come home."

"No. I've thought it through. I just wanted you to know what I was doing so you didn't worry when I didn't show up at school."

"Didn't worry? Are you out of your mind? Don't do this. It's illegal. You're breaking the law. Stop it now."

"No. I've got to get him out of there."

"Where are you now?

"I told you. Portsmouth."

"No, I mean, where in Portsmouth?"

"The diner. You know. The one at the circle right off 95."

"Stay there. I'm going to call your parents. You've got to talk to them before you do anything."

"No. I'm doing this."

"Okay, okay. Look. Wait then. Stay there. I'm going to drive up. We'll do this together. I want to go with you. It'll be safer if there are two of us."

"No way. You can't get involved in this."

"Then please call your parents. Maybe they'll go with you."

"There's no time. He's got to get out of there now. I've got to get going or I won't be able to get him on that flight."

"What flight?"

"To Ecuador. I found a flight he can get on today."

"Oh, God. Please, Luke. Slow down. You're not thinking this through."

"No. I've got to go. I'll talk to you from Boston after I get him on the plane."

"Luke. Please."

"Love you." Luke hit the off button on his cell phone.

Gwen thought for a couple of minutes and then called Luke's parents. Her call went to voicemail.

Chapter Twenty: Closed For The Season

Luke made the drive from Portsmouth to Sparta without incident. Text messages from his parents and Gwen went unanswered, and their telephone calls went to voicemail. He rehearsed what he would say to any member of the Defenders he encountered and what he would say to his brother. By the time he entered the dirt road into Camp Liberty, he felt prepared and confident that his plan would work.

It was almost nine when he reached the camp's gate. The gate was shut, there was no guard, and a hand-lettered sign said, 'Closed for the Season.' Surprised, Luke got out of the car, walked over to the gate, released the latch, pushed it open, returned to his car, and drove through. He wondered what was going on. Had everybody left?

He drove the rest of the way into the camp and parked in front of the office where he had first met Gordon McKnight. As he got out of his car, the office door opened, and Barry Stark came out onto the porch. "Didn't you see the sign? We're closed."

"Yeah, I did. Hi. I'm Luke Perry. My brother works here, Mark Perry. I've got clothes and stuff for him."

"He's not here. Turn around and leave. I told you, we're closed."

"Gees. I drove all the way up here from Connecticut. Did he go to Iowa? Look, I've got his passport and some other papers he may need besides his clothes. Can I at least drop them off in his cabin or something?"

"I told you. He's not here. Now get going."

"Can I at least give them to you?"

Barry Stark thought for a minute before saying, "Look, I have no idea when he'll be back, but if you want to leave the stuff here, you can leave it here on the porch. I'll hold on to it for him."

There was something about how Stark said it that Luke didn't trust. "I can bring it over to his cabin. No problem."

"Cabin's locked up for the rest of the winter. Just leave it here. I'll take care of it."

Mark and Lenny Pratt were having breakfast in the kitchen wing off of the dining hall. With only three left in camp, they were responsible for their own meals and cleaning up. When Lenny heard the car drive past, he went to the window and looked out. "Heh. There's someone here. Take a look."

Mark went over to the window. He saw his brother's car. Then he looked over to the office, where he saw Barry Stark talking to someone. Mark couldn't see his face, but he knew it was Luke. "Oh, fuck. What's he doing here now?"

"Who?" Lenny asked.

"My asshole brother."

"Your brother?"

"Yeah, Luke. That's Luke."

"Stark's not going to be happy."

"No shit. I'd better get out there."

Mark grabbed his jacket, put it on, and started to walk out of the dining hall. Lenny got in his way. "Wait a minute. You sure you want to talk to him? You'd better let Stark handle this. No one's supposed to know we're here."

"I know but…"

"Don't be stupid. Stay here. I can go find out what's going on."

"No. I don't want any trouble like last time," Mark insisted.

"Stark's going to be really pissed."

"No shit."

Mark walked around Lenny, out of the dining room, and headed towards the office.

When Stark saw Mark coming their way, he said to Luke. "Go in the office."

"Let me get the stuff from the car." Luke turned towards the car and saw his brother and another man walking towards them.

"Mark, what the..." He turned around and said to Stark, "What's going on?"

Mark shouted, "I'll handle this. Luke, come with me."

Stark responded, "Oh, no."

"Don't worry, Barry. I've got this." Mark started walking towards his cabin. He turned and said to his brother, "Come with me."

Stark shouted. "No. No. I want you here. Inside. Both of you, get in the office. Now."

"I said I'd handle this."

"And I said get in the office. Now." It was a command.

Mark paused, turned, and started toward the office. Luke followed him without saying anything.

Stark waited until they passed him, then followed them into the office. He nodded at the two chairs facing the desk. "You two sit down. Just sit there and don't get up. I need to make some telephone calls."

He left the office and went back out onto the porch. Lenny was still waiting there. "You stay right here and make sure they don't come out. I'm going around to the back office. I want to hear what they're talking about."

"Got it."

Barry Stark walked behind the building and quietly entered through the back door. The room in the rear of the building had been initially designed as the nurse's office for Camp Nebizun. Gordon McKnight now used the space for files and as a break room since there was a sink and a refrigerator. There was also a small bathroom. The walls between the spaces were thin, single layers of inexpensive pine paneling. Stark walked over to the wall between the two offices. He could easily hear the

211

heated conversation coming from the other side of the wall.

"We've got to go now," Luke said. "There's room on the flight to Ecuador, and we can book it on the drive down."

"I'm not going anywhere."

"Jesus, Mark. Are you crazy? You fuckin' killed a United States Senator. If I could recognize you, others will, too."

"Recognize what?"

"That phony Spanish accent and your run. Your damn run. Don't be stupid. Every FBI agent in the country is working on this. At some point, you and your bunch of crazies are going to get caught, and when you do, you'll get the death penalty."

"No one recognized us."

"If I did, someone else will."

"Who?"

"I don't know. Someone from home. Maybe someone you served with. Someone. They're going to be looking for you."

Barry Stark had heard enough. He burst into the room. "Perry, leave. Go to your cabin and stay there. Now."

Luke got up and started running towards the door. Stark went after him and caught him from behind. He spun him around. "You're not going anywhere. Sit."

"Fuck you," Luke said in almost a whisper and turned away from him.

Stark swung and hit him in the back, right over his right kidney.

Luke screamed in pain and fell to the floor.

Mark started to move towards them.

Stark took a pistol out of his holster and pointed it at Mark. "Don't take another step." He shouted, "Pratt, get in here."

Lenny Pratt came into the office, and Stark told him, "Go get some zip ties and a roll of duct tape from the workroom and bring them back here, and hurry. Go to the armory, too, load up an M4, and bring it with you."

Lenny Pratt left on a run.

Mark shouted at Stark, "What the hell do you think you're doing?"

"Sit down and don't say a word. You're lucky I don't shoot you both." Stark waved his gun toward the two chairs. "Now sit."

Mark helped Luke over to a chair. His brother was crying from the pain. "You're going to be alright. It'll be gone in a couple of minutes. Trust me."

Luke didn't respond.

After he settled his brother in the chair, he sat down in the other one. "What're you going to do," he asked Stark.

"I don't know, but neither of you is going anywhere until I've talked to McKnight. So sit."

When Lenny returned, Stark took the rifle from him and said, "Use the zip ties on both of them. Hands behind the back then tape them to the chairs."

"Both of them?" Pratt asked.

"Yes, both of them."

"Oh, come on. This is stupid," Mark shouted and started to get out of his chair.

Stark walked over behind Luke and pointed the pistol at his head. "Sit your ass down or I will blow your brother's brains all over this office."

Mark sat back down.

"Mark," Luke shouted.

"Shut up. It's going to be okay. Just shut up."

Lenny put the zip ties on both brothers and used the duct tape to fasten their legs and arms to the chairs. When he finished, Stark returned the rifle to Lenny and said, "Stay here with them. I've got to make some calls. No talking. If they start to talk, tape their mouths shut."

"Why don't I just do it?"

"Okay. Do it."

"Blindfolds?"

"Not for now. I'll be back in a couple of minutes."

Stark left the office and walked rapidly to his cabin. Once inside, he called Gordon McKnight. His call went to voicemail, so he texted Gordon with instructions to call him immediately and sent an email with the same message. Attempts to communicate completed, he sat on the side of his bed and started imagining scenarios. None of them led to a desirable outcome. He was sure that Luke had told someone his plan to send Mark to Ecuador. That could be the solution. Send them both. Get them the hell out of the country. Send Lenny with them to make sure they arrived there. Once they got there, maybe an accident occurred, or perhaps a drug shooting in Ecuador. Ecuador had drug gangs. Maybe that would work. They could both be taken care of. He kept going over scenario after scenario. Every one of them had problems. He stopped. It was McKnight's problem, not his. McKnight had hired Mark. McKnight had roughed up the brother last time he was here, not him. Why the hell didn't McKnight get back to him?

***

Luke had been right: His father wasn't concerned when he walked into the kitchen and looked out the window to see if it was raining or snowing and saw his son's car wasn't in the driveway. Jim Perry wasn't thinking about either of his boys as he put coffee and water into the electric *Mr. Coffee* and turned it on. He sat at the kitchen table and watched the dark liquid fill the carafe. He wasn't thinking, just watching and waiting. It was all automatic. Another weekday morning. Nothing special.

When his mobile telephone started to ring, it came as a surprise. It took a couple of rings before it registered with him that it was ringing. He picked the phone up, looked down at the number, and didn't recognize it. Another spam call, he thought. He pushed the button on the side of his phone to silence the ringing and put the phone back on the table.

A minute later, the notification chime went off, telling him he had an incoming text message. He picked the phone up, opened the messages, and read: *It's Gwen. I have to talk to you. Luke is in trouble.*

214

Twenty-One: Preparation

The sun had just come up, and I was taking Blackie for his morning walk. I wondered when the snow would finally melt. It was cold and overcast, but despite the conditions, I tried to convince myself that it would not snow again. Then Anita Perry's call interrupted me

When I first met the Perrys, her husband had done all the talking. Anita had been a background figure to me, almost an 'extra' in the Perry family drama. That changed when we met in my office, and she took the lead, asking me for help in finding someone to de-program her son from the cult of "these terrible people in Maine who have taken over her son."

Now she was crying, trying hard but failing to restrain the tears so she could tell me what she couldn't believe was happening. I kept encouraging her to take her time and slow down. It wasn't working.

"There is no time," she scolded me.

I stopped asking her to do the impossible and just listened. Finally, I told her I had to ask some questions, and she seemed okay with that, barely, but I started asking.

Five minutes later, I had the gist of what she was trying to tell me. Her youngest son, Luke, was convinced her older son, Mark, had "killed that senator up in New Hampshire." Now Luke was driving to Maine to get Mark to fly to Ecuador before Mark got caught by the FBI. Her husband, Jim, had learned Luke's plan from Luke's girlfriend, Gwen, and now, Jim, her husband, had just left to drive to Maine to bring both sons home. He had taken a gun with him. Some kind of rifle. Would I please go to Maine and make sure they were all safe? No, she didn't want to

215

call the police. She knew Mark would never kill anybody, but other people in 'that group' might have. If they had, who knows what they might do to her boys and her husband?

Whenever I suggested she call the sheriff's department, she told me she couldn't. She had promised her husband. When I offered to make the call, she pleaded, "This is my family. Please don't. I don't know who to trust." She seemed to trust me and was clear about what she wanted from me – to bring her family home safe and sound. I didn't ask her, "How the hell am I supposed to do that?" I refrained from saying, "What if Luke's right? What if your son is a murderer? What do you want me to do then?"

Helping Mark Perry avoid the law was not on my preferred list of activities for the day. On the other hand, perhaps he was with the Defenders in Iowa. If Luke was right, this was a group of fanatics; kill one candidate so they can protect another – it felt like theater of the absurd. What a mess. What a colossal, fucked up mess. Why the hell was I thinking about getting in the middle of this? And then there were her tears and pleas. I told her I would think about it and get back to her. That brought on more tears and pleas. I hung up.

I did think about it as I walked back home. Since the assassination, there had been all kinds of theories that ran counter to the initial belief that MS-13 had assassinated the senator. Especially telling was the widow's statement that there was something very strange about the accents of the perpetrators. Then there was MS-13. They denied having anything to do with it – not a very MS-13 kind of behavior, given that they had previously threatened Perez. Why weren't they gloating?

My encounter with Gordon McKnight at Camp Liberty and his lying to me and Heng about Mark's membership in the group troubled me. Were these merely "weirdoes," to use Jackie's word, or were they a far-right extremist group capable of murder? McKnight had pissed me off with his militaristic dismissal of me and Heng and his lies. Could I imagine him leading this group in a plot to take over the presidency through assassination? Was I thinking that? Seriously? Here in the United States of America?

Finally, there was the damned *Militia Manual* that Jackie had given me. According to the manual, violence was acceptable to 'defend liberty.' It was the 'Christian' thing to do.

I called Anita Perry back just before Blackie and I reached our condominium. When Anita answered the phone, I said, "Okay. I'll go to Sparta again, but I want you to understand something. My focus will be on making sure Luke and your husband are safe. If something happens where I wind up believing Mark was involved or knows anything about the assassination, I will be notifying law enforcement. Those are my ground rules. There's no negotiation about them. Do you still want me to go?"

She paused, but not for long. "Yes. I understand. Thank you. I know Mark had nothing to do with what happened. Thank you."

"I need something from you. I want to know about both Luke's car and Jim's. What kind of cars are they driving, and what are their license plate numbers?"

"I don't know their license plate numbers. Jim is driving a Ford. He always bought Fords. It's a four-door, and it's a kind of gray. Luke has an old Toyota. I think it's a Corolla. It's light green. Would the license plate numbers be on the insurance papers? I can look for those."

"Yes. They should be. Call me back when you find them."

"I'll go look for them right now."

"Good. Okay. I'll stay in touch. You do the same. If you hear from anyone, call me right away. Okay?"

"Yes. I will."

Then my doubts started – again. What was I getting myself into? Why not just call the sheriff's office and let them handle it? I had committed myself, though, to a terrified woman who was worried about her family. I tried to imagine what she must be going through. One son was convinced that the other son was a murderer and wanted to send him out of the country where he could avoid extradition. Her husband and her youngest son were heading into a nest of what? A bunch of losers playing dress up or a disciplined militia plotting to hijack of the government of the United States of America?

217

If I was going to do this, I was not going alone. It was now seven-thirty, and I knew Vicki would be up. I called her and described my conversation with Anita Perry.

"What are you going to do? No. You're going, aren't you?"

"Yes."

"You're not going to go alone this time, I hope."

"No. That's why I'm calling."

"Okay. Who do you want to bring with you? I think I already probably know."

"Probably. Pat, Butch, and Jackie."

"Of course. You know I might be able to help."

"No. First, your parents would kill me. Second, you need to stay in New Haven and mind the shop. You okay with my pulling those three offline? They all report to you."

"Of course. What about the law? FBI, sheriff's office. You know..."

"This could get very messy. I know."

"And even get you arrested."

"Honestly, I'm hoping no one's home when we get there."

"That's going to be your excuse?"

"Well? Why not? It was all over the news. The Defenders are out in Iowa defending General Pope."

"Good luck with that. Just stay safe. Have you talked to Eve about this?"

"Not yet."

"That may be scarier."

"I know."

"Be careful."

"We will."

After I got off the call, I texted Jackie, Pat Brady, and Butch Stofani and told them to get ready for a road trip. My explanation of where we were going and why was cryptic. I asked Jackie and Pat to go to our warehouse in Bridgeport and get the van, communications equipment, and anything else they thought we might need. I added, "Pat, this is an armed encampment. I have no idea what's going on there. I trust your judgment about what to bring." I simply asked Butch to meet us there. I told the three of them to be ready to leave in an hour. Jackie didn't like my cryptic reason for going. She texted me right back, "What's up?"

"The Defenders in Maine situation. The whole Perry family's gotten involved and are there or on their way there. The mother asked to get them home safe and sound."

Butch texted, "Law enforcement?"

I answered, "Not yet. May not be needed."

Pat texted, "Extraction? How heavy?"

It was a military term: 'Extraction.' I hadn't been thinking of it that way. But that might be what we were about to do. I didn't know how to respond specifically, so I answered, "I hope we won't need anything, but I want to be ready."

Bringing the three of them felt like overkill to me, but I was in a 'better safe than sorry' mode, and I knew having them with me would make my trip to Sparta an easier sell to Eve. I also felt safer with these three than if I was going alone.

I had worked with Butch Stofani before, when we were hired to protect the son of a Turkish diplomat who was studying law in New Haven. I had gotten to know him well and had a great deal of respect for his common sense and skills. Whenever Nutmeg had a protection assignment, Butch was in charge. He had been part of the governor's protection detail for the Connecticut State Police before he retired at the grand old age of forty-five. Sam had started recruiting him a year before the retirement, and Butch was only too glad to make the change to the private sector. He was not a fan of the governor. Quiet, unassuming, Butch seemed at times to slip into a deceptive everyman countenance. Son of a Cuban mother and an Italian father, people were stumped guessing at his ethnicity. He was average in build, height, weight, and any other item on a physician's chart.

As a firm that often provided security services for large gatherings of important people, Nutmeg had specialized communications equipment that was not unlike what was used by law enforcement agencies. Our founder, and until a few months ago CEO, Sam DeRosa, would say our equipment was significantly better. What was also unique about Nutmeg was our cache of a wide variety of weapons. Eve asked me once why we needed them. The only answer I could come up with was, "Because Sam wants them." I thought of Sam as a hobbyist when it came to firearms. He would reject that nomenclature. "I'm prepared," he would argue.

His partner in this endeavor was Pat Brady, one of Nutmeg's first hires. Sam used to say Pat was a cross between John Wayne and Sylvester Stallone – Rooster Cogburn meets Rambo. Pat knew firearms, practiced with firearms, repaired firearms, and was an excellent shot. His Special Forces background was not unlike that of Mark Perry. He was just older and wiser. Where Butch could disappear into a crowd without notice, you always knew when Pat was present. Everything about him was triple X in size, from his voice to his neck and shoulders.

Texts completed and arrangements made, now I had to face Eve. I dreaded that conversation. I was right to do so.

"A paper cut. Remember? You said that's the biggest danger of being a private detective. You might get a paper cut."

"I know. I did say that."

"And now this. You're walking into the camp of an armed militia that may have assassinated a United States Senator, and you're going to try to get the assassin's family members to leave with you when they're trying to get the assassin out of the country. Do I understand all of this correctly? Am I missing anything?"

"No. Well, there are a couple of things. There may be no one there. They may all be in Iowa. And we don't really know for sure that Mark Perry had anything to do with Perez's murder."

"Jesus, Frank."

"Yeah. I know."

"Do you? Do you really?"

"I'm not going alone. Butch and Pat will be with me. Jackie, too."

"What will Jackie do, throw a computer at someone? Pat and Jackie were with you when you got shot. Remember. You still got shot."

"Chances are there's no one there and it will be a wasted trip. The only reason I'm taking them is…"

"So I'll feel better? Don't you dare go there. I know you better."

"You're right. I'm being cautious. If you could have heard Anita Perry, though, you would be making the same decision. I'm sure of it."

"Oh, just go. I know I can't talk you out of it. Just go. Be careful and have Jackie ready to call in the cavalry if something doesn't feel right."

"I will. I promise. Although I'm not sure who the cavalry is up there.

"Whatever it is there. Promise?"

"Promise."

With that, Eve knelt next to Blackie, who was standing next to me and started talking to my dog. I knew, then, how much trouble I was in. She said, "Take care of him Blackie. Take care of this idiot like you did last time. I want him home in one piece. Okay?" She gave Blackie a hug, and he licked her face, which had tears on it.

***

As I drove away, I wondered whether she would still be there when I returned. Sure she would. She understood. I kept telling myself that as I drove to the warehouse to meet the others.

Bridgeport, Connecticut had once been an industrial town with many large brick buildings that housed machinery and people who made everything from waffle irons to 'Tommy' guns and bullets. By the 1990s, companies had left the city, and many of the buildings were torn down. The remaining ones were repurposed and often included several organizations under one roof. A regional center for the arts occupied a section of one building and drew students from around Fairfield County to study everything from dance to jazz.

Some of the buildings were used for storage, and that is how Sam DeRosa came to rent several thousand square feet on the ground floor of one of the existing brick buildings. Always the entrepreneur, he then sub-let space to different entrepreneurs trying to get their dreams going.

The space Sam and Meg kept for Nutmeg functioned as the attic for both their personal goods and those of Nutmeg Security and Investigation. By the time I arrived, Jackie and Pat had packed everything into the van and pulled the van out into the parking area. Butch was standing by the garage door, waiting for me to drive in so he could close the door and lock everything up.

When I joined them outside, Pat gave the four of us protective vests to wear. He had loaded three HK416 assault rifles to bring with us. Each rifle had a magazine that held thirty rounds and had an effective firing range of just over three hundred yards. These were very powerful weapons. In addition, three of us wore Glock 21s. Jackie would not be armed. She hated guns and wanted nothing to do with them. She would stay with the van and manage our communication equipment.

Butch climbed into the driver's seat as we closed up the van and took seats. Butch and Pat in front; Jackie and me in back. We had removed the third row of seats to make room for the equipment, and that is where Blackie settled in.

Jackie said, "I packed a few extra things I thought we might need."

"Like?" I asked.

"Drones, an audio amplifier, and a thermal imaging detector."

Pat asked, "We have that shit?"

"Sam and his gadgets," Jackie laughed. "I added the drones. Actually, we have three of them."

"Three?" Butch said.

"Yeah. Battery life. You only get about thirty-five minutes on these small guys. You want more time; the drones get bigger and are easier to spot. These are small, but they're excellent. Three cameras on them."

"Oh," said Butch, not questioning Jackie's expertise about such matters.

"I also have a layout of the camp."

"How did you get that," I asked.

"Old brochures still online from when it was Camp Nebizun."

"Great. Let me take a look."

222

Jackie opened her iPad and turned it on. A few keystrokes later, we were looking at a map of the camp.

"Does it look familiar?" Jackie asked.

"Wish I had paid more attention when I was there, but yeah, from what I remember, this is it." I pointed to the parade ground in front of the office. "This is where we drove in and talked to McKnight. We drove around in back of this building, and that's where Perry's truck was."

"Assuming the brother and the father are there, and they're inside someplace, where do you think they'd be?" she asked.

I pointed to the office. "In here, or maybe here in this building." I pointed to the building labeled 'Dining Hall.'

"Do you have a plan?" Butch asked.

"Sort of."

"Sort of?" Pat chimed in.

I paused before saying, "Well, we have five hours to figure it out. If there's no traffic, we should get there by two."

"How far ahead of us are the Perrys?" Butch asked.

"Not sure about Luke. Jim. Maybe one to two hours. That's rough. Could be more. Could be less."

"Plenty of time for them to get into trouble if there are people at the camp," Butch said.

Chapter Twenty-Two: Threats

Holding his mobile phone out in front of him, Barry Stark was on speakerphone as he paced back and forth on the parade ground in front of the Camp Liberty office. This was his third phone call to Gordon McKnight since the arrival of Luke Perry. He stopped listening when he heard a car and looked up to see a gray Ford come rapidly down the last hill and onto the camp parade ground. Surprised by the sudden intrusion, Stark told McKnight he would have to call him back and started walking towards the car that had appeared as if out of nowhere. "Who are you? What the hell do you think you're doing?" he shouted at the man who was getting out of the car.

"I've come to get my sons," Jim Perry shouted and started walking towards Stark, carrying a rifle pointed at Stark.

"Whoa. Hang on. Easy there. Who are you, and what makes you think your sons are here?"

"That car over there, for one thing." Perry pointed his rifle toward Luke's car, which was parked in front of the office. "Now, where are they?"

"Okay. Now, hold on. How about pointing that rifle toward the ground? There's no reason to get upset or anything. You've got to be Mark and Luke's dad. I'm Barry Stark. I work with Mark. Good to meet you."

Stark walked towards Jim Perry and held his hand out as if to shake it. Confused by this friendly gesture, Perry relaxed and pointed the rifle barrel toward the ground. Cradling the rifle in the crook of his left arm,

Perry held his right hand out to return Stark's offer to shake hands. He wasn't prepared for Stark to grab the rifle, twist it away and slam the rifle's butt into his mid-section sending him sprawling onto the ground gasping for air.

"Idiot!" Stark shouted at him.

Perry couldn't respond.

"Pratt! Get out here."

When Lenny Pratt came out of the office, he saw Stark pointing a rifle at a stranger who was lying on the ground trying to catch his breath. "Dad here has come to get his sons. Isn't that sweet?"

"Jesus Christ," Lenny said.

"Drag him inside with the other two. I don't think he can walk on his own yet."

"What are we going to with...?"

"Just do it."

"Okay. Just ask..."

"Don't. I don't know. Okay? I don't know. Just do it."

"Alright." Lenny Pratt helped Jim Perry to his feet and pushed him toward the office's front porch. Perry slipped and fell. Pratt knelt beside him and pointed the assault rifle he was carrying at Perry's temple. "You get up by yourself and walk into that office on your own, or you will die right here. Do you understand?"

Struggling, Perry got to his knees and then stood upright and walked toward the office.

Lenny Pratt followed him.

Barry Stark got back on his mobile phone and called Gordon McKnight.

"This is going from bad to worse," he reported. "The fucking father just showed up. What are we going to do?"

"I don't know," McKnight answered. "First, you've got to harden the camp down so no one else can get through."

"What! With two people? How the hell am I going to do that?"

"Figure it out."

"Shit, Gordon. Don't give me that."

In Iowa, Gordon McKnight was also pacing, but in a hotel room the Pope campaign had assigned to him and another Defender. "Okay. You're right. You're right. You can't. Sorry."

"Gordon, this is serious. What the hell are we going to do?"

"You hang tight. I'm going to call Washington. Talk to my brother. I'll get back to you as soon as I can."

Stark didn't have long to wait. Fifteen minutes later, Gordon McKnight was on the phone giving orders. "Okay. I talked to Doug. Here's what he wants you to do. For now, you're going to get out of there. Use the panel van. Put all the cars into the maintenance barn and lock it up. Turn the power off for the whole camp. Lock everything up. When you leave, make sure the gate is closed and locked. Also, make sure the 'No Trespassing' signs are obvious."

"He wants us to leave? To go where?" Stark asked.

"You're going to go East, almost to the Canadian border. Josh Whitman has a fishing camp there. When I get the address, I'll email it to you. Pick up some groceries on the way and hang out there until we figure out what the next steps are. Too many people know about Camp Liberty. You need to get out of there now."

"For how long?"

"I don't know. Just get going." McKnight's impatience was irritating Barry Stark.

"What about..."

"What about what?"

"The files? Computer?"

"There's nothing in the files to worry about."

"You sure?" Stark challenged.

"Just personnel files and camp stuff."

"Okay. What about the computer?"

"It's password protected and encrypted."

"Yeah, but..." Stark started.

"Barry, think. If the father knew his son was there, others do, too.

Just get the fuck out of there and do what you're told. The camp has to be completely shut down. Remember, all the Defenders of Liberty are in Iowa protecting General Pope. Got it? All the Defenders."

"Yeah, yeah. Okay. I'm on it."

An hour later, the Camp Liberty van pulled out of the driveway and onto Sparta's main road. Barry Stark was driving. Next to him, holding an assault rifle, was Lenny Pratt. Jim, Mark, and Luke Perry were sprawled on the floor in the back of the van. They were blindfolded, and their mouths were covered with duct tape. Their hands were fastened behind them with zip ties, their ankles were bound together with duct tape, and their arms were taped to their sides.

Left behind was an empty Camp Liberty.

***

We had several different identifying banners we could use on the sides of the Nutmeg van, depending on the situation. These banners attached to the van's sides with strong magnets so they wouldn't blow off when driving on the highway. It was Jackie's idea to attach the ones for the 'Church of the Divine Spirit.'

When we reached the locked gate into Camp Liberty, Butch stopped the van. Jackie got out, went to the back of the van, opened it and within a matter of minutes we were watching a monitor receiving visual signals from a drone flying above the trees making slow circles above the camp.

Jackie said, "No cars or trucks. No movement at all. It looks vacant."

"Can you go lower?" I asked, looking over Jackie's shoulder at the screen.

"Sure." Patiently, she reduced the drone's altitude to just above the rooftops of the camp's buildings. "Still nothing. What me to look in windows?"

"You can do that?"

"Sure." She maneuvered the drone from building to building, stopping to hover outside a building's windows before going to the next building. Twenty minutes later, she said, "I want to retrieve. I've only got about fifteen more minutes of battery time."

"Do it."

When she retrieved the drone she asked, "Want me to set up another one?"

"No. We're going to go down there and take a look. Let's set up the com."

"We all going?" Pat Brady asked.

"No. Jackie, I want you and Butch to stay here with the van. Pat and I will bushwhack up this hill and around the gate. If anyone comes from the main road, tell them you were surprised that the camp was closed. Use our cover story if they ask why you're here."

"Got it. We're just simple God-fearing people looking for a place to hold a summer retreat for our congregation."

"Be sure to remove your com sets and cover the equipment with the tarp if you hear someone coming. If you have to leave, do so. Pat and I'll hike out and meet you about a mile down the road, south of the driveway. From the map it looks like a trail comes out there."

"Will do," Butch said.

Pat and I gathered our weapons, climbed up the hill next to the gate, and started heading down towards the camp. Ten minutes later, we were standing on the parade ground. There was still no sign of life.

"Where do you want to start?" Pat asked.

"Let's start with the office and then do the cabins."

"We breaking in?"

"Possibly. We'll play it by ear."

Looking in the office windows, it was obvious no one was there. I started looking for things that seemed out of place. I didn't know what I was looking for. I was just looking. Neither Pat nor I saw anything that grabbed our attention. We walked around back to the entrance labeled 'Nurse.' It was the same. The room was spartan. No one was there. I was about to leave when something caught my attention. "Pat, look at the coffee maker. It looks like there's still coffee in the carafe."

"Shit. You're right."

"Either they're slobs or people left here in a hurry."

"Are we..."

"Do it."

Pat slammed into the door. There was no deadbolt, and the jam gave way easily. I went over to the coffee carafe and felt it. "It's still a little warm. Someone or somebodies were just here. I want to check out the office again." We went into the office.

Pat said, "Duct tape. Here on the desk and some electrical ties. Couldn't see them from the window."

"Let's keep looking."

Able to hear our conversation, Butch asked, "Do you want us to come down?"

"No. I don't think anyone is here. For now, stay where you are."

"Okay."

Pat and I looked more carefully now. We pulled out file drawers. We didn't know what we were looking for; we were just looking. "The computer's still here," Pat said.

"Desktop. Too much trouble to move if they were in a big hurry."

"Probably."

Finding nothing that caught our attention, I took my phone out and snapped a few pictures, then we decided to move over to the dining hall. Looking in the windows, we saw that whoever had been eating breakfast there had not cleaned up after themselves. We saw two plates and accompanying forks and knives set out on the corner of one table. "Two people at least," Pat said.

"Yes," I confirmed. "Let's try the barn."

We walked around behind the dining hall to the barn. There were no windows and a padlock held the doors together.

Pat didn't ask this time. He went around to the side of the barn and returned with a small boulder. Five strikes later and the screws holding the latch on one side of the door gave way. I slid one of the doors open. Five vehicles were in the barn. I knew the owners of three of them.

I took pictures of the two I did not know, along with their license plates. I texted Vicki the images with a note. *Can you pull your strings and find out who belongs to these, and let me know?*

Sure, she responded. *Everything okay?*

Yes and no. The camp is empty, but all three of the Perry cars are here. My hunch is that they've been taken someplace else and against their will, at least for two of them.

She answered: *Time to call the sheriff's office?*

Not yet. But getting close. I'll keep you posted.

Pat and I looked around the barn for a while but found nothing to help us figure out where the Perrys were.

"Pat, let's check out the cabins."

Looking in the windows, we saw that most of the cabins were not only empty but also tidy – military tidy. Beds were made, and no clothes were scattered about. Two cabins were different. We broke into both.

The first bedroom had one unmade bed and an open drawer. There was no suitcase or backpack. In the bathroom, there were a few toiletries but no toothbrush or razor. "Somebody packed in a hurry," Pat said.

"Yep. And didn't leave anything behind to tell us who he is."

"Cops could get DNA."

"Yeah, but we can't. Let's keep going."

Two people had occupied the second cabin we broke into. But there was a difference. One of the bureaus was practically empty. The other, though, was still filled with clothes.

"Mark Perry?" Pat asked.

"That's my guess. Looks like he didn't leave of his own accord."

"Definitely. Look. His initials are on this backpack."

A story was beginning to frame in my mind. I had no idea if the narrative I was creating was true, but the few facts we had supported it. With his brother and father's arrival, Mark Perry was now suspect in the minds of the two Defenders who had been left behind at Camp Liberty. What if Luke was correct and his brother was one of the assassins. Was Mark now a liability? Had Luke's accusation now created danger for his brother?

Convinced there was nothing more for us to learn at the camp, Pat and I retraced our steps and rejoined Butch and Jackie at the van. We were loading our gear into the van when Vicki texted, identifying the cars in the barn as belonging to a Barry Stark and a Leonard Pratt.

Jackie immediately went online and found information about both. "Stark is ex-state police, Massachusetts. Nothing much. There are a couple of complaints of excessive force. No discipline record, though. There is almost nothing on Pratt. His brother, though, is a different story. He's a mercenary. Not a nice guy."

"But nothing on Leonard? Absolutely nothing?" I asked.

"Nothing unless you count a couple of speeding tickets and one DUI he got nolled."

"Shit."

"Where do you think they went?" Butch asked.

"I haven't a clue," I answered.

"There was nothing on the desk," Pat added.

"Computers?" Jackie asked.

"A desktop. Wasn't on," Pat said.

"Doesn't matter. Let me at it."

"No power," Pat said.

Jackie looked at Pat in a way I had never seen her look before. It was dismissive. "So we turn the power back on. It doesn't matter; it will have a battery backup unless they were too cheap to put in a UPS."

"UPS?"

"Uninterruptible Power Supply."

"Let's go," I said.

"Gate?" Butch asked."

"Pat?" I asked.

"Got it," Pat answered.

Ten minutes later, the power was on at Camp Liberty. Jackie had fired up the computer and was looking at it. She didn't say anything for a minute. Then she said, "Take a look underneath the desk and in the drawers. See if anything is taped somewhere. People do that with passwords. This is McKnight's, right?"

"As far as we know," I answered.

"Let's assume it is. Jackie got out her mobile phone and started working the keypad."

"What are you doing," I asked.

"Accessing the file I have on him." Jackie put her phone down next to the computer and started entering data into McKnight's computer where it asked for the password. Periodically, she would pause and then give it another try.

"I'm in. It was his mother's birthday."

"You had his mother's birthday?"

"Of course."

Jackie started typing on the computer's keyboard. Periodically, she would stop and then start again.

Impatiently, I asked, "Well."

"Strange file directory. Some areas are encrypted, and I can't get into them with his mother's birthday. It'd take time and a lot more guesswork to access them. Today's emails haven't been encrypted and moved. Wait. Kaboom! I think I know where they're going. Take a look."

I took a picture of an email with an address. The email said: *This is Whitman's camp. Key in wood box.*

Still at the keyboard, Jackie started typing.

I said, "What now?"

"Give me a sec." I waited.

"Joshua Whitman is the owner. Washington, D.C. Super conservative dude. Donates to all the wrong people."

Butch said, "Let's go. They can't be too far ahead of us."

"No, no, no. I need a few minutes." Jackie scurried under the desk and started disconnecting cables. "We're bringing this with us. This could be a gold mine. Who knows what else is on here?" She began handing components to us. "I want to take everything."

"Even the printer?" Butch asked.

"Yes. The printer. We have no idea what's in its cache."

With the four of us working, we had everything loaded in a matter of minutes and were on our way out of the driveway. The power was back off, and we closed the gate behind us. No trespassing signs were back on the gate, and Butch had entered the address for the fishing camp in Pine City Township into the van's navigation system. It was close to the US border with New Brunswick.

In the back seat, Jackie and I went through files. In the front, Pat napped, and Butch, at the wheel, hummed along to Zac Brown on the van's radio:

I got my toes in the water, ass in the sand
Not a worry in the world, a cold beer in my hand
Life is good today
Life is good today.

Chapter Twenty-Three: Reel Escape

The sign said *Reel Escape*. Stark came to a stop on the state road, looking for a road or driveway, but couldn't find one. The area was heavily forested, and the snow all around the sign was undisturbed.

There were mounds of snow on each side of the main road pushed there by plows over successive snowfalls. Stark drove a little further down the road, going slowly, stopping occasionally to peer into the dense forest. Seeing nothing, he sped up, looking for a place to turn around. He had to go three miles before a crossroad allowed him to reverse direction.

Returning to where they had seen the sign, Stark stopped, then started up again. "It's got to be here somewhere," he said to Pratt. He stopped the van, got out, and started walking back and forth on the road near the sign. Returning to the van, he backed up twenty yards. "That's got to be it."

"Where?" Pratt asked.

"See where there's a break in the trees? Gotta be it. That's where the driveway must go."

"How we gonna get in there with the snow?" Pratt asked. "The van'll never make it."

"We'll have to walk."

"What the hell was McKnight thinking? I'll bet no one's plowed it all winter," Pratt said.

"No reason to. No one's coming up here fishing in January."

"Fucking snow got to be a couple of feet deep."

"Maybe a foot."

Stark got out of the van and walked back and forth in front of the area where he assumed the driveway to be. When he returned to the van, he said, "We've got to get the van off the road. If I can get past where the snow plows have piled the snow, maybe we can make it up the driveway. I'll give it a try."

Stark pulled the van to the opposite side of the state road and stomped on the gas pedal. The van shot across the dry pavement and into the mound of snow made by the plows. The van went in a few feet and came to a stop, its rear wheels spinning on the bare pavement of the main road. He backed out and tried again. On the third try, he got past the snow mound, but as soon as the van got past the mound and the rear wheels got onto the snow, the wheels just spun. With all four wheels now on snow, he tried to back up again to get a running start, but even in reverse, the rear wheels spun. He tried going back and forth, but it didn't work. "Fucking rear wheel drive piece of shit," he said to Pratt.

"What are we going to do? Can't just leave it here."

"We're almost through. Get out and push when I put it in reverse. I think one more try, and we'll make it."

Pratt got out of the van and walked around to the front. He put his back up against the van, and when he heard the engine rev up in reverse, he started to push. It was just enough, and the van shot backward, leaving Pratt lying on his back in the snow.

"Shit," he said and walked back into the middle of the road where the van was waiting for him. He climbed into the van next to Stark. "Next time, you do it."

Stark didn't reply and again aimed the van at the snow mound, almost demolished from his attempts to get through it. He again floored the van, and it sped forward across the road. This time, he was successful, and the van made it through the mound and onto the undisturbed snow on the other side. The snow was barely a foot deep there, and with the slight downward incline towards the break in the trees that Stark had spotted, the van could move forward.

As they approached the area where the trees separated, the terrain became level then rose slightly. The van's momentum stopped. Without a downward slope, the rear wheels could no longer get traction in the snow. "We'll have to walk in from here," Stark said.

"How we going to do that with them?" Pratt said motioning to the back of the van where the Perrys were.

"We'll have to free their legs and remove the blindfolds."

"None of us have boots."

"You're sounding like a wuss. You want to stay here? Move it."

Stark and Pratt exited the van and opened the two back doors. They removed the blindfolds of the father and two sons, cut the duct tape that bound their ankles, and ordered them to slide out of the van.

"How are we going to carry all of this stuff?" Pratt asked, pointing to the grocery bags and their backpacks and suitcases.

"Free their wrists and arms. They'll carry the stuff. We'll tie them up again when we get to the cabin."

"With what?"

"I don't know. There'll be something there. It's a fishing camp. There'll be rope or something. We'll use fishing line if we have to. Let's get going."

The minute they removed the bindings from Mark Perry, he ripped the duct tape off his mouth and lurched towards Stark, reaching for his pistol and knocking him down into the snow.

Pratt pointed his assault weapon at Jim Perry and said, "Cut the shit or your father's dead, then your brother."

Looking up, Mark saw the assault rifle pointed at his father's head and rolled off Stark.

Stark got up.

Mark started to get up, but Stark kicked him in the ribs, and Mark went back down into the snow.

"Asshole," Stark shouted at him and kicked him again. He handed

Mark the duct tape he had ripped off his mouth and said, "Put it back on."

Unloading the van and getting the backpacks, luggage, and groceries distributed among the three Perrys took a few minutes. The snow covered their feet and was halfway up their shins as the five men walked towards the tree break that Stark assumed was the driveway into the fishing camp.

Stark ordered Mark Perry to take the lead since he was the biggest. Mark was followed by his brother Luke and then his father. With his assault rifle at the ready, Pratt was next in line, followed by Stark.

Their feet were cold without boots, and Stark began to wonder about frostbite. The weakest of the group, Jim Perry, fell several times. Stark ordered Mark to give Luke the groceries he was carrying and help his father up each time.

With no idea where they were going or when they would reach their destination, Pratt said, "I think we should go back to the van. We can push it back out onto the road. This is nuts."

"And then do what?" Stark said.

"Keep going."

"Keep going where?"

"I don't know. Better than freezing our asses off."

"Maybe we'll do that if we don't find the place in the next fifteen or twenty minutes."

They struggled walking up the incline. When they reached the top, the break in the trees turned to the right and started down a hill. In the distance, they saw a cabin and a large lake.

"That's gotta be it," Stark said.

"I don't give a shit if it is or it isn't," Pratt said. "That's where we're going."

Going down the hill was easier, and ten minutes later, the five were standing on the porch of a simple, rustic cabin twenty yards from the shore of the lake. Barry Stark left the porch and went to the side of the cabin, where he found the wood box described in McKnight's text message.

Without gloves, he leaned down and used his arm to brush the snow off the top of the box to open the lid. He found the key, returned to the porch, and opened the cabin's door to let them in. There was no difference between the temperature inside the cabin and outside.

The cabin was nothing more than one big room and a sleeping loft. In the middle of the room were two fifty-five-gallon barrels arranged horizontally, one on top of another. Metal stands held the bottom barrel off the floor, and a set of additional stands held the top barrel over the one below it. A metal chimney went from the bottom barrel into the top barrel. A second chimney went from the top barrel through the roof.

"What's that?" Pratt said.

"Barrel stove."

"That's a stove?"

"You build a fire in the bottom barrel; smoke goes up into the top barrel and heats it. It'll work. Just takes time."

"So, there's no electricity in this dump?"

"Doesn't look like it. Two burner propane stove on the counter. Looks like a propane refrigerator over there. Get a fire going in the stove."

"We got to tie them back up," Pratt said, pointing at the three men whose mouths were still covered with duct tape and who were standing together in the corner of the cabin, having been guided there by Pratt's assault rifle.

"First, get a fire going. Give me the rifle."

Pratt handed Stark his rifle and looked around the cabin for some kindling. He found a bag of fatwood in one of the cabinets, rich with dried, highly flammable sap. He took out three sticks to use as kindling and laid them in the bottom barrel of the stove. Using a butane lighter from the same cabinet, he started the fatwood and added small logs from the bin next to the stove.

"Good work. Now, find some rope so we can tie them up again," Stark commanded. "Try that shed down near the dock."

"Here. Give me the gun. You go look," Pratt answered.

"Watch yourself," Stark said. "I'm still in charge here."

"Of what? Everything's totally fucked up, and you know it. We should just shoot them, torch this place, and get the hell out of here."

"We're not going anyplace until McKnight tells us what he wants us to do."

"How's he going to do that?"

"What do you mean?"

Pratt showed Stark the front of his mobile phone. "No bars, genius."

***

Sam DeRosa was a passionate man, and Nutmeg Security and Investigations had been the focus of this passion for twenty-five years. His family came first, of course, but Nutmeg was not only a business to Sam; it was his creation, and nothing was too good for Sam's Nutmeg. That extended to the van we were driving. It was a Mercedes crew van with added back seats. Powered by a diesel engine with all-wheel drive, the van had every option Sam could imagine using, from the comfort package to the high-end navigation and sound system. While its primary Nutmeg use was transporting equipment and people from site to site, wherever Nutmeg had security contracts, it also found its way into use as an occasional weekend camper for the DeRosa family. Because it was winter, it was, of course, dressed with snow tires on all four wheels.

The sky continued darkening, and I was sure snow would begin any minute.

Butch said, "What do you think? Flurries or the real thing?"

Jackie always had information. "Flurries. Nothing more." She was looking at her mobile phone. "Another thirty minutes or so. Then, clear as a bell. Almost a full moon tonight."

"What time will we get there?" I asked Butch.

"GPS shows an ETA of 1805." Military time. Of course. We were on a mission. "Going to be dark in a little while."

Jackie and I went back to work on the files. Thankfully, Sam also had regular power outlets in the van along with Wi-Fi.

The files were interesting but not startling. Every Defender had a file. For the most part, they were like the personnel files of any organization. We expected the Defenders to be mostly ex-military and police, and they were. There were a lot of divorces and few children. There were several arrests and complaints of domestic violence. DUIs were not uncommon. Educational attainment was typically twelve or fewer years.

The camp records were also what one would expect, with a few exceptions. The receipts for the Defender arsenal were extensive, and I was surprised at some of the items McKnight had been able to purchase. He had established himself as a licensed collector and had applied for and received several specialized permits. The Defender arsenal included a bazooka and several small cannons. From the back seat I reported what I had just found.

"You mean we might be facing a fucking bazooka?" Pat asked.

"If they brought it with them. I guess it's a possibility. I didn't see anything like that in the barn, did you?"

"No. But we didn't check out all the buildings."

Butch didn't say anything.

A few minutes later, Jackie said, "You know what's missing? Bank statements. We have receipts for stuff, and they were spending a fortune, but we have no bank statements. Where did all this money come from? We know where the money went, but where did it come from?"

"We must have missed something at the office."

"I don't think so. Certainly not in the file cabinet. I'll bet all the banking was done online, and they didn't want to have any paper statements."

"The computer?" I asked.

"Probably. I hope so. We're talking millions."

"You're right."

"You know what this means?"

"Yeah. If Luke Perry's right and Mark was involved in the assassination, and it was a Defender operation, that means…"

Jackie interrupted me. "Some one or some group is financing the overthrow of the United States' government."

"If that's the case, they won't think twice about getting rid of the Perrys." I didn't add, "Or us."

In the front seats, Pat dozed, and Butch hummed. Now, it was Bob Seger. Whenever the chorus came, he would join in: "*Against the wind. We were running against the wind. We were young and strong; we were running against the wind.*"

"Speak for yourself." It was Pat waking up. "I've got to piss, and I'm hungry. Anyone else?"

"Seriously?" Butch said.

"Seriously," was Pat's response.

None of us had eaten anything all day, and I was hungry, too. I also needed some 'facilities.'

Route #9 in Maine doesn't have a lot of places to stop, so it was another twenty miles before we saw the sign for Crossroads Grocery. Like most of the 'grocery' stores in rural Maine, Crossroad Groceries would make you sandwiches, sell you groceries, and was stocked with an abundance of snack foods. Want a fishing lure or bait? They had it. Outside, they had fuel, both gas and diesel. They even had a pump for kerosene alongside the building. You got the key to the restrooms from the clerk and had to walk around back to access them. Fortunately, they had an array of sandwiches already made and sitting in a cooler. We each grabbed one and a bottle of soda or water.

As I paid for everything, I asked the clerk, "Seen anyone else tonight? We're supposed to meet a couple of friends – wondering if we're ahead or behind them."

He responded, "One other van stopped. They bought plenty of groc'ries. I'ma guessin' you'll all eat well."

I nodded, thanked him, and put everything in the van.

Biological needs were addressed, and we were back on the road in fifteen minutes.

"Seems like we're on the right track," I reassured the group.

Forty-five minutes and three turns later, Pat instructed Butch to slow down. A few seconds later, the GPS announced, *In one thousand feet you will reach your destination.*

We pulled in at the sign for the *Reel Escape*. It was easy to find since it was the only place where the snowbank had been disturbed. We drove as far as we could until the Defender van blocked our path.

"I don't want to go in blind. Jackie, would you…" I asked.

"On it."

"There enough light?" Butch asked.

"With this moon – plenty."

Five minutes later, the second of the two drones followed the path someone had made in the snow through the cut in the trees. As we watched on the monitor, Jackie maneuvered the drone higher to get an overall view of the *Reel Escape* cabin and how it was situated on the lakefront. We were able to see the dock and the shed next to it, as well as another outbuilding a short distance from the cabin.

"What do you think that is?" Jackie asked.

"Outhouse," Pat said.

Jackie maneuvered the drone lower and we could see that tracks were going back and forth to the shed by the dock.

When she raised it again, Butch pointed to the curling white smoke coming from a metal chimney in the center of the roof. "Looks like they've got a fire going."

"Can we look in the windows?" I asked.

Jackie didn't answer. She simply brought the drone to hover first outside one and then another of the two windows on the side of the cabin facing us. We could see one man standing at what looked like a sink with an old-fashioned pump. In another corner, a man sat holding onto what looked to be an assault rifle. We couldn't see into the area that fronted the lake.

"I could bring the drone outside the porch windows," Jackie said, "But I'm afraid of bumping into something because of the roof supports. I'll lose the moonlight, too."

"Don't. How about the back of the cabin?"

Jackie brought the drone up and over the roof of the cabin. "Too many trees. Same problem. Afraid I'll hit something. Branches all over the place up close to the building."

"Okay. Bring it back."

Jackie retrieved the drone and returned it to its case in the back of our van. The four of us got back inside.

"How do you want to play this?" Butch asked.

"The Perrys have to be there," I said. "Just two people didn't make those tracks in the snow."

"I agree," Pat said. "So, we're dealing with at least two guys with weapons. We know one has an assault rifle. The other probably does, too."

"And we don't know what else they've got with them," Butch added.

"And we don't know where Mark stands at this point or what they plan to do," I added.

"Not a lot to go on," Jackie said. She voiced what we were all thinking.

"So, what's our goal?" Butch asked. "Get the Perrys home safe and sound. Right?"

"At least two of them: Luke and his father. Mark? I don't know about Mark. He sounds like he's pretty far gone. He may have turned on his family."

"Don't forget the cabin back at their compound," Pat said. "That was Mark's stuff that was still there."

"You're right. We don't know about Mark."

"We've got to treat him as a hostile until we know he isn't," Butch said. "Remember, if his brother's right, Mark hacked that senator to death with a fucking machete and did it right in front of the guy's wife."

"You're right," I said. "We have to get him under our control. Question is, how do we do all of this without anyone getting hurt?"

"Especially you," Pat said. "I don't want to get Eve on my bad side."

We all chuckled at that.

"I've got an idea," Jackie said. It may sound crazy, but it might work.

243

You remember those old Western movies? You know, the ones where bad guys are holed up inside a cabin, and one of the good guys climbs up on the roof and stuffs something down the chimney so the smoke can't get out. Cabin would fill up with smoke and force the bad guys to come out. You know. The bad guys come out all choking and stuff."

"You volunteering for roof duty," Butch asked. "As I recall, the people in the cabin fired up at the roof, and that was with ancient Colts. Can you imagine what an assault rifle would do to that roof?"

"No, not me. The drone."

"You serious?" I asked.

"Yeah. Might not block the chimney totally, but…"

"Enough to make the cabin very uncomfortable," Pat said. "A fucking drone. What a wonderful, nerdy idea."

"Thank you very much."

"Think you can do it?" I asked.

"I have absolutely no idea."

Butch said. "Even if they just heard the drone, one person might come out to see what's going on."

"We could grab him, and that would be one less to worry about," Pat said.

"Anyone have any better ideas?" I asked. I looked around from one to the other.

No one said anything.

Chapter Twenty-Four: Shots Fired

Lenny Pratt found some rope in the shed by the dock. First, he bound Mark, then Luke, and, finally, their father. Pratt made the three of them sit on the floor. Their mouths were still covered with duct tape, but at least they could see. There wasn't enough rope to tie their ankles together.

One hour went by. Then two. Stark and Pratt said little to each other. They took turns pointing a rifle at their three prisoners. When he was off duty, Stark found an old *Field and Stream* magazine and started reading an article. When it was his turn, Pratt dozed. They each left the cabin at different points to use the outhouse in the back of the building.

After his outing, Pratt said, "What about them?"

"Yeah. We'd better."

By nodding his head in his father's direction, Mark insisted that his father be the first to make the journey to the outhouse. When they returned, Mark noticed Pratt wasn't paying much attention to what he was doing. He was tying a granny knot to hold the rope ends together. He saw that repeated when they next took Luke. When it was his turn, Mark used his strength to push against the ropes when Pratt retied them. Pratt wasn't paying attention and didn't notice Mark's wrists weren't flush together when he pulled the rope taut before he tied the finishing knot.

Mark waited until Pratt was finished and walked away. When Pratt turned his back, Mark started to wiggle his hands and wrists. It worked. He was able to loosen the rope. It wasn't easy, and the rope cut into his wrists, but the continuous movement, as painful as it was, loosened the rope to where he could begin slipping it down his wrists and onto his fingers.

Periodically, Mark looked over at his father and his brother. They were responding differently to what was taking place. Mark thought his father looked defeated. At one point, he was sure his father was crying. His brother, though, seemed angry. Luke would start moving about, and Lenny would tell him to stay still or he'd come over and make him. When that happened, Luke would look at Mark, and Mark was sure his brother was filled with fury at him. Hate. Mark was sure his brother hated him.

Barry Stark and Lenny Pratt ignored the Perrys, paying attention to them only when they made some noise or the one time they had to take them out for their outhouse break.

As time went on, Pratt became increasingly convinced that things had become truly fucked up beyond all recognition. He said it to Stark, "This is FUBAR, man. We've got to kill them, burn this place down, and somehow get the hell out of here."

"How we going to do that? The van is stuck. We can't exactly call AAA."

"No shit. We can't call anyone."

"McKnight'll handle it. Gordon'll take care of it. Stop your whining."

"Yeah, right. What makes you think he and the people behind him aren't goin' just disown us?"

"How the hell they going to do that? They're every bit as involved in this as we are."

"Bullshit. Think about it. McKnight can just say we went rogue, and the Defenders had nothing to do with anything. McKnight didn't go to Montana. We did. McKnight didn't go to New Hampshire. We did. Use your fucking head. It's the smart move for them. Come on, Barry, think, will you? Ask yourself, what's the smart move for them? It's to get rid of all of us, these three idiots and us. Maybe that's the plan. Maybe that's why they sent us here. There could be people on their way here right now."

"Stop it. You're being paranoid."

"Am I? Think about it. It'd be the smart move, wouldn't it? Eliminate all of us. Who's to know?"

"Shut up."

"Yeah. 'Shut up.' You go 'shut up.' Why don't you make us something to eat? What the fuck else are we going to do?"

"Shut up."

"Fuck you."

Stark thought about the comment McKnight had made to him about leaving the camp: "All the Defenders are in Iowa." Was Platt right? This fucking cabin. No internet. No power. Who would know? No, McKnight would never kill his own men. He got up and started opening one cabinet after another.

Pratt got antsy watching Stark rummaging through cabinets. "What are you looking for?"

"Something to cook with." Two cabinets later, he found a couple of pots and cooking utensils. He brought them over to the stove. He removed his pistol from its holster and placed it on the counter next to the sink where he could easily reach it then went over to where his assault rifle was leaning against the chair he'd been sitting in. He moved it alongside the cabinet under the stove. Knowing he could get to either weapon in seconds, he walked over to the propane refrigerator, where he retrieved some of the groceries they'd brought with them. A few minutes later, he had the propane stove going and stirred a mixture of chopped meat, onion, and red peppers together.

"How much longer?" Pratt asked.

"Just a few minutes. You got someplace you need to be?"

"Fuck off."

"Pratt, what's your goddamn problem?"

"I'm hungry. That's my problem."

"You sound like a two-year old." Mockingly Stark added, "Daddy. I'm hungry. When will supper be ready?"

"Stark, you're an asshole."

In the corner of the cabin, Mark Perry kept working at the ropes that bound his hands behind his back.

Stark stood at the stove, stirring the food, trying not to pay any attention to Pratt. About five minutes later, he stopped stirring. He stood still and sniffed. "It's getting smoky in here. Check the damper on the stove. Make sure it's open."

Lenny Pratt went over to look at the chimney. He fiddled with the damper, opening and closing it. "It's all the way open."

"Crack a window. We may need to create a draft."

***

It didn't take us long to get our gear on and begin to follow the trail that led away from the Defender's van. From inside the Nutmeg van, Jackie tested our communications equipment. There were no problems. When we started to walk, we walked in a single file. I didn't have to tell Blackie what we were doing. He had multiple scents, all going in the same direction, in addition to a trail. I followed him. Pat was behind me, and then Butch. The snow was sufficiently trampled that Blackie only had to jump on occasion to make it over a small area where the snow had not been beaten down by the five men whose trail we were following.

The almost full moon was behind us, and we had no difficulty seeing. From the indentations in the snow, we could see where people might have fallen. The snow was trampled for a few yards around those areas rather than moving in a straight line.

I was glad I was dressed appropriately and wondered what it must have been like for Jim and Luke Perry. I doubted they anticipated they would be traipsing through the snow when they left West Haven, Connecticut that morning. I also wondered what plans this Barry Stark and Lenny Pratt had for the Perrys. Nothing I considered made any sense to me. Were they hostages to be bargained for? Were they simply on a death march that would end when they reached the cabin? Perhaps a chopped hole in a frozen lake would be their burial place.

When we reached the top of the rise, the trail turned to the right, and we could see the cabin and the lake about two hundred yards down a fairly gentle slope. Yellow light glowed from the cabin windows.

Behind me, Pat said, "Probably kerosene lanterns. No power lines."

"Generator?" Jackie asked from our van.

"I think we'd hear it. No wind. It's very quiet," Butch said.

We paused looking down the slope at the cabin. A Christmas card. It looked like a scene from a Christmas card – moonlight, snow, cabin, soft yellow light coming from the windows.

Someone in the cabin opened a door.

I motioned to the others to drop low. "*Platz*," I whispered to Blackie, the Schutzhund command to lie down. Behind him, we all did the same. The light from the moon was strong enough that if someone had looked up the hill, they would have seen us. We'd appear as dark shadows, but they would be able to tell we were people and not trees or bushes.

Two people came out of the cabin, walked across the porch onto the snow, and went behind the cabin. We lost sight of them. They reappeared as they walked towards the outhouse. We could see that one of them was carrying a rifle. One person entered while the man with the gun stood guard. A few minutes later, the prisoner exited the outhouse and was escorted back to the cabin. We stayed crouched down in the snow and watched the ritual repeat itself two more times.

"Looks like Mark's a prisoner," Pat said.

No one responded.

We waited a few more minutes to see if anyone else left the cabin. When no one did, I said, "Let's get going." I didn't want Blackie going ahead of us as we worked our way down the hill. "Blackie, *komm*." Blackie came to me. "*Fuss*." He took up the 'heel' position, his right shoulder to my left knee, only a couple of inches away from me. He struggled to maintain a perfect position walking in the uneven snow, but he did his best.

Pat pointed out a group of bushes about ten yards from the porch. "Let's set up there. We'll be able to see one side of the house and the porch. We only have to deal with one entrance."

249

"Good idea," I responded.

Slowly, we worked our way down the hill. We stayed on the trail the others had made until we were close to the bushes Pat had pointed out. We veered off.

Butch, the last in line, did his best to kick snow back over the new trail that we were making. You wouldn't notice it unless you were looking for it. A small animal could have made it.

When we were in place, I asked the others, "Suggestions?" I was really asking Pat. I knew he'd already have a plan.

He did. "Butch and I will work our way onto the porch and station ourselves on either side of the door. Once Jackie gets the drone in place and the cabin starts to fill up with smoke, they'll probably send one person out to check on the chimney. Someone comes out, Butch'll grab them. I'll go in and take out the other person."

"Take out?" I asked.

"Remove as a threat, if you prefer. Remember…"

"I know. They have assault rifles."

"And they assassinate people."

"What about me and Blackie?" I asked.

"You stay here until you see me go in. Then you and Blackie run like hell and come in. Hopefully everything will be under control at that point. If it's not, do what you can to control it."

"But…"

"I watched you get shot once. Not going to happen again. Now you do the watching. Jackie, you all set?"

"Give me a sec. Just gotta open the van's back doors." A few seconds later she said, "It's in the air."

We watched the sky.

Butch said, "That it?" and pointed up.

We all looked in the direction he indicated. As bright as the moon was, it was hard to make out the drone. When it turned, we would get a glimpse of it as the moonlight reflected off a shiny surface.

We watched as the drone circled the cabin's roof and came lower a little bit at a time until it settled on top of the cabin's chimney. It hung there, not quite on top.

Jackie said, "Want me to try again?"

"They might hear it," I said.

"Could be a squirrel," Jackie said. "I know I can do better. Practice makes…"

Pat was impatient. He said, "Let's move."

"Leave it where it is," I said. I watched Pat and Butch head toward the cabin. Given where the drone hung off the chimney, it would take a while before any noticeable smoke buildup would occur, if ever. I started thinking of other scenarios that might draw Stark or Pratt out of the cabin. Perhaps Blackie barking. I also didn't like staying where I was. I understood and appreciated what Pat had said, but it didn't feel right. I had gotten us into this situation. I started to slowly move my way towards the porch. I planned to position myself behind Butch.

When Pat saw me move onto the porch, he motioned me to stay several feet behind Butch, so I didn't crowd him.

We waited. We could hear muffled voices inside the cabin but couldn't make out what people were saying. We waited some more. No one opened the door. I was getting impatient. Maybe we should shift to plan 'B.' Except there was no plan 'B.'

I watched Pat leave his position and slowly move off the porch and around to the side of the cabin.

"What are you doing," I whispered into my microphone.

"Quiet," he answered.

A few minutes later, he was back on the porch and in position. "It's working," he said.

We continued to wait. Five minutes later, a window on the side of the cabin opened. Still, no one opened the door. Finally, the door opened. Whoever opened it didn't come out onto the porch, though. He just stood in the doorway, holding the door open to let the smoke out.

Pat motioned to Butch to grab him.

Butch handed me his rifle, and I strapped it onto my back, flicked the

251

safety off of mine, and got ready to rush in the door.

I tapped Butch on the back that I was ready. He reached into the doorway, grabbed the man, pulled him out onto the porch, and flung him onto the porch floor.

"What the..." the man screamed.

Butch dropped down on top of him, put one hand over the man's mouth to shut him up, and with the other, he took out his knife and held it at the man's throat.

Pat was already going through the door and moved off to the right. I followed him and moved to the left. As I did so, I saw Mark Perry, rope hanging from one wrist, charge at the counter where there was a gun. The man who had been at the stove got to it first and started firing.

Three bullets ripped into Mark. He stopped moving and slowly fell forward.

Seeing people coming through the door, the man turned his pistol toward the door, but he was too late. Pat had him in his sights and fired over and over again. One slug after another tore into the man's body and threw him backward into the wall before he slumped to the cabin floor, his torso riddled with holes.

I went over to check on Mark. I put my hand on his neck, trying to find a pulse. There was one, but it was weak and intermittent. Then it stopped. I rolled him over and saw the three bullet holes grouped neatly together in the middle of his chest. Blood had already pooled on the floor under where he had fallen. I looked over at his brother and father and shook my head. I looked back at Mark. There was nothing I could do for him. Looking back at Luke and Jim, I was equally helpless to do anything for them.

In my headpiece, Jackie whispered, "Is everyone okay?"

"We are," I said. "But we have two dead. Mark Perry is one of them."

"Jesus," Jackie said. "Do you want me to call someone? Sheriff? FBI?"

"No one yet. We've got to figure out what's going on. I don't know who's Pratt and who's Stark."

"That guy is Barry Stark." It was Pratt. Pushed into the cabin by Butch, he was pointing at the man Pat had shot. Pat pointed to the rope on the floor where Mark Perry had freed himself. Without talking, Butch pushed Pratt in front of him and kicked the legs out from under him. Pratt fell face down onto the floor.

"Watch him," Butch said to me.

I wanted to attend to Jim and Luke Perry. I gave Blackie the 'guard' command, "Blackie, *pas auf.*"

Blackie stood in front of Pratt, barking loudly in his ears.

Terrified, Pratt shouted, "Get him off me."

Blackie kept barking.

"Don't move, and he won't bite you," I said.

Blackie kept barking.

After removing the rope from where it was dangling from Mark Perry, Butch commanded, "Arms."

Pratt knew exactly what he meant and put his arms behind him. Butch tied them together.

Seeing Pratt was under control, I released Blackie and told him to stand where he was. "Blackie, *steh.*" Blackie stopped barking but remained close enough to Pratt that Pratt could feel his breath.

I went over and started untying Jim and Luke Perry. I handed one of the ropes from Luke to Butch, and Butch tied Pratt's ankles together.

When I untied Jim, he went over and knelt beside Mark. Slowly, he lifted Mark's body and brought it towards him, cradling his dead son. He was crying uncontrollably.

Luke didn't move. I don't think he could. He just watched his father.

I didn't say anything to either one of them. I didn't know what I could say.

Pat said into his microphone, "Jackie, get the damn drone off the chimney. You did good, girl. It worked, but we gotta get rid of this smoke."

"Consider it done."

Butch rolled Lenny Pratt onto his back. He put his knife against

Pratt's throat. "You're fucked. You know that, don't you?"

Pratt shook his head 'yes.'

"Good. You have nothing to gain by bullshit. What was your plan?"

"We didn't have one. We were just told to come here."

I went over to Pratt. "By who?"

He didn't say anything.

Butch increased the knife's pressure against Pratt's throat.

Pratt shouted, "I want a deal."

"You want a deal?" I said.

"Yeah. I want a lawyer and a deal."

Pat came over and knelt on Pratt's chest. "Do we look like cops to you?"

"McKnight sent you, didn't he? Shit. I knew it."

Pat looked at me and I came over. "No. McKnight didn't send us. Are you expecting someone?"

"I don't know. McKnight sent us here. Then you show up. I don't know, maybe."

"Well you're going to tell us everything you know from beginning to end if you want to save your sorry life, including who might be on their way."

It didn't take long for Pratt to tell us everything from the trip to Montana and threatening the governor to the assassination of Senator Perez. When he finished, I told Jackie, "Call the nearest FBI office. Probably Bangor. If not, there should be one in Augusta. Do you have cell coverage?"

"I've got two bars. Should be enough."

Pratt said, "Wait a minute. You said you're not cops."

Pat ignored him.

"How long 'til someone gets here?" he asked me.

"Who knows?" I answered. "If it's Bangor, it's probably a small field office – one or two people on call at this time of night. If that. Calls might go to Portland or Augusta. It could be three or four hours."

"Sheriff's office?"

"Absolutely not. Who knows what sympathies some local deputy might have? Pratt said they didn't have a plan. We only know there's some group behind this."

"Pratt could be right. They're all a liability at this point. Why not get rid of all them," Butch said.

"Could be on their way here," Pat said.

"Jackie," I said. "We need to get her down here. She's too vulnerable where she is."

"With the snow tires, the van can probably make it," Butch said. "I'll go back up and get her."

Jackie said, "Guys, you know I can hear you. I can drive down and call from there."

I looked at my phone. "There's no cell coverage down here," I said.

"I brought the satellite phone with me. No problem."

"Okay. How are you going to get past their van though?"

"If I can't drive around it, I'll push it out of my way," she said.

"You watch too many movies," Pat told her.

"Got a better idea?"

I shrugged. No one else spoke up.

"Okay. If Sam sees any damage though, I'm going to say it was your idea."

Jackie just laughed.

I turned to Pratt, who Butch had dragged over to one corner and had sitting up against a wall. I had Blackie sitting directly in front of him. "You said you were worried that McKnight would send others to eliminate you, Stark, and the Perrys. Who and why?"

"It's what I'd do."

"You're not answering me. Who and why?"

"I don't know who, but why is pretty fucking obvious."

Pat said, "We'd better get ready. Just in case."

"We know the camp in Sparta is empty. Defenders are out in Iowa," Butch said.

Jackie chimed in on the comms. "There are a lot of idiots in Maine.

Could try recruiting some of them."

"Pay attention to your driving," Butch said.

"I am. I am. I'm almost there. Their van wasn't a problem, but this untouched snow is making it slow going."

Ignoring Butch's parental caretaking of Jackie, I said, "And who knows when the FBI will arrive? Okay. Pat, why don't you organize us for visitors of all kinds? I'm also going to call my son. We're going to need legal representation. The FBI is not going to be pleased with two dead bodies and our involvement."

"You think?" Jackie said, coming through the door. She had the Satphone in her hand.

"We'd better…" I started.

"Already done," Jackie said.

Of course she had texted Vicki to let her know everything was okay. Butch, Pat, and I used the Satphone to text our spouses.

Telling Eve I was fine might have been premature, but I didn't think so. Finishing my text to Eve, I looked at Jackie and realized I didn't know who Jackie would text to let them know she was okay. She was pacing back and forth, staying as far away from the bodies as she could.

I said to Butch and Pat, "Can you guys hold down the fort for a couple of minutes?"

Pat said, "Sure."

I turned to Jackie, "Let's get some fresh air."

Blackie left Pratt and came with us.

When we got outside Jackie asked, "How much trouble are we in?"

"I don't know. I guess it all depends on the FBI."

"Do you trust them?"

"The FBI? I don't know. I don't think we have a choice."

"Do you think others are coming? I mean militia types."

I paused before I answered. "I don't think so. But I don't know. Sorry. You going to be okay?"

"I don't know."

"Not what you signed on for, is it?"

"No. Not really."

I took in a deep breath of the cold air. "Sorry Jackie. I never should have involved you."

"You needed me."

"We did. And you sure came through. Did you let people know you're okay?"

"Yeah. My dad."

"Good. We'd better get inside. See what Pat wants us to do."

***

When we came back in, I noticed that the two bodies were now covered with blankets. I hoped Pat's planned rotation of lookouts and Jackie's periodic surveillance with the three drones guaranteed we would not be surprised by any uninvited guests.

There was little talking. Butch cooked us up some breakfast foods that had been brought by the two Defenders.

Neither Luke nor his father wanted anything to eat.

Jackie found some more blankets and gave them to the father and son. Wrapped tightly and sitting against the wall opposite where they had been held captive, they looked like mummies.

Ben arrived first. It was three o'clock in the morning, and he did not come alone. His boss, Emily Harrison, the managing partner of Lawton, Chase, and Harrison, Heng Pho, who was with Ben when I called, and a Maine attorney whom Emily knew from their time together at Yale Law School also walked through the door.

Emily's opening words when she walked through the cabin's door were, "What mess do we have to clean up this time, Frank?" She was only half kidding.

By the time they arrived, we had finished eating. Our lawyers assured us the food would not be considered part of the 'crime scene.' Butch started a second pot of coffee.

The three lawyers grilled us. Timelines, motivations, who did what. At one point I thought they were being overly harsh, treating us like criminals. Emily's response caught me up short. "The FBI will think you are. Be prepared to be accused of being vigilantes who have broken several laws. If we don't play this right, you might be leaving here in handcuffs and detained until they're satisfied you're not the bad guys." The grilling continued.

When the FBI arrived, it was eight o'clock. They were not alone. In addition to two FBI agents, there were six members of the sheriff's department. They told us the state police and a representative from the Maine AG's office were on the way.

Chapter Twenty-Five: Unraveling

Rather than a Christmas card, the front of the cabin now looked like a parking lot for law enforcement SUVs. The Washington County Sheriff's Department cars had all their blue lights flashing. The lights of the FBI SUVs flashed from inside their vehicles. The Maine State Police cars were blue with, of course, blue lights. I have no idea how the representative from the AG's office got there. She was the last to arrive and came by herself.

The FBI took command. The deputies from the sheriff's department and the state police officers did as they were told by the FBI agents, that is until the county sheriff himself showed up and tried to take command. The FBI agent in charge took the sheriff outside. I couldn't hear what they were saying, but when they came back inside, the sheriff organized his men to secure the scene and arrange for ambulances to come remove the bodies of Barry Stark and Mark Perry. Then he left.

The ropes that had bound Pratt were removed and replaced with Washington County Sheriff's Department handcuffs. Even the choice of agency handcuffs had to be negotiated.

As far as I could tell, all the state police officers did was stand around. I thought they might have been waiting for somebody, but I didn't know who. It was clear that the FBI would do any interviewing that was to be done.

When the FBI agent in charge, Nathan Drum, tried to take Lenny Pratt out to an FBI SUV to interview him, Pratt refused to go.

"I'm not going anywhere without a lawyer and a deal."

Since everyone in the cabin heard him say this, there was nothing the agent could do. Pratt had already tried to get Ben, Emily, and the lawyer from Maine, whom we now knew to be Edlon "people call me Ed" Pelletier, to represent him. They had all refused.

At one point Drum confronted Emily, as he pointed to the remnants of our breakfast. "You and your clients contaminated a crime scene."

Her response was a chilly, "You've got to be kidding me."

He didn't follow up and we didn't hear anything more about 'crime scene contamination.'

The FBI agents were methodical. Each of us was interviewed separately. Emily or Ben always accompanied a Nutmeg employee.

An FBI agent would take us out of the cabin for our interviews, which took place in one of the two FBI cars. Our attorney sat in the back with us while the agent sat in front.

Ed Pelletier stayed with Luke and Jim Perry and refused to allow the agents to interview them since they did not have their own attorney and would need an attorney of their choice. Luke wanted Ben or Emily to represent them, but Ed suggested they wait until they got checked out at a hospital, then got home and had an opportunity to think about it.

Fortunately, the two lawyers representing us created a narrative – mostly true – that absolved us of any wrongdoing. We tried to convince them we were simply trying to fulfill the obligations of our contract with a client who was concerned about their son. We had broken no laws. While we might have suspected something nefarious was occurring, we were not obligated to report our suspicions to the FBI. After all, somebody had hired the Defenders to protect a candidate for the presidency of the United States. So, didn't that make them legitimate, at least in someone's eyes? Besides, anyone who had done a modicum of research into the Defenders would know as much as we did. We did, however, tell them everything that Lenny Pratt had told us. We did not talk about any duress that might have occurred to extract this information.

Pratt, committed to silence, was not about to complain about how we treated him. It appeared to work.

To the extent we and our lawyers felt comfortable, we avoided saying too much about Luke's suspicions about his brother. Pratt's recounting of the assassination he had provided to us was sufficient for the agents to understand that Mark was one of the assassins. We saw no reason to cast shade onto Luke or Jim. They were suffering enough as it was, not just the loss of Mark but also who Mark had turned out to be.

When the FBI finished interviewing us, I asked if Jackie could be our technical liaison to the FBI in deciphering what was on the computer we had taken from Camp Liberty. They said no. The Defenders' computer was evidence. Later, I learned that while we were having breakfast, Jackie had been busy copying files from the Defender's computer onto a thumb drive.

Butch, needing to occupy himself, kept making pots of coffee for the mob that had assembled. The bag of coffee beans was all but exhausted when we were allowed to leave the *Reel Escape* a little after eleven o'clock. The two bodies had already been removed by the representatives of the sheriff's department. Three of the state police troopers had left. One would remain until a forensics team had taken pictures of the cabin, inside and out, and had mapped everything that had taken place. The only other law officials remaining were the FBI agent in charge and the state attorney general's lawyer. Once satisfied that she would not be filing state charges against Nutmeg employees, she left. Pratt was a prisoner of the FBI and would receive federal charges.

I liked the FBI agent in charge. He was direct, competent, and saw the big picture all too well. He was kind to Luke and Jim Perry. He offered to have another agent accompany them to the hospital then drive them to their home in West Haven once they were cleared. He told them they would not be able to retrieve their cars because Camp Liberty was now considered a crime scene, and the other FBI agents who had been with us were now there, along with others, securing the camp.

He was not so kind to me. "You know you came really close to breaking a host of laws. Why the hell didn't you just call us?"

I repeated what had been said numerous times by now. "We didn't actually know anything, and I had a client contract to respect."

Hearing the exchange, Ben said, "We've covered that territory and my clients have cooperated fully. You're badgering."

It was clear our narrative did not satisfy him, but he had to accept it. He knew he had a much bigger problem to address.

***

Jackie's relationship to data and technology is one that I do not comprehend. She claims it is similar to my love of sailing. She examines computer programs the way I study sailboat designs. It is an aesthetic sensibility that goes way beyond a concern for function. She has informed me that she is fascinated with how the program creator has solved problems requiring many tradeoffs. It was on the drive back to Connecticut that she told me she had copied files from the Defender's computer.

Pat said, "That's our girl."

I said, "Jesus, Jackie."

"I don't know who to trust."

I let it go. I wasn't sure I did either.

***

Someone won the race to discover what was in the files, Jackie or the FBI computer forensics experts. I knew the FBI was not about to tell me if they had opened them up. They weren't telling me anything. As far as they were concerned, the people from Nutmeg Security and Investigations were nothing more than irresponsible vigilantes who had broken all sorts of laws and endangered our democracy by not notifying them that we suspected there was evil brewing in the hearts of the Defenders.

I continued to wonder if one of the multiple law agencies involved would change their minds about pursuing some legal action against me and Nutmeg. It became apparent, though, that there was an embarrassment factor involved. The last thing the FBI wanted was to illuminate our actions in contrast with their inaction. At least, that was my assessment of why neither the FBI nor the sheriff's office did anything more than confiscate Pat's weapon. The sheriff departments throughout Maine were not enforcing Maine laws regarding their homegrown militias. They were not about to do anything. After a day of legal inaction, I started to relax.

Jackie texted me at ten o'clock that night when I was getting ready for bed: *I'm in. You're not going to believe it. See you in the morning.*

How the hell was I going to wait until morning? Was she nuts? I texted her back: *Headlines please!*

She texted back. *Verbal. Only person to person. Tous Les Jours. 0830.*

I felt like I just entered a John Le Carré novel, but I knew Jackie was (A) very concerned about what she had found and (B) was not about to budge. *Okay*, I texted back.

Eve was still downstairs while this text exchange was taking place. Since the events at the *Reel Escape,* we had talked very little. I assumed her day was consumed with meetings and preparing for a new semester. I had given her the *Cliff's Notes* version of what took place at the *Reel Escape* from when we arrived until we left. She asked questions about details but didn't probe, which surprised me. But then we each got so busy that I didn't pay much attention to her seeming nonchalance. I focused on navigating Nutmeg and its employees back to normalcy and ensuring everyone understood that we could not talk about anything that had taken place. The FBI had made it clear that any reluctance they had to prosecute us would disappear if we started talking about what we knew. I also took a nap. I was exhausted, physically and emotionally. So was Blackie.

When Eve came upstairs, I assumed it was to get ready for bed. I was still wondering about the text exchange with Jackie and what she had found when Eve said, "Hon, we have to talk."

That got my attention. "Uh oh," I thought. Here it comes. She's made up her mind. She's leaving. When I left for Sparta with my crew, I knew it was possible. Out of fear, I rejected it. No, she won't. I was sure she wouldn't. She was here when I returned, so I stopped worrying, but here it was. She was going to leave me. Even though I hadn't gotten hurt, others had. For Mark Perry and Barry Stark, it was more than a 'paper cut.'

"I've been avoiding you," she said.

"Honestly. I haven't noticed. I've been so caught up in…"

"Protecting Nutmeg. I know. I've got a fire going. Come on downstairs. I've poured a glass of Baileys for each of us. It's important. I needed to be sure before I said something."

"Okay."

She turned and walked out of the bedroom and down the stairs to the living room. I followed her. I felt like a student on the way to the principal's office. I prepared myself to be suspended from school, from our marriage.

We sat next to each other on the couch. She handed me my glass, picked up hers, and pointed it towards me. "A toast."

I raised my glass to meet hers. "To?"

"Here's to the next chapter in the story of Frank and Eve."

I was totally confused and must have looked it. "Now that I have your complete attention. Dr. Francis Xavier Kelly, let me tell you how I've spent my last couple of days."

I just looked at her and waited. I had no idea what was coming.

"I spent some time with Elizabeth." I knew Elizabeth was her spiritual advisor and a colleague at the University of St. Joseph in Hartford. "When you left on your adventure to find the Perrys, I didn't know how I felt."

"It wasn't really an adventure."

"Shush. Of course, it was. Let me finish. Something had changed, but I didn't know what or why. I knew you felt like you had to go."

"I did."

"I know. And I was surprised at how I reacted. I didn't say anything to you at the time."

"You were crying."

"And I wasn't sure why or what it meant. Anyway, Elizabeth told me a story. I vaguely knew it but hadn't thought about it in a long time. It was about a sister of the Sisters of Notre Dame de Namur. Her name was Dorothy Mae Stang. Ever hear of her?"

"No."

"Quite a woman. You need to look her up. There is a book, documentary film, and even an opera about her. They call her the Angel of the Amazon."

I had no idea where this was going.

Eve continued, "Dorothy went to Brazil, the Amazon, in 1966. She went to save the rainforest from extinction and to serve the poor farmers who were dependent upon it. Among other things, she helped them learn how to farm without destroying the rainforest. She got a lot of attention in Brazil because of her work. Not all of it was good. Her life was threatened over and over again by loggers, but she never left. Eventually, they hired people to kill her in 2005. They assassinated her for what she believed in."

I still didn't know where this was going.

"In Brazil, they consider her to be a saint. So," Eve continued, "I spent some time reading about her as Elizabeth suggested, and then all the pieces I was struggling with came together."

"Eve. I'm sorry, I don't..."

"Know how this applies to a new chapter for us? I know. I'm trying to get there. Dorothy Stang had a mission, Frank, and she had to live it out. That's who you are, my love. I know you don't think of it that way, but that's how you act. Look at your life. Think of why you sought out being in the military police when you were in the Navy, and then you went to graduate school and got a doctorate in criminal justice. Then you taught courses in criminal justice, and now you catch bad guys and help people who are in trouble. And it can be dangerous, but it is as much who you are as Dorothy Stang was who she was."

"Hey, I'm no Saint."

"Hmm. I won't comment on that, but you never know. Anyway, all of the members of Dorothy Stang's community had to learn to live with the danger Dorothy was in. They could do that because they loved her and believed in her mission. That's what I must learn to do with you, and I'm well on my way. What you do is your mission in life, and it was for a long time before I came into it."

"I thought you wanted me to go back to teaching."

"It wouldn't satisfy you now. I know that. You know that. Not now. Maybe some time in the future when you and Blackie get too old to kick ass, but not now."

"You're serious?"

"Very. Please don't misunderstand me. I don't want you to do anything foolish, and I'm still better with you getting paper cuts rather than getting shot."

I didn't know what to say, but I did know she was right; something had changed in her.

"To a new chapter." She held her glass up again, and we joined glasses to celebrate the new chapter.

I must have had my idiot smile on.

She asked, "What are you so smiley about?"

I laughed.

"Are you laughing at me?" she asked.

"No. No. At us. At me."

"And why, may I ask?"

"Oh, Eve. I love you so much. I'm sorry I put you through this." I started laughing again.

"What is so damn funny, Frank?"

"Us." I stopped laughing. "On the way back from that Godforsaken cabin, I kept thinking, 'Kelly, you're an idiot.' I had just spent several hours with an assortment of FBI agents, sheriffs, and troopers. I had watched two men be shot to death, and I was probably going to be spending a lot more hours unraveling the mess I had gotten myself into.

"Just before I left, you were sitting on the floor crying. Remember. Blackie was licking your face. And then we left. 'Idiot.' The word fit. So, what did I do during the long drive home today? I got on my phone and started looking up information about the criminal justice program at UNH. Guess what? They have a master's degree program in investigations. A master's degree."

"Wait a minute. Are you saying you're too old to kick ass?"

"I didn't say that."

"So, what are you saying?"

"I'm saying I need to make appointments and explore options."

"You're considering…"

"Making some changes."

"Are you telling me that after all I went through to get on board with…"

We are far too old to wrestle like a couple of teenagers in heat, but I didn't let her finish her sentence. We wrestled our way onto the floor, started laughing, and one thing led to another.

Later, over ice cream, Eve wanted to know more about the events at the *Reel Escape* and the aftermath with the FBI, as well as the assorted players. I told her about the work Jackie was doing on the files.

She asked me what, if any, involvement Nutmeg would have going forward. She wanted to know. She really wanted to know. Eve had asked questions before about cases, but they were 'polite' questions to show she was interested. She had even introduced me to colleagues like Henry Gore when she thought they might be helpful, but this was new. There was nothing polite about this inquisitiveness. She wanted into this new world we were creating together.

We didn't know its shape, but it would be ours. That included coming with me to meet Jackie for breakfast.

I didn't know what Jackie had found and was concerned about any legal ramifications that might be involved, so I texted Ben to ask if he was available to join us.

He said he was and asked if it was okay if Heng came with him.

Of course, I said, "Sure." When I ended the call, I turned to Eve and said, "Ben asked if Heng could come."

"I doubt she's driving down from Storrs just to meet us for breakfast."

"You think…"

"That your son is shacking up with a lovely young woman? Inevitable is the word I would use."

Chapter Twenty-Six: Tous Les Jours

Meg DeRosa is a fantastic negotiator. The real estate market in New Haven had been down, way down, when Meg negotiated a very long lease for the Nutmeg offices at 129 Church Street. It is an amazing location. Although the DeRosas lived in Fairfield, Sam wanted an office in New Haven, the 'Gateway to New England.' Parking could be a pain, but my office looked out over the New Haven Green, which more than compensated for walking a couple of blocks twice a day or sometimes more often. We were right next door to the United States District Court. Three blocks away was the FBI office. Jackie didn't want to meet at the office. I wondered if she was being paranoid. Did she think we might be bugged?

We were not a small group. Jackie had called Vicki. That made sense, I told myself. After all, Jackie did report to Vicki.

Vicki, though, had invited her parents, who had recently returned from their jaunt to warmer climes. Their consulting contracts were part of Sam and Meg's payout for selling Nutmeg. I understood why Vicki invited them, but I was anxious about the size of the group.

Assembling chairs and small tables for eight at Tous Les Jours during their breakfast rush – the best pastries in New Haven – was difficult, but it was managed thanks to a cooperative staff who knew us to be frequent customers.

I was surprised to learn that Heng had recently been there several times. When I started describing how good the croissants were, she said her favorite was the *pain au chocolat.*

Had she moved in with Ben? What about her fellowship? I reminded myself that I had other things to worry about.

When we assembled with our various coffees and pastries, Jackie had us huddle together as if conspiring to take over the restaurant.

"Why the intrigue?" Sam asked too loudly, given the look Jackie gave him.

And then she started. "I don't know who to trust. I thought Lenny Pratt might have been putting us on with some of the things he told us, but he wasn't. They're trying to take over the presidency. For real."

Ben and I looked at each other. Ben said, "I think we may have a problem, folks. The FBI has cautioned us to be very circumspect about what we discuss with whom and where we do it."

Sam took Ben's admonition personally. He did not want to be kept out of the loop. Emotionally, Nutmeg was still his. He did not like Ben setting boundaries around what he could and could not know. He said, "I know how to keep my mouth shut."

Meg said, "Ben, you've spoken with them. Perhaps you could stop Jackie if you think what she shares is inappropriate."

Not wanting to get into a pissing contest with Sam, Ben said, "I don't have a problem with the who. The problem is with the where. I suggest we keep things light here, then we meet up at my office."

"Good idea. That okay with everybody?" I asked.

No one objected.

We kept conversation light while we ate, but we were all in a hurry to learn more. After eating our pastries, and taking our coffee to go, we all went to the office of Lawton, Chase, and Harrison and settled in one of their conference rooms.

Jackie has a very organized approach to storytelling. She began with her guesswork to open the encrypted files. McKnight had not been very creative. Rather than using his mother's birthday for everything, he used his first wife's birthday for some and his second wife's for others. She described the money flow from *The Committee* to the Defenders of Liberty and thus to the threats of assassination. When she started to tell us about Mary Olson, the governor of Montana, and the threats to her and her husband, Ben stopped her. "Folks, we're starting to deal with names now, and I think we must stop."

Meg put a hand on Sam's arm, but he didn't say anything.

Ben continued, "This is dangerous territory. I'm not sure we all want to know this information." He looked around at us as if to check that it was okay for Jackie to stop. No one said anything. He asked Jackie, "Have you communicated what you found to the FBI?"

"No. I…"

"Are you worried because you downloaded the files?" Ben asked.

"Yes."

"Do you think their forensic people will have already opened them?"

"I have no idea."

"Okay. Here's what we're going to do. For many of us here, we already know much more than we should."

I was impressed watching Ben take over.

"Do you have your computer with you?"

"Yes. It's right here." Jackie pointed to her bag.

"Good. As soon as she comes in, which should be any minute now, you, Dad, and I are going to meet with Emily and discuss how we proceed from here. I'm pretty sure we'll call the FBI and invite them for a chat."

Vicki asked, "Is Jackie going…"

"To be in trouble? Probably not. Especially if we invite them and take the first steps. In the best of worlds, their people will not be as clever as our young friend here and they will be grateful. I'm sorry to be the downer here, but I believe this is the best course of action."

"I want to be there, too," Sam said.

"Sorry, Sam, but you're no longer an officer of Nutmeg. Dad has to do this."

"Wait a minute here. I …"

"Sam, shut up," Meg told him with a glare.

"Dad, cool it," Vicki told him. "The three of you do what you need to do. The rest of us can head out. I should get to the office anyway."

"Heng," Eve said, "I have to be in Hartford today. I can give you a lift to Storrs if you'd like."

"I've got my car at Ben's, but thank you."

"I can give you a ride over there."

"That would be great."

As they walked out, Emily was coming through the door. She looked perplexed, then her eyes found the rest of us in the conference room. Without stopping, she approached us, entered through the glass door, set down her coffee and portfolio, shrugged off her coat, and said, "Fill me in."

***

Ben's assessment of the situation was accurate. The FBI came to the conference at Lawton, Chase, and Harrison with no sign of belligerence. Even the agent in charge who'd been on scene in Maine came.

The agents did ask Jackie about her decision to copy the files from the Defenders of Liberty computer. She answered honestly that she did not know who to trust given the depths of the conspiracy.

It was not a complete answer. "I wanted to satisfy my curiosity" would have been more complete, but the FBI agents appeared satisfied with her "I didn't know the extent of the conspiracy" response.

What happened next surprised me. The agent in charge, Nathan Drum, said to Jackie, "I want you to take a minute before you answer my next questions: What information from the Defenders computer have you shared and with whom?"

Jackie thought for a minute before saying, "The owners of Nutmeg – former and current, Ben, Eve – Frank's wife, and Heng. I was just explaining the passwords, then some stuff about the money flow. I think that's it."

Ben added. "Jackie was about to share more information when I stopped her."

"Okay, good. Next question. And, again, think before you answer it. Does this information exist in any other place other than your computer?"

"Yes. A thumb drive."

"Do you have it with you?"

"Yes."

Drum opened his hand and reached toward Jackie. Jackie went into her bag, pulled out the thumb drive, and handed it to Drum.

Drum asked, "I need to be clear about something. Is one of you representing Jackie?"

Emily said, "Ben is attorney of record for Nutmeg Security and Investigation." She then spoke directly to Jackie. "Jackie, Ben can represent you in this matter if you would like, or you could employ a different attorney to represent your interests."

"Do I need one?" Hearing the anxiety in Jackie's voice, I felt sorry for her.

"Yes," Emily said. "I believe you do."

"Ben, then."

Ben said, "If there comes a time when there is the potential for a conflict of interest between Nutmeg's interests and yours, I will be sure to tell you and help you get another attorney."

"Oh. Okay." Jackie's usually confident voice was shaky."

"Great," said Drum. "If it's okay with you, Ms. Harrison, may we use the conference room or should we move to our offices? I need to do some paperwork with Ms. Forrest and her attorney."

Emily told them they could stay there. She and I left and went to her office to wait.

When we arrived, I asked, "What's that all about?"

"My guess is they want a formal signed statement from Jackie about both custody of evidence and a confidentiality statement about contents. What's on that damned thing that Ben stopped her talking about?"

"She was about to tell us something about the governor who dropped out of the race, then – I'm guessing – who was involved in planning and

273

bankrolling the assassination and the conspiracy to take over the presidency."

"She knows all that?"

"Yes."

"Poor kid."

An hour later, Drum invited us back to the conference room.

When we arrived, an FBI agent finished gathering Jackie's computer, her thumb drive, a paper where Jackie had written down the passwords she had used to gain access, and signed documents. They promised to return her computer and the thumb drive. When Jackie asked about the Nutmeg files on her laptop, Drum asked whether they were encrypted. She answered, "Of course they are."

"I assume you have them backed up."

That earned him a dismissive, "Yes, they're backed up."

Drum said, "Well, at some point, we may need to access any Nutmeg files pertinent to our investigation. Will that be a problem?"

Jackie did not get a chance to answer.

Ben said. "In principle, no. However, to protect Nutmeg and its clients, we may require prior authorization from our clients and possibly a court order."

"Of course."

"Dad, Agent Drum wants you to sign an NDA as well. You probably should have stayed for this discussion, but I wasn't sure. Sorry."

"Not a problem." I signed the document Drum handed me.

There was no discussion about Jackie possibly having committed a crime, nor was there any discussion about me for not reporting our suspicions about the Defenders of Liberty or my knowledge and support of Jackie's activities.

We never did learn whether the FBI forensics people had already been able to access the encrypted files. Drum made it very clear: as far as Nutmeg and its employees were concerned, it was 'case closed.' They thanked us for our cooperation. We thanked them, for what I wasn't sure. Neither the bottles of water nor the coffee service had been touched.

When they left, I said, "Talk about an anti-climax."

"The best kind," Emily said.

Jackie asked, "So what do we do now?"

"Nothing," Ben said.

"Nothing? That's it! You're kidding."

Emily laughed. "Nope. At least for now. As far as you and Nutmeg are concerned, that's it. The FBI knows to contact us if they need anything more from Nutmeg. But for you two, it's all over."

I said, "I still want to know what was on that damn computer."

Emily said, "Well now you can ask away, but I'm leaving. I do not want to know."

There was a lot of detail. Jackie filled me in on the planning, the reasoning behind it, the threats, and then the enlistment of Mary Olson as a potential vice-presidential candidate.

"Did she know about the plans to assassinate Juan Perez?" Ben asked.

"No, I don't think so."

I said, "Can you imagine what must have gone through her mind when Perez was assassinated? She must have been terrified."

"Yeah, but she didn't say anything," Jackie said.

"What about Pope?" Ben asked.

"Not as far as I can tell," Jackie said. "They must have deliberately kept him in the dark. You know. Plausible deniability."

Jackie kept telling the story. The chains of emails – there were several – provided names, dates, plans, and actions. When she told us who was on *The Committee*, I had to ask her to repeat herself. I was having a hard time breathing.

***

Vicki and I went to the funeral for Mark Perry. It was small. Family and a few friends. Sally Gwynn was there as was Gwen, Luke's girlfriend.

Anita Perry thanked me for my efforts. It was generous of her.

Jim Perry did not say anything to me, or from what I could tell, anyone else.

Luke hung on to Gwen like a tree branch in a river flowing to only God knows where.

I did not envy Anita the task she had in front of her.

There was no eulogy for Mark, just prayers of petition:

Let us pray for the soul of Mark that he may rest in the peace of Christ and be welcomed into the eternal embrace of God's love.

Let us pray for the soul of Mark, that God may grant him eternal rest and receive him into His heavenly kingdom, where he may live in peace forever.

Redemption. Was Mark's final act enough? Mark had freed himself from the ropes Pratt and Stark had tied him with. The rope burns on his wrists where he had struggled were deep and raw. He had rushed to get Stark's pistol that was on the counter. He would have calculated what his chances were of getting there first. He must have known they were small.

Enough. What is ever enough? That damn word. It had plagued me my entire adult life. I had failed the Perry family. They counted on me to bring Mark home alive. I failed.

There was no collation after the service. Vicki and I drove back to the office without stopping for lunch.

***

When the headlines came, they came in waves. One week after our meeting in the conference room at Lawton, Chase, and Harrison, Gordon McKnight was arrested for conspiracy to commit murder and as an accessory to murder. The following day, John Pope held a press conference. Eve and I watched it that night on the evening news. Dressed informally and wearing his trademark field jacket with its NRA emblem on the breast pocket, Pope strolled up to the microphones and said:

Because of recent events and the arrest of Colonel Gordon

McKnight, there have been rumors and speculations regarding the private contractor our campaign employed to provide security. I ordered that contract to be terminated.

Olin Matthews, my campaign manager and trusted friend, has chosen to leave the campaign. Several people recommended the group to Olin, and he believes he was misled, actually betrayed, but that it was still his responsibility. I asked him to stay with the campaign, but he convinced me that this was the best course of action, so I have accepted his resignation.

Sidney Twarog has agreed to assume the role of campaign manager. I look forward to working with Sid as we take back America and right the Ship of State so it may sail confidently into the future, embodying the principles upon which this great nation was founded. Thank you.

Reporters shouted questions at him, but Pope responded to only one: "Who will provide security now?"

"The Secret Service."

Twarog came forward and said, "Sorry, folks. We have to stay on schedule. There will be no more questions." He then turned and followed Pope as they headed for the SUV cavalcade that awaited him.

I turned to Eve. I was incredulous. "He's not dropping out."

"Did you expect him to?"

"Hell, yes. He had to have known what kind of group the Defenders were even if he didn't know all the plans."

"Optimist."

My telephone rang. It was Henry, so I put it on speaker.

"Can you believe this shit? What the hell does it take to get rid of these animals?" he asked.

I couldn't say, "If you only knew." Damned non-disclosure agreement. Instead, I said, "We were watching. Do you think there's a chance..."

"Of his getting elected? Yes. There's a damn good chance this son-of-a-bitch will get elected. He's a shoo-in to win the primary."

"Maybe there's more that will come out. You never know," I said. Then I immediately wondered if I had gone too far. I was looking at Eve when I said it. She gave me a look and reached out her hand for my phone. I gave it to her.

She took it off speaker. I could tell from her end of the conversation that she and Henry had proceeded to engage in a conjoint bemoaning of the state of American political life.

When she got off the phone, I said, "Something good has to come out of this. Two people died. The Perry family. Look what they have to live with. There has to be something positive that comes out of all this."

My phone rang again. This time it was Ben. As I had with Henry, we discussed our disbelief that Pope was staying in the race. As we finished expressing our incredulity at Pope's decision, my lawyerly son added, "Don't forget the NDA, Dad. I know you're going to want to tell the world. You can't. We signed it to protect Jackie and Nutmeg."

"I know. I know," I answered.

When I got off the phone, Eve asked, "What is it that you know?"

"Just some legal stuff we have to deal with."

"Remember you said there had to be something good that came out of all this."

"Yeah."

"Well, what about Ben and Heng? They came out of this."

I smiled. "Yeah, I suppose you're right."

"No supposing about it. This is the real thing."

"You're sure?"

"That we may be adding her to this growing family? Absolutely!"

I smiled first, then laughed. "You're right. That would be a good thing. I like her."

"So do I." She stopped there, but I sensed she wanted to say something else. She did. "When are you seeing Stu?"

"I have an appointment next week."

"And you'll…"

"Tell him about this? Of course. What I can."

"Good. There's something else."

"What?"

"Jackie. I'm not worried so much about Butch and Pat, but she's..."

"Young. I'll talk to her about how she's doing and suggest she might want to see someone. I can tell her that it's mandatory for cops when they're involved in a shooting."

"Good."

***

One month later, a federal grand jury was charged with deliberating whether there was sufficient 'probable cause' to indict a group of leading Washington insiders who referred to themselves as 'The Committee.'

Four months later, Jackie received a FedEx package from Nathan Drum. In it were her computer and thumb drive, both of which had been wiped clean.

279

Acknowledgements

I have many people to thank: Cheryl Katon for her help understanding the ins and outs of camp construction and camp life; my granddaughter Jackie Scholl and grandson Forrest Keller for allowing me to blend their names into Jackie Forrest as well as protecting me from making egregious technical computer technology mistakes; my reading and writing colleagues – Judy Campbell, Kalina Vendetti, Abigale Bottone, Tess Baumberger, Karen LeBlanc, Florence Noonan, Marc Olivere, Sasha Rucinska – who provide encouragement and feedback; Rachel Green, Ron Clarke, and David Minnick were kind enough to read the manuscript in draft form and provide comments and suggestions.

I am grateful for the ongoing work of scholars and organizations who illuminate the world view and the activities of those who would dispense with democracy. The rage described in this book is real.

Stephanie Blackman, my trusted copy editor and publisher, makes things easy for me, and I am indebted to her for that.

Finally, my partner in life, Melody Barlow, who puts up with me, my frustrations, and me getting up in the middle of the night to work. That is in addition to reading, editing, and commenting on draft after draft.